Missir

by

L Penn

A _real_ love story

For
Zoé

13th of 2008

Mature content not for easily offended

This book is dedicated to my mother's memories

First published by cdben/L Penn February 2018 (version 1.0)

ISBN 978 19857 48774

Visit the website:
http://anovel.wix.com/strongwords

L Penn

Chapter One

"Do you miss him?"

Do I miss him?

These are words I thought would never be asked of me. The coming of his smile with slightly crooked incisors from unchecked teeth; teeth that should have been checked when in infancy by more astute parents who could have pushed him to being sporty too, you know, engage in some sort of physical activity to help stave off that approaching beer-belly but I happily cuddled it in the end. And nothing could be done about that mop of curls sweeping his crown before starting to recede from his cute forehead? Nice. And what about that laugh! A laugh whilst clapping those large hands of his creating a sound so startling you'd flinch and could not help but laugh also. Then there's his shock at your suggestion he get acquainted with modern appliances that could hold more than last night's take-away and a couple of canned beers. Yeah, he could use your help. And a lot of it, some might say. Like? Well, for instance, reminding him to wash his pert backside after the magazine-reading, number-two dump stinking out your bathroom for the next three hours unless you sprayed a powerful poison-neutraliser before attempting to drop a load yourself. Least the toilet seat is comfortably warm - got to give him that. Oh, and don't forget the small introductions for cooking Sunday dinners he'd at last start to eat well. Vegetables, roast joints, meaty gravy: all the good stuff to ease him off fart inducing beers to a palate pleasing medium-red. White he would choke at. The gurgling of his pink tongue from the acidic hit of a white - no way! And afterwards came that laugh followed by the large clap of hands which always made you jolt before matching his infectious smile.

Do I miss him? Yes, I miss him.

~

Toby McGuire and Sean McGee held my hands behind my back while they dunked my head in a basin full of cold water. I couldn't escape as they were holding me pretty tight and I wasn't going to fight back with my fifteen-year-old bones looking to challenge these sixteen-year-old's.

"Listen shit-face, give us the Walkman or we'll bash you!"

Now how could I give them the Walkman received on my birthday from my good old mum when I couldn't free my hands? Boys were so illogical.

"Not so brave now are you, Pearsy, come on, give it us!"

Emery Pearson was the name bestowed me. Most people loved it cos it sounded rich but my family were far from rich. Somewhere between doing-alright and wanna-be-doing-better, who knows, but we weren't rich. My parents had bought our home and smartened it up so once you're in that 'ownership' bracket the customary extended brick-porch is built which just sneaks outside the local authority's building-line making you look regal amongst the ordinary set of houses. Dad was good with his hands and helped put up the porch, and with Uncle Robert supplying most of his talented labour and materials, it didn't cost much. To everyone it appeared well grand so the kids at school thought we were rich. No, we weren't.

"Hand over the Walkman, Pearsy!"

It was neatly placed inside my sports bag; side pocket with the long zip. Go on, have a look, take it, it's yours. No, they were too dumb to grasp that fact and more interested in dipping my head in water whilst crunching my arms behind my back.

"Please," I spluttered, "just stop it will you, you can have the Walkman!" before Toby grabbed a chunk of my hair and dunked me beneath the cold water again. Seconds later he let me up for air, however, it was pre-planned to allow Sean to sink a solid fist in to my stomach.

Shit! Boys were dumb but jeez they knew how to make you hurt.

"You're a bloody pain, Pearsy!"

They let me go and I slumped to the floor. I couldn't stop them from taking my sports bag and ransacking the entire thing before finding my prized annual gift.

Toby, his brand forever wicked, rasped, "Got it!" followed by a hard mocking slap to the back of my head. Thanks, boys.

Now I'm left thinking couldn't they just take it and get lost? No, I guess they really wanted to emphasise their mean-spirits and dishing out 'adventure playground' pain was a part of it.

"You need to give up things right at the off, Pearsy," dug the devil's double, Sean, "and stop being such a flipping twat!"

Sure, while I struggled to catch my breath as Toby gleefully pulled me up by an ear and Sean got me round the throat and the two slung me up against the wall. Oh great, they're gonna hit me again.

Bang.

The toilet doors swing open and in walks someone I cannot see but hear. Too busy trying to make a decent breath for my lungs after my throat grab and hit gut.

"Hey, you two, what are you doing?! Get your hands off her!"

I remembered he sounded tough. Like nothing could scare him. Not anyone from those endemic 'stalk-and-slasher' movies to the grand three-hour mafia epics. My dad loved watching them.

"Hey, I said get your hands off her!"

Sean's hand instantly unhooked from around my neck while Toby let go of my ear. Starting to splutter again, I sank to the granite floor of the *boys'* lavatories. Yes, it was easy getting yourself dragged in there from a soundless corridor whilst making your way to another lesson of uninspiring Geography after arriving late from morning break - and no - I wasn't smoking behind the bike sheds.

A quick glance from my tear-filled sight caused by my rough treatment, the stalwart boy was busy grappling Sean and Toby out of the toilets and before I closed my eyes to suck in oxygen, the two pain-loving lads disappeared under the controlling hands of this never-before-seen-saviour, returning with my Walkman.

Yeah, now I could dig that alright.

"Hey, are you okay?"

Did I look okay?

Feeling his ample hand gently stroke my wet hair, I suppose I was okay but I sure didn't feel it.

"Here's your stuff."

He kindly placed the Walkman back inside my bag and I thought, gleaning from the situation that my dad had miraculously stepped from outer-space.

Aiding me to my feet the Samaritan coolly rubbed my right arm then placed the sports bag in my left. I barely gripped it when he lifted my chin and saw I these fiery green eyes under a blanket of scraggly dark curly hair.

"Hey, I'm Jack, Jack Charles, just moved here. You gonna be okay?"

I tried to straighten up and look as if I could take a good gut punch but so wanted to double over and heave.

"Yeah..." I said gasping, "I'm fine."

His beam was joyful, "Well, look, I need to take a piss."

Of course, why else would he be in the boys' toilets.

"Yeah, yeah...go on, I'm okay."

With his burning greens hatching on to my hazel-browns - my mum said they were hazel-brown - I let his playful punch admirably scrape my chin before watching him leave to step inside a private cubicle.

I would not encounter difficulties with Sean or Toby after that, nor would I have a conversation with Jack Charles until years later.

~

"Why do you think you miss him?"

Wasn't that obvious?

No, apparently not, according to Susan James. Why do therapists ask these mundane questions? Isn't it obvious I miss him but thinking why I do is even clearer, no?

Why does anyone think they miss someone, isn't there this void that needs filling? You create a hole and want to fill it with something, don't you? Holes needed to be filled in I thought, maybe, I don't know, I could be wrong. Dig a hole in the back garden you don't necessarily want to leave it for placing deceased pets down there. You might want to plant flowers, grow vegetables, or build a pond and watch kids play. Holes, voids, same thing, they always needed filling, didn't they!

Susan continues, "Emery?"

I answer her, "Yes."

"Your thoughts," she presses nice, "on why you miss him?"

Well, my mind takes to wandering to his warm crumpet led hands on a cold winter morning slicing up under my

11

cotton vest to stay across my belly. His palms were so wide he could cup one side of half my ribcage and play the piano on it.

"Em..." her continued probe, "do you want to say why?"

Again, there's his long grizzly feet that plush bath water in to my face as we dined pizza inside our candle-lit cast-iron tub, surrounded by beautifully glazed terracotta floor tiles listening to drip, drip, drips, splash on the floor. His grinning mouth would be fleecing away the Italian pepperoni special; pleasurable.

"Are you afraid to tell me, Emery?"

I liked it when he towelled me dry and scooped me up then carried me to the main bedroom before flinging me cave-man-style on to our bed. The king-size mattress made it safe to play-wrestle as he would pin me down snarling and folding my legs until my laughs made him laugh before his collapsed torso smothered mine. And then he'd take me. He would take me to where I had not gone before and return me to a place I long wished to keep.

"Is it too hard to think about?"

Christ, too hard? His manhood was *always* too hard, too prominent too distinct. Each morning it was there staring up at me wanting to enter. Like an uncontrolled beast of epic size wanting to dip forth and spring wetness drowning my cunt. Oops, should I say that to Susan? Still not sure, and besides afterward I'd get my downtown area rubbed dry with those hands of his scented from caressing my arse.

Could I tell Susan that?

"You've always opened up before, Em," she attempts to link, "You know I'm not here to judge but to listen to you."

I lift my lolling head and make in to her eyes. She's extraordinarily gorgeous. I think that helps you play in to her hands, her being so affording and tempting. I couldn't see a ring. I wondered if she took it off when she addressed her clients, you know, mould you round in to thinking she was open to any and everything because she had all the time in the world to give you, and only you. No man sat waiting for her to be mother-and-whore when she got home. Wonder what her place is like? Detached eighteenth-century cottage with all modern trimmings and acres of land? Sounds good; it should be where she does her therapy sessions not inside this clinical office space but panoramic scenery overstretching the grounds of a Royal Park. Okay, fine, this view across the country greens offered some relaxation in order for the distilled among us to feel a little freedom therefore we should open up each pore of emotional tide we were all drowning in!

Come on, Susan, here are my thoughts, tell me what *you* miss?

She doesn't. "Maybe you feel like a drink now?"

A drink: "No."

Damn. I replied too quickly. I was off balance and she knew it. Come on, got to change this.

"Err, sorry," my feeble apology, "I'll have a coffee. Black please, no sugar."

With her broad smile she got up and left the room.

Hadn't caught on before but she's got a great backside. She was wearing a white pencil skirt and navy blouse so I hadn't noticed it in the pants suits she always wore.

Tease.

I wonder how many male clients she tailored. Wondered if they'd like to caress her arse and massage her cunt dry?

You crude fuck.

Hell, I was here about my arse, my feelings, my massages, couldn't let Susan's fine bottom get in the way of all that.

Shit, I'm side-tracked. Must focus; Being left alone, no matter how briefly inside her smart office, she knows her things are safe with me. I proved that time ago.

A flash return sees her place my cup of hot black on the desk. She sleekly moves round to her seat while taking a sip of her own coffee leaving a perfectly lined froth of milk to lace her upper lip before licking it clean. Her succulent mouth made me think how would it feel to have her lick me, or me lick her? What would it be like sleeping with a woman? Apparently the latest popular monthlies surveyed seventy-five-percent of women experiment with another woman. I still remain in the twenty-five-percent. I like cock. I like *big* hands. I like to be picked up and carried some place. I like men. I miss my man. I miss him.

~

"Hey, all A's and B's well done girl!"

My dad looked overjoyed. His little darling came through. Damn right, I had. Wasn't about to let the old man down with mediocre exam results. I saw the way he got up every morning doing a five day week, sometimes six, and come home reeking of burn and molten steel. He had a good career in the shipbuilding yards and mum's precision typing saw her manage the yards administrative offices. It's where they met. Amongst iron, glass, and the smell of a north-west sea, we did okay. The well-to-do community saw a rich history slowly dwindling, so when the opportunity came to buy your own home, mum and dad grabbed it.

Seeing their determined efforts I set out to ensure my grades from secondary school were nothing short of amazing. It was the summer of '85. I made my parents proud and my siblings were chuffed for me.

Jamie was my younger sister by two years, and Lucas, my brother, two years senior. We got on okay. We shuffled the usual blood-rivalry at times but mostly we were fine. Our parents did a good job of us, if I say so myself. There were no serious social problems elevating our household though we could see a sense of issues rising throughout the community as the shipyards were being squeezed out of existence. For me, leaving my home town would take priority and heading off to college emulating my brother would become my next goal.

~

The aromatic Brazilian beans were mouth-watering as they steamed from both our cups. "Strong enough for you?" said considerately.

I nod yes but the water was too frigging hot and needed to cool. Those bloody urns could leave a scold if you weren't careful; should have asked for cream.

"Emery?"

Oh, yeah, back to me again.

I'm supposed to be opening up right, that's where we were, something about missing him too, of course. I shift to watch the formal grey blinds covering the window behind Susan's chair. It looked like they had been dusted free since our previous meeting. Last time I checked I recalled seeing a film of particles layer each slat. Shouldn't matter whether a place is private or state run as keeping the therapeutic office hygiene clean would always see a patient at ease. Maybe that's why I'd been on edge and out of sorts; my having noticed the film of dust had gone. Yeah, you dodger, who the hell are you kidding? You're required to participate, so participate. You managed to avoid the group sessions so be happy. Christ, stop being difficult. Anyone would think you actually wanted to be here. Ah, but then again you do, don't you. You *want* to be here. Susan's been great, you get time off the regular landscape, and you can at least try to understand yourself. No, now wait a second, who really *does* understand their self? Aren't we afraid to! Are we ever prepared to reveal all, to expose every inner feeling that is akin to the moment of conception? Damn, that explosion! That wonder of a finite being beginning to grow: I mean, wasn't it incredible how it formed, it felt, it thought. Some called it scientific others a holy plan. I didn't know what to call it except it gave rise to magical moments.

~

"He's sitting over there."

I craned my neck to catch a glimpse of him chatting away amidst a smart young group only he appeared dishevelled and mismanaged. Slinging his college bag on to the canteen table, he drew in the discerning crowd to words of his political romp.

"Don't you want to go over?" Carla said to me. She looked childishly hypnotic among the creative rush which besieged us in the vast corridors of Somerfield College. I'd hit the slopes and travelled down to this Middle-England Edwardian plot to further my life's interests. Not sure what I really wanted or where I planned to be in life but hoping a few years meandering inside these educational corridors seemed like a perfect place to start.

Carla plates, "Everyone says he's looking to mess up the Student Union."

I exalt, "Student Union?" My ears pricked up as I settled eyes upon him. He commanded those sat round with the ease of painting a studied nude. The air-strokes of his hands trailing intrigue.

"Well," my good pal forces me to listen up, "you're just going to sit here?"

Making Carla eat my friendless look she pretends to swat an invisible fly.

She smiles, "I'm going over."

Now my smile, "You want to see his good looks."

"Well he's not exactly hard on the eyes is he?"

She started to make me feel all fuzzy.

16

"Come on, Emery, you might like what he has to say."

"I already know what he has to say."

She looks fruitful, "Yeah, and how's that?"

"Well…" I turned away from my friend and watched the table seating the next generation about to make their own stamp on the country, and said casually, "The first thing he'll say is… 'I'm Jack, Jack Charles'."

Chapter Two

"I've allocated you more time today so you can prepare for next week."

Next week, yes, my last session, or so they tell me! What if we could go on and on? I'm sure we could. Susan wasn't bored yet, I fascinated her, I could tell. She didn't want this to be our penultimate session and neither did I. Why would anyone want to give up a good friend? Good friends were hard to come by so having one as an instructed professional geared toward helping, 'you-be-you', and to understand things better was someone you did not willingly give up. They had to be pried from you. The need for a good friend naturally clung tight. We could be friends forever; I get that feeling from her.

"There's a lot we have to get in today, Em."

Was that a mild warning I was being lazy and not trying to make the most of it?

I sipped my black coffee. It cooled sufficiently to make me sip it again and find Susan's distinctly blue eyes. They were like a mixed-turquoise blue, very distinct. There were blue eyes then there were Susan's. What on earth played hind those eyes of hers? I should be her therapist for a day and check what lay at the back of her spectacle. Identify her sorrows and joys and wield out every emotive shield she let hide. Yes, allow me to be your therapist for once.

Oh no, no, I couldn't. I was simply too afraid. What lay behind my own eyes was difficult enough, so perhaps no, I wouldn't want to poke at the back of someone else's mind.

"Ginger nut?" she offered, reaching to inspect inside her large black handbag resting by the leg of her chair.

I shook my head no and added a smile and she immediately replaced the branded biscuit pack back; couldn't take watching her lick ginger crumbs off that mouth of hers. She took a drink of cream caffeine enticing my look to that 'white line' highlight her lush upper lip. Mm, okay, all part of getting the client to open up, I guess. Shit, why did all these niggling little traits of hers prove so bothersome? As the one supposedly revealing everything why do I feel I've read something *else* in to it? You never felt these idiosyncrasies appeared natural from the get-go but were carefully construed and coolly spun. And what a construct it was, intricate yet precise, so, yes, lace your mouth again with cream, Miss James, and I'll see.

"You've come a long way, Emery," she glides, "I don't think you want to see all the hard work thrown away."

Well, I wouldn't let it.

"Nothing will be thrown away," I say informative, and take two more sips from her hot Brazilians. I shy from her brilliant eyes. It was getting harder to look at her.

"I can't force you to talk, Em, so I won't, but it would be nice if you could think over everything these past few months."

Emotional blackmail, such crap! Yeah, all the hours you've given me with the right words to help ease my sorry arse and a caring hand reach out to my own. Yeah, I get it.

"The group sessions you didn't want to take part in and I've tried to assist you every other step of the way."

I light up, "So you think I got spoilt?"

She tilts her head, nice.

Why was it so?

I suppose doing work this important allowed a lot of time to make your tresses reflect an auburn glow, like that of a sprinkling dusk. The stuff we were given to lather our heads barely supported limp locks to be presentable. Pah! Absolute rubbish! All down to having good genes the university's dorm mistress would say.

~

"Caroline and Emma, you look considerably unkempt today."

The provost tried to encourage prim-self-managing of us nubile set her priority: A wonderfully educated and glamorous individual whose charms were continuously flicked away by the rugged boys from the rowing team. My two room-mates, Emma and Caroline, were looping student loans and rent fees so they didn't have time to think about appearances only.

"And your dorm could do with a bit of a clean."

"Oh, fuck off!" muttered Emma, upon the provost's exit from our quarters.

"What a stuck-up cow!" delectably added Caroline.

I watch both girls fiddle round with sorting books before starting to undress right in front me. These unashamed days during the very inviting Nineties meant nothing was out of bounds or off limits. Carlton University's open and honest irreverence made no secret of it.

"So," Emma's query of me, unlacing her frilly bra, "is he coming round or are you going over to his place?"

The girls were captured by a relationship that held bonded from three years previous at college to furthering during the start of uni. I didn't reveal much to them except this beau's name was Jack Charles.

"Can't be really serious if he hasn't let you meet his parents yet?"

I didn't want to meet *them*. I was seeing *him*.

"So, did you follow him here or did he follow *you?*"

I gave the two an un-answering smile.

"Oh, you bitch, tell us!"

Half way through their getting undressed they decided my smile wasn't honourable enough and leapt on top of me on top my bed unveiling a bungling mess of semi-nakedness and cheap wool pullovers getting dragged down over cotton briefs, crotchet my helpless form, they then began to joyfully batter me.

"Come on, Em, spill the beans!"

Amidst playful punches and rib tickles I could hardly get a word out.

"Okay, okay!"

Caroline sat back on my stomach and Emma had a hold of my hands pinned at the top of my head.

It was kind of scary.

"I think I followed him here but really it was more of a mutual thing than anything."

"You liar, he followed you! Come on, tell us everything!"

Another brash moment of serious tickling and a punch to my sternum made me give.

"Okay, alright, shit! It was me, I followed him!"

Slowly they unwillingly released me and allowed me to sit up while feeding one another this mischievous look.

"So you're *only* here for him then?" scratched Caroline.

"Told you," Emma echoed, "She's not serious about having a career but getting a husband."

I suppose such lame thinking bothered some people but the two lassies were wrong. I *did* want a career. I also wanted Jack Charles.

~

"Emery, I really would like you to try and engage a bit more," Susan lassoed me. "I'd like it if you could tell me something, really, anything today, especially as to why you've closed yourself off, particularly as this is our last but one session, considering everything." Musically done, a tiny strand of her auburn hair is brushed sideways. "Look, Emery, will you try and be-"

"Try and be what?"

My response startled her. I usually didn't snap. I usually did everything she asked of me.

So she cards down heavy, "If you want to leave it all till the last session, then that's okay. If you don't want to talk today, that's okay too. I just think you should use the time wisely and make the most of it."

I flounder, "Most of what...what...my last moments with you?"

For goodness sake, why was I trying to rile her? She was a friend, an only friend, and a good one too. Fuck, stop being silly.

"Em, do you want to just sit here, say nothing and stare at the walls for another hour? Do you think that will help anything?"

Well what was anything anyway? Anything can be *anything*, right? This 'anything' to help me stop feeling awkward and help settle my growing nerves and finish this black coffee while feeding you all the words you want to hear? Do I think that will help anything? Oh, Christ, not now! The sky brightening outside called to me. I should be out there, among the clouds, flying with the birds, free as a bird, just let me fly.

~

"Want a drink?"

"Just the one, okay, I've got a test in the morning."

"You'll be fine, kid. Since when have you failed any test?"

History: More of studies that didn't seem fair or relevant as many students thought the writings of past were geared toward the minority rule over the masses. Student Unions plagued with the same old faces that governed with impunity, and when there come discourse, the regulars always seemed to end up on top. Nothing appeared to really change. We went out on protest marches and petitioned the alumni, put signatures to express dissent, and still nothing changed. The same old universities rode the same old corridors filled with the same old teachers and students. Except nowadays there fell a sprinkling of colour allowed in some of the halls as ethnic groups were stowing their shining light, oh, and several of the female kind were attending courses previously dominated by all-male fields. I always thought it strange being among a specified lot why any would want to be the first to challenge the stiff-upper-lip halls that would continue in secret to gnaw and whisper harshly behind your back. Throw them some crumbs, keep them nibbling, we'll still maintain our order. I didn't want to break down those doors, just be unchallenged to open a few of them, like Jack did.

"What's your paper?" he asked, handing me a bottle of opened beer.

"French revolution to Charles de Gaulle abandoning his Foreign Legion."

"Abandoning?"

"Weren't there mishaps during the independence of certain African states?"

"You're writing about *that?*"

"Not all history's grand and all conquering. Some of it's pretty nasty bullshit. In fact it probably all is. We just get taught about how great our country became."

"Boy, you don't fuck about, do you?"

"And you don't have to swear."

"I thought you liked it when I swear?"

I'm smiling, "Only when the time's right."

"And when is that?"

Like now, another passionate evening where his hand, grabbing the front of my crotch so rough it was like a fired canon-ball.

This is when you swear.

The beer bottles dangling from our palms clanged together after he gripped me fierce and flung me against the dorm door and pulled my hair hard banging my head in to the pine-wood panelling. I reached and put my bottle on top the drawer next to my unmade bed piled high with several hardbacks then grabbed hold of his curled strands and yanked his head backward as though I were trying to snap his neck. Tough, he jerked free and we stopped to watch one another. I smiled. He grinned. Now is when you swear, you fuck, fucking do me, and his beer-bottle-holding-hand came swinging down from my mouse-brown locks and slammed hard in to my midriff. I gasped loudly, enjoying its soft-hurt sensation and my open mouth was quickly covered beneath his beer drenched lips hovering doth that brought a heat to the back of my throat. I felt my hit belly shoot wet from between my legs. Jesus, this shouldn't be happening, but God, yes, it was.

"I want to see your cunt!"

He didn't need to ask.

Instantly pushing the bottle between my legs my vaginal lips felt the circle of the green bottled top. Okay, yeah, I didn't want to piss in it but he held it with such accuracy and flaunt that I would not have had trouble doing so. I opened my legs allowing him to do anything and he used his left hand holding me tight against the dorm door, his forearm manoeuvring toward my neck keeping my body still. His eyes stuck to mine before slowly closing then he met my lips with a hurried kiss that cooled my mouth before surprising me by pouring beer inside my jeans front.

What the...?

I heard the thud of the bottle beside my leather booted foot and the next thing was his hand thrusting down my jeans, moving aside my panties to probe my vagina. He knew how to work those fingers. Craftsmanship! My Lord, he saw in to me, felt in to me, and I could do nothing but welcome his desire spread across to my own.

Suddenly he stopped everything.

Now what!

You bastard!

No, I was wrong.

His fiery greens penetrated my browns and he again made me gasp as his wide palm clubbed my abdomen. The brief leave of wind made me shoot further wet from below and he lifted up my checked-shirt to once more palm hard my belly before tearing down my denim to rest at the base of my beer-soaked thighs.

You fucking animal.

God's animal. Mankind's fucking animal. My animal!

My panties were inhumanly yanked down. Yes, they had that *Friday* emblem knitted across them. Mum gave me two sets for my twentieth birthday and they fitted comfortably, so with the smell of beer rising they smelled good too. Jack's smell smelled good. Mingled with beer from the scent of my mornings-washed vagina everything smelt good.

Mm, God's given animal.

Yes, now see my cunt.

~

"I'm not trying to be difficult today," I said honestly.

"Okay," she smiles.

I try to breeze free, "Just that...some things are playing on my mind."

"Things?" she slices in, "You think you can tell me about them?"

Easing the cup from her mouth again, that creamy foam line was left behind. A white cupid's arrow sat blissfully above lips which could hold any ones gaze. Christ, had such beauty been bestowed in me would I have been a successful career woman? But weren't you? What I had wasn't enough. It's never enough, I don't think.

My spike's alarmed, "Am I meant to gather everything up and make sense of it all? I mean, talking with you, spilling life's beans, trying to bring it all together and say done, a final farewell, everything's fixed inside me."

Susan responds, "Some things can't be fixed, Em, but I think most things can."

"So what am I doing here?" I practically snapped, "I should have been fixed already?"

"Don't you feel a part of you has?" she measures surprised, "You came here in trouble and needed to talk. You talked and I think we fixed some things, don't you?"

Some things?

Did I really need an answer; no, but looked for one anyway, "My messed up head?"

"You weren't messed up, Em. Depression and anxiety aren't messed up, they're conditions, illnesses."

"I wasn't depressed," my feeling so, "I wasn't anxious."

"Then what do you feel you were?"

Good question: If having done what I'd done isn't messed up or an illness then what is? What am I? What did I do? What did I *really* do?

"Do you think our sessions were a waste of time, Em?"

I asked Susan to call me 'Em' after our first meeting. The way she said Emery was almost sexual. Like a pretend seductress who cast your name in such a way you only ever imagined having sex. I saw the way she used her words. She probably wasn't getting any so doing this job made up for it. Talk about everybody else's sexual hang-ups and forget your own cos you know that you're getting off on everybody else's - in this - the perfect place to get off on morbid fantasies. We were a rich pool to pick from; young and old, black and white, mad and bad, good and great. The choice was phenomenal. The weird and wonderful all in one place for these *experts* to devour our thoughts. Hell, they could never get bored.

The coffee cooled enough so I downed the lot.

My head was spinning.

I felt a good masturbation was needed.

No dildo, just hands. If it wasn't the real thing I didn't need it. When it has human character, such as the flop, the half-way boned, the veins emerging and that fold of skin; that was something to play with. A stiff painted plastic rod emulating a cock could never be an alternate with me.

Wonder if Susan used one?

"I've learned a lot during my time with you," said filtering something for her to feel good, "I don't regret it."

"But you have doubts about today?"

"No, not really, I'm just not feeling sure about what I want from it."

She consoles, "Try and see it as any other session, Em."

This convention of office dialect I had always objected to. "Session?" said not unkindly, "It was our *time* wasn't it? Session sounds so...formal."

"Okay then," her remedy satisfies, "see it as any other...*time*."

Coating her words with a smile, I smiled back. I was again warming to her. How could I not fail to warm to her?

Chapter Three

The guy's hands were around my neck squeezing the life from me. Fuck, I couldn't get up, I couldn't breathe, and I couldn't shake him off. Shit.

The demonstration for greater equal rights got out of hand. With Christmas holidays approaching the university had grown more chaotic than ever. Protests were held over singles and same-sex parties prolifically allowed, and this new 'uncivil rights' movement was gaining momentum. Rebel-rock-bands and gay-pop-star songs were being played loudly and daily throughout campus. Open sedition, could it be? Social change could take years, decades even, maybe centuries, and so my trying to help bring about this 'new' change I was getting the life choked out of me by this gobby fat git sat astride my torso showing total exuberance as his chubby hands looked to crush my larynx. Well, no, screw that.

I kicked and twisted with no success until I thought I must have succeeded somewhere cos the fat slob was no longer sat on top and I could breathe again after a few turbulent seconds coughing up my guts.

Damn.

Amidst all the pounding and scrapping and some worldly-girls judo-throwing boys over their hips, I saw the fat sod hobbling helplessly after receiving a perfect head-butt right in the face. Well I thought, yeah, though never one for violence, that head-lick was something to behold. The fat lad was further left paralysed with a perfectly placed kick to the groin and he dropped to the ground disappearing beneath a swarm of fleshy, floundering hands, and trainer-dressed feet.

My breath almost back, I got hauled up, soldier straight, and held close to a familiar body: My bloody hero.

"What the hell are you doing here, I told you not to come? This lot are just spoiling for a fight, can't you see?"

Now I could see. Peaceful demonstration marching toward a busy town centre on a Friday night was no place for a budding revolutionary. We were bound to greet hostilities at some point from a booze-fuelled bunch.

"Look, are you okay?"

I saw in to his petrified eyes as he saw in to mine dazed. Just hold me my knight in shining armour.

He crushed me to him and I felt planet biceps caressing my arms. Big strong, Jack.

"Come on, let's get outa here!"

He navigated shoving aside several protesters still engaged in fighting and heralded me to a quiet side street. Instantly there were flashing police car lights and sirens igniting the roads. I knew I was alive.

"Don't do this again, kid, leave that to other people, you'll only get yourself trampled."

I clambered back my breathing and found his searching look. Okay, so I wouldn't do it again and not without him being there and not without having belief in the cause. Well, no, this one *was* a cause.

"Jack, we have to stand up for those who-"

"Hey, I'll come with you, okay! Caroline and Emma ain't no bodyguards."

Caroline and Emma, my friends who were teaching me about the disenfranchised, the downtrodden, the abused, and we, the more privileged, should be helping. Yeah, I get that, but we weren't going to be much good if we got the crap bashed out of us trying to achieve it.

Yes, Caroline and Emma. Hell, where were they?

"Jack?"

I spun round and checked out the melee before my eyes. Police and people waylaying in and I glimpsed my two girl-friends being manhandled among the flailing mess.

"Jack, help them!"

"You stay here!"

Like a maverick-hero from a rebel comic-book he ran in to the mire of fists and feet. My neck would stay bruised for a couple of weeks to come but Jack's tendered kisses and sublime finger strokes took away my reminding of this naïve, ill-judged, Friday night.

~

"You know the saying 'time is money'," Susan fluffed out, "well it isn't here. I won't push you ahead of schedule if you don't think you've had enough time."

Enough *time*, was that our fixed word? It covered a lot of scope and could be our word for these final minutes together. Time! It meant money for some and years slaving over a job most of us hated. It was holding your precious first-born and seeing years disappear down the pipeline as you grew wrinkles, got diminished eyesight, and frail bones. Time: You make it reward-*less* or reward*ing*. Nevertheless, so much of it just seemed to get lost.

"We can extend our time if necessary, Em," Susan begins kind, "that's not a problem. I can put you on a furtherance programme and no one will ask questions that I can assure you. But what I do need is for you to give me a reason, what more do you think you need from all this?"

As she took another sip of coffee I mused a second's thought. If I masturbated in front of her that could cover my needs. I would have preferred to masturbate in front of him but that was not possible.

"Emery, we don't have to reach any final conclusions today, just so you know."

Conclusions, didn't they come at the end of an orgasm? No, that *was* the conclusion, Susan would say. Metaphors, rhetoric, semantics, confusing stuff at times even for my university educated arse. Our campus not being of the elite table but broadened enough to assist early juniors who were sufficiently grammar school finalists: Hang-ups about that sort of trivia made no difference to me. As long as I could say what I meant, that was okay.

My eyes glued to her coffee-cup sat next to some type of hand therapy stress-ball. "So I know?" I ask, as my eyes plane in on that palm-held thing you squeezed occasionally cos you hadn't done an honest day's labour in your whole fucking life. "What would you conclude for me, Susan, if we were done today?"

She smiles easy. Stunning!

"Now you know I can't tell you that don't you, Em? My report will go to the supervisor's office and they'll make their own summary and have it read and assessed by another professional then you'll be made aware of their findings."

"Findings," I feel my ears move, "What's there to find? Did I act maliciously or didn't I?"

For a moment she allows those shimmering turquoise rounds to halo over me. I was no angel. If she had been a man I do think we would have slept together by now and I'd be enticed in to revealing all and show them everything I had up my sleeve and more.

Sly dogs!

This system wasn't here to help conclude and find anything but to keep me down and to stay down.

Findings! Just what the fuck did they *want* to find?

~

"Jesus," I complained to Jack, "the New Testament mixes some of the Old, just not enough for us to figure out this whole translation in to the rights-and-wrongs of certain passages."

"It also speaks of a shitfaced revelation that will consume each and every one of us in the final days."

"Don't you think they're here already?"

Lying on his stomach, Jack turns his head and gives me one of his lasting inquisitive looks. He smooths away some of his curls so I am free to stare in to his eyes. Religion and politics should never be discussed when you're laid on top of a bed: Especially my bed.

"You shouldn't believe every word you read, Em."

"I wasn't."

"Well I think you were."

"Well I wasn't."

"Oh yeah, so you're gonna give me that now are you?"

"Yeah, I'm gonna give you that."

"You sure?"

"Yeah, yeah I'm sure."

Snapping his teeth at me like a crocodile readying to feast, I kicked his legs with my thick lined slipper-socks and it flicks him to land a sugary punch in my ribs so I roll over to prevent him hitting me again but he makes a sneaky angle and hits me right in the gut. After an escaped breath I try not to laugh as he effortlessly roles me vulnerable and sits on top my groin. Grabbing hold the loaded theology book, he slams it shut above my face.

"Give?"

I marry those eyes of his and appear sheep-like, my false *give* soon forgotten as I lash out and slap his chest.

He's outsmarted, "Oh really, Emery?"

"Yeah, Jack, really."

Attempting to take command of my hands I evade his sharp move and grab him round the head pulling him toward me and flip him all the way over on to his back. He's momentarily stunned by my expert body toss and I sit back on his chest, however he easily reverses my take-down and gets on top of me again, this time compelling my ruin and I cannot escape.

"Give?" his second demand, but refusing to answer, I turn my body and wildly scrap to get free. "Emery... Hey!"

My strength surprises him and he's forced to use his-all to effectively pin me down and hold me still.

I felt myself get wet.

"Are you gonna give now?"

Hell no.

But he thinks that I have.

So I sprout him puppy eyes, my hazel saucers, and he releases me, big time turkey.

The moment my legs allocate space I angled my body and kicked him off to fall in a bungled heap by my bed. I'm sure his body thumping the floor alerted the dorm beneath but I didn't care as I foolishly rush him but he's too agile and just picks me up, hurling me back on the bed to regain his dominant position and rips my shirt.

"Oh shit!" my slight alarm but he's simply smiling.

"Yeah," the grinning couldn't get any bigger, "and you'd better frigging give."

Another attempt to make myself free saw him literally take my fumbling arms and fastidiously pin them under my body so I could no longer do a thing.

I struggle, "You big git!"

"My little fuck," wetting his lovely lips over my lain form, "Give?"

Defiant, I shook my head no so he reached over my face and comes back with the seven-hundred page theology book spread wide open.

I watch him carefully.

He was flipping heavy applying enough pressure so I could breathe okay but I didn't like this losing shit and was determined to not give-in.

"You're stubborn, Emery Pearson," making his self really comfortable on top of me, "I like stubborn...I like your fucking stubborn."

"Yeah," I grate, "You ain't gonna like it so much when I fucking get out of this."

Loving it, he keeps on smiling, "Yeah?"

My not so smiling: "Yeah!"

Holding the ghastly thick book in one hand he used the other to ravenously rip open my shirt, along with my bra, and slowly, easily, waved the beast of a book over my left breast.

"You give?"

Shaking my head no, he opens the book right down the middle.

"Give?"

Again I shook my head no.

Unbeknownst, the sudden snap shut of the theology pages clamping round my hard nipple was something totally unexpected.

I cried out.

"You bastard!"

He grinned, this time snapping the book shut across my right nipple and the wetness down my groin increased.

"Jack?"

"Em?"

Christ, how could I admit it was turning me wetter? "Okay now, enough!"

His eyes were having none of it, "Hmm."

To my further delight he opened and snapped the pages shut across each breast this time, firm enough to secrete more juice from between my legs.

How could he do this? How did he know to do it?

I moaned and he simply looked at me. I think he understood because I sure as shit did.

Re-opening the thick hardback, he looked to snap the pages around my nipples again only now he paused, and for a studied moment, just held my glazed expression.

"My little stubborn," he uttered, and spread his tongue to moisten those full lips, "Emery Pearson, my fucking little stubborn."

Was I?

He reached behind and pressed his hand inside my jeans to find *Thursday's* panties and touched my creamed vagina.

I was not ashamed of my wetness.

He again wet his lips and leaned down to wet mine.

~

"Does this thing work?" I asked, reaching for that hand-held stress-ball.

"Yes," Susan answers readily, her eyes eager to engage me, "You should try it."

I roll the bloody thing in my palm and take in all the colours circling it. Lusciously swirled in the rainbow shades creating a Jupiter-style moon within my hand, God-like, putting the finishing touches to a solar-system only I understood. The power afforded the Mighty One could be shared, no? His understanding, his greatness, his all-seeing, could that not afford in me? I could get up and walk out this staid office, take the stairs, leave each step behind crumbling as I go, and after my entrance outside this building, outside the rules and merits and goals, they would crumble with the rest of it bringing about complete erasure of everything avanious that constantly sought to control. Yes, I could at last be me.

Susan shines, "Anything?"

Was she kidding? I rolled the damn ball for a brief moment and she thinks I have all the answers? Yeah, I did, for a second or two. But I wasn't going to tell her, was I? Previously in my world I missed out the part where only Susan James floats up beyond the crumbling walls, a lone survivor in my universe, in my ideal solar-system, in my own everything.

I say to comfort her wish, "It feels relaxing."

"You want it," she beams, "it's yours?"

I grip her eyes and she grips mine.

Did I want this ball of colours belonging to me after I guess so many of her clients had rolled it around their troubled palm? No, I didn't. Her gesture was nice though, or was she attempting to hold on to me in some kind of far-spiritual embrace. I liked the idea of it.

"No, it's okay," I mutter, re-placing the round swirling rainbow beside this four-inch high curving statue made of bronze, and which, if I'm honest, I had always thought resembled liquid mountains. The offer of that as a final meeting gift was far better; another palm-size distraction or attraction, whichever way you chose to see it.

"Thanks anyway," I add.

She checks out the returned stress-ball with this look a little hurt. "I meant it, you know," her followed words.

"Yeah, I know you did," my reply, making to soothe her shot pride.

Christ, don't take it to heart!

Again, she flows, "Emery?"

Why couldn't I just say it out loud? Now we'll skirt around it for another minute or so. Shit, I tell myself, say what you mean, woman.

~

"Do you realise there's a human style detonation equal to a nuclear bomb going off if you were to get pregnant?"

Jack's eyes flick up from between my crotch and I'm upset his mop of thick dark hair has disappeared.

I suspend reasoning, "What, eh?"

His smile spreads wide with a shimmer of teeth from his eating me grandiose whole.

"A detonation," he continues smug, "The creation of life."

"Oh fucking shut up and stop teasing me!"

"I'm telling the truth."

Was he really, did I care? No, I wanted him to keep munching away not raise his big head and start some deep discussion about child birth.

"Fuck it, Jack!"

He grinned even bigger.

"You know your hole leads to something magical, Em."

Yeah: flipping period pain, ejaculations, to brats, and warm fuzzy feelings, so get on with it, will you.

"Aren't you in awe of what your body can do?"

Right now I wanted it to swell with pleasure and spurt a feeling only he himself knew could not be beaten, not by anything.

"This pink thing that you have-"

"Jack!"

He flicked my labial with an accurate forefinger clipping my growing clitoris at the same time, and my word, this millisecond, this blinking millisecond of an incredible explosion smite me. Yes, a frigging nuclear one!

"It doesn't always have to be rushed, you know."

On fucking fire was I that a salt tear entered my eyes and I covered my mouth to stop the sound of crying.

He knows: "Emery?"

My swollen clitoris like a door had been slammed shut on it. Dear God!

"Hey, girl!"

His worried voice smoked around me low and a cry escaped my throat.

That was it.

Peering at my vagina another guy-smile filled out his chock lips.

Before the chance came for me to turn away or say any words, he crashed in to my crotch with a ravenous take of my swollen clitoris that I thought the ceiling had fallen down on us. What then followed was the kind bashing of my devoured pink organ too great to understand or lurch back from, that I burst out tearful as the swelling threatened to leave me of life.

Seizing his mop of great swirls I thrusted his head away. Could take no more, no, I was dying, truly fucking dying.

"Em?"

My crotch burning red, a deep heat penetrated every part from my mid-section down and I nearly threw up.

Jack's manly palm circling my waist stopped me from vomiting as I foetus my frame and could not - no - *would not* move.

"Hey, are you okay?"

Gasping low, I tried to recapture normal breathing for his words could not help, not when I got hit like that, not when I came from a second of blazing hot to ravishing hellfire that consumed my entire being. No, neither when it felt as though a thumping fist had crushed my insides and I fought to find air. No, not when he made me orgasm like that. No, no I was not okay. I was extremely fucking *more* than okay.

Recovering parts of my breathless body, I manage to say, "Jesus, Jack!"

He scrambled aside me and held a palm over my left cheek. "Hey, are you alright?"

His hand is warm.

I avoid this night's saddened green eyes and give him a weak nod yes.

"I'm sorry," he says, "I thought I'd hurt you."

I let tears fall. I did not want to stop them falling.

No, Jack, you hadn't hurt me. I don't think you could ever hurt me.

~

"Look, thanks, but I'm not interested in your stress-ball."

"Okay," Susan, tapering off, "Something else then?"

A present, oh good, more bribes. But it wasn't necessary as she already won me over by saying my forename like that airy sex she brandishes about. Invisible but it was there. A constant no doubt, these special therapists had to be aware of it. Peculiar that bloody word also, broken in two it spelt, *the-rapist*, had to be a peculiar formation. The raping of one's mind, emotions and thoughts, coated over with an open sense of sexuality: The raping therapist.

"Is that bronze?"

I point to her rolling miniature mountain.

"I like that," said I.

Reaching with her right hand Susan takes the statue graciously. She hands it to me and our fingers brush tentative. I solemnly try to keep mine looking graceful but with the cheap nail-files wc were allowed they looked nothing like the super manicured, crimson painted elegance of hers.

I take the statue quick but she captures my hand and closes brilliant fingers around it.

"I never noticed them before," she says.

Notice what, my scraggy extremities after years of unattended trap. Who'd even want to notice!

"We do our best," I mention, trying to pry my enslaved hand from hers, but she, for some unknown reason, holds on to it. So I let her.

"You avoided the dumb-bells?" she asks polite.

I didn't *need* physical therapy, I was in good shape. Or so everyone told me. Having been brought up to eat scrambled eggs and oats instead of sweet-laced cereals for breakfast kept me in shape. A lot of women round my age were similar in structure than the younger, increasingly overweight set. The late Nineties saw a rise in obese generates budding from sugary foods that came out of the last decade. I wasn't about to let that happen to me. Mum and dad kept us active and eating well and they still looked good. So too my siblings, Jamie and Lucas, and I wasn't about to let them down by piling on the pounds just because I was stuck in here. No, I was going to continue looking trim because it caught Susan's eye and I appreciated her noticing. I know I didn't belong among her social-set but keeping trim and healthy was just as good. They owned power and control yet their hidden envy of the seen-lesser-brigade who captured their convenience held power in me. Bet it made Susan feel humbled mooting out that comment.

"This carving was given to me by my father," she lets out, "When I started this job," I'm sure unintentional, "It's usually never come up in a discussion before."

She releases my hand.

"Discussion?" Pretending I'm interested in the bronze statue but I keep her eyes more, "Is this now a discussion?"

She leans back in her leather hand-crafted chair that could match any presidential office making the words sublimely fit for her.

"We were discussing a possible present for you," she says squarely.

Possible present, ah, yes, put a fist between my legs, your other hand gripping my throat, then prance your long hair over my face while your mouth plays about my neck and your teeth leave their impressions searing my flesh. Yes, a present.

"I couldn't take this," I said, "Your father gave it to you."

I peruse the bronze thing and as mentioned before I did like its curving structure and unnamed presence.

"If you like it, Em, I want you to have it."

"Have it? No, no, I couldn't."

"Okay, I'm *giving* it to you."

Now I play around with it in my hands. It's smooth, enchanting, and silken. Silk wove from the perfect web.

~

"He's over there, playing centre-back."

I strain my eyes at Emma's finger-point to see Jack near the back of the volleyball court.

"What's he doing there?" I queried.

"Lanky bastard can get the balls back there, saves a point, you know."

"He isn't lanky," I protest.

Emma comes back, "He's over six-foot isn't he?"

I shift fast to nudge her hips, my contention evident at her debasing of him.

"He should be at the front scoring points," remarked I, as Caroline engages us from her visit to the side-bar with three plastic cups of vodka-orange.

"It's for fucking charity, Em, take it easy will you!"

Several alumni glance horrified at Caroline's remark but she bats them away with a flash of dazzling red hair.

I take my drink and nearly finish it before Caroline makes comfortable and screams with glee as another point is scored on Jack's team.

"You're getting the next lot," Emma scolds me nicely.

Derisory, I glance at my cup and proceed to finish it then playfully crush it in my hand slicing Emma to make a flash of kittenish-eyes.

"Pearson, you're so fucking sexual."

She fondly post-war's me her brown eyes that sparkle with delight through her blonde locks. It was a luscious combination and she knew it too. Fellow students flirted and made no attempt to hide their sexual want of Emma's gamine looks flaunted along with this curvaceous body. Had she wanted to be an escort she would have made millions off either sex, then out of the blue, in an extravagantly deft move, Caroline sweeps Emma's head round and delivers one of those, 'You're mine' kisses to her blonde girl's lip-gloss. Don't worry I wasn't anywhere interested in getting between their sheets although they made no secret of wishing to get between mine.

We had our attentions diverted when the whistle blew and a rushing stream of sweaty bodies hurtled over and smashed in to us supporters sat on the benches next to the court. Jack, among the prime, amateur athletic set, near left my cheek swollen as he measured to kiss my lips.

Show off.

Caroline and Emma ensured they would not be outdone and cautiously held on to their drinks while beginning to heavily make-out.

It was half-time.

"Did you see those cheats?" panted Jack.

My friends saw nothing as they failed to respond while tasting each other's tongues.

He reached for my crushed cup but it was empty. One of his team mates snaked a hand round my head and handed him half of a peeled orange. Starting to watch him munch on the fruit, he continued his watch of my friends' blossom.

"Don't you ever think about wanting to be amongst that?"

He'd better be joking right.

"Everyone loves Emma," I informed him bland.

"Yeah?" he moved to get comfortable as the hassle of half-time provoked, "You want to hear what they say about *you*."

"Say about me?"

The coach yelled for his team to gather round and Jack eased away with a realm-like look while shoving peeled orange in to his mouth.

The git! He says that and leaves me hanging. How unfair was he? I swing round to air my disappointment on my two friends but they were swamped inside one another's mouths busy painting a masterpiece with their loving moves as they entr'acte a growing crowd to pleasingly view the canvass being brush stroked.

Whew! Yes! Everyone just had to love that, hadn't they?

~

"It's a nice offer," I say kind, and meant it, "But I couldn't possibly take it."

Praying Susan isn't offended I carefully place the miniature statue alongside the hand-held stress-ball. Grandeur, they complement each other on her beech-wood desk.

Like her. All four pieces; the desk, the chair, the statue, the ball! One big fucking complement!

Isn't that what all this was?

A big fucking one-off compliment: Yes, you've done well in your sessions, you're showing improvement in your life, you're seeing things more clearly, accepting others, making positive changes. Get lost.

I liked being me. I'm okay being the other me. I like me.

"My offer will stay open to you, Em," I hear her say, using a pristinely manicured hand to re-fix the statue facing toward me. "You can have it anytime you choose while I'm still available to see you."

How nice. I may take her up on that later. We'll see.

Making to leave the half-pound of bronze behind, I re-focus, "Suppose my present is you helping me, you know, all the help you've given me so far."

"I'm here to give you more if necessary."

"I don't think I need any more."

"We have to consider next week."

"Alright, but you said earlier I could take longer if I needed to."

"Yes, we can, that's still open, but I have to plan for next week if things are to conclude between us."

The path we shared lingered to broker an end. "So I should be okay?" I ask succinctly.

Her ears go up like the dog from the TV kids' cartoon, *Rhoobarb and Custard*. "Don't you want to be okay?"

Then I respond like the cat. "I always thought I would be," said matter-of-fact, "Just because I'm in here doesn't mean I'm without hope. I always felt I'd be okay. Walls don't stop you thinking outside them."

She garners me like I've said some prophetic shit. Well I hadn't. Anyone inside this God forsaken place could tell you that. Any one of us could.

~

I thought they were asleep, as lord, I was looking to get there.

Having switched off the lamp on the bedside drawer could they not see I was trying to fall sleep? Wasn't that a bleeding indicator I was attempting slumber or indeed already had? No, of course not, cos two grown women who were busy inside the hot frigging throes of bad-ass heightened sex couldn't give a fig a third party in their dorm room was asleep.

Okay, I was *trying* to get there as I had a busy tomorrow prepping my thesis paper in beautiful order for my theologically presented piece to Mrs Hadfield. I'd completed it and wanted to go over it again in fine detail sharpening anything that may need sharpening. I knew nothing did, it's just that I wanted to re-check, but as soon as I heard Caroline would be returning late from her English Literature study, I believed her and Emma would gossip some before retiring to bed.

Yes, retire late in to the night would be fine not stay up till the early hours and end your wayward selves in to an absolute shit-faced-grunting-fuck. Sure I could, and should, moan sometimes, but I wanted to get good grades all round no matter the blinking class, despite these horny two not believing so.

Now, goddamn it, the gummy smell of marijuana floated across to my side of the room pummelling my senses.

Those two could be annoying.

They could also be riveting.

My tiny digital clock read one-thirty in the morning and I was unable to drift further in to the tired abyss for I listened Caroline go under the sheets to pay Emma an intimate groin visit.

The deep of winter calm ensured one was certain to hear the linking of bedclothes swishing around with two amour beauties beneath.

Their low voices merged in to giggles and kisses, and their touching flesh like white-water-river shifting current so fast I had trouble telling which way up either girl was.

They made a sound different from Jack and me. Not better not worse, just different. It made me think of our sounds, sounds which we made while we understood no one would be around for the next hour or two. Man, we didn't bother Emma or Caroline with our frolics but this duo of girls another code bode, one like the cold-war spies had to mess up the enemy and make sure the read of the situation would be deciphered incorrectly. Well, I'd deciphered these two alright but pretend I hadn't. Could I really rise and reveal my shock at such a brazen display of ignoring all the rules? I was no peeping-tom but I got the feeling they were wanton exhibitionists. And why shouldn't they be? Attractive, maverick, and finger-licking good: Yes, finger-licking good.

Oh God, Pearson, Emma elatedly chastised, rules were meant to be broken, and Caroline would relish grabbing my arms and pin me in a grappling half-nelson happily watching Emma play around throwing punches at my fat-free middle. Yeah, you two break the rules when it suits, I needed my sleep.

After ten minutes of heavy breathing and shit, I swear I could hear Emma say my name or at least whisper it, there then followed a series of murmurings and giggles before that damned medley of female flesh started to vigorously dance again.

I was forced to admit it sounded better than any musical composition I heard coming from violin enthusiast, Benjamin Knowles' room next door.

~

"You were placed in here to help you understand what you'd done, Emery," Susan dishes out naturally, "About what really happened. You at least must come to terms with why you are here."

Yes, of course I understand. It's so I am not permitted thought, unless approved by you, that I have to face up to my crap each and every day and pay for it in provisional time spent with your psyche-analysis and stay closed-away from the world until I admit or figure out what the hell was wrong with me. Did I sum it up properly because I'd hate to think I haven't learned anything?

Her voice sweetened, "Em?"

Me, me, me! Don't show dissent. You'll be crossed off otherwise, so, don't show dissent. If any of this were secretly recorded by the powers that be I'll be screwed. So, don't show dissent.

Ever sweeter called, "Emery?"

I was in a game, *their* precious mind-fuck game, so play by their rules. Just shut up and play.

"Sorry," Susan refreshes, "I know you prefer to be called Em. Sometimes I forget."

No you don't. You like Emery. *I* like Emery. Just that you saying it bears heavily on my messed up mind, right.

Emery Pearson, what has become of you? Once a bright future lay mapped out, a happy home, a good career, a wonderful partner...

I remember the question. *Do you miss him?*

Susan James, Mum and Dad, Jamie and Lucas, my friends and associates, a watching world of peers and professionals...I answer you as before...yes, I miss him.

Chapter Four

"You know Jack Charles, don't you?"

My mouth full of oats and warm milk I answered the query nodding my head in the positive.

"You know he's got a theology test coming up, right?"

I stop taking another spoonful of filling breakfast and watch the young man hovering at my canteen table.

"You've got one as well, right?"

He made me nervous. What our upcoming test had to do with him a complete mystery.

"Well I do too," he continued, "and I was wondering if you'd share it with me?"

I put my stainless steel spoon down and stayed watching this, 'ragged-lead-singer-of-a-rock-band', looking chap.

He comes across surprised, "Come on, Pearson, it is Pearson, isn't it - you know!"

I am now not certain of anything, I know that.

"Look," he slides down his bundle of books and sits opposite me, "I know Jack can get a hold of the test papers so he'll know the answers, right."

Swallowing everything which remained in my mouth I swallowed again that nothing was left before I practically gagged in shock.

Hell, "You what?!"

He threw away bewildered eyes and got serious.

"Come on, I just want to see, I won't tell."

Now I was pissed off.

"What are you on about? I don't know anything about any 'test papers'."

"Look, if I don't pass this test I could get thrown out. My grades are shit and I just need a little help with this one paper, that's all."

Christ, he had to be pulling my leg. Cheat? In theology of all classes, no frigging way!

Pushing aside my unfinished bowl I gather up my books and jump to leave.

But he sears, "Oi?"

The lead-singer snatches my arm and spills a couple of dreary novels I'd tucked among my study work.

"Listen you, you'd better get me those test papers or I'll tell the Dean."

Unimpressed with his lame threat because I knew Jack - nor I - would ever cheat on an exam, and I did not care that several students stopped their chomping break of fast and fiddled to watch two conflicted growing-ups instead.

"Get your fucking hands off me!"

Being from a northern town I was not one to cower from the clutches of a strange male squeezing my flesh a crisis red. No, he had to let go, right now.

So I spray, "If you don't fuck off there's gonna be trouble!"

We both turn and see another male coming for us. He looks ready to sling this guy off of me and stomp a hole through him but I dug my hand free and gestured I was okay putting a halt to any scrap that could ensue.

The lead-singer fervently tossed, "You tell your Jack he'd better watch out cos it's just gonna take one little word for his scam to come out."

I hastily reached down to pick up the fell novels tucking them between my other books and made off to find Jack.

My drilled enquiries to locate him see me enter the boys' toilets with a stride of officialdom and he's surprised - though thoroughly turned on - by my presence amidst his mates before my tirade explodes without any thinking process behind it. I guess the lead-singer got me rattled enough that my first few sentences were brash and harsh and apart from the mortified human screen facing me, Jack's boys cloak hurried from the scene leaving us to unravel the tale.

For tale it was, I were shew informed, as I recalled Jack saving me from Toby and Sean during that scuffle in the lads' toilets at secondary school and I never thought I would be challenging him over rumours about stolen test papers because I never got the chance to press things further as he smiled a delectable smile and viciously snatched my shirt front and commanded himself a witching kiss of my lips.

My foolishly aggrieved thump of his chest went unsigned as I floated in to him and he simply waved control over me.

The following crash-bang of a UPVC toilet door opening then locking shut as the force of my head slapped against the partition wall and my jeans were round my ankles sharing the floor with torn pages from spilled books. As sure as life and death, I forgot the *cheating-on-test-papers* rumour and let my vagina become Jack's focal subject.

~

"Anyone ever tell you you're quite something?"

That had to shake Susan up.

"What do you mean?"

"You know," I lean a tad nearer the crest table and play my right forefinger along the edge of polished wood, "People must fall for you," I try to glean, "you know...give you everything they have emotionally and hope you'll return the favour in some way."

Susan makes her *Susan* smile and I show my teeth.

"We're here to get you ready for next week, Em, and more if necessary, so I don't think my love life is where we should be heading."

Why not, I had no objections?

I stop playing my finger along the lavish wood and sit back in the patient's chair. She always knew what to say and even better *how* to say it, especially my damn name.

"Love life?" said to myself, and she hears, and in her turquoise eyes she wants more.

"Lots of things happen around love," she simplifies.

Beginning to shine I spark for extras then say like I'm some kid, "Are you asking me that?"

The bright glimmer of auburn hair bounces off my hazel pupils. We're re-connecting.

"What do you think, Em? That nothing happens around it?"

Oh, Susan, I know I'm a patient of yours, but really, I haven't been simply twiddling my thumbs over these past few months. The whole world revolves around it: Money, sex, relationships, family, everything. No story, no news, no country could be formed without it. So, love. It covers all.

Feasting do I to investigate; "It would be interesting to hear something about your love life."

She smiles again. I want her to open her closed door and show me *some*thing; reveal a new price to her stunning puzzle that pricks my fingertips every time I try to piece it together. Figuring I get to know Susan then she gets to know me: *All* of me. Even this late on.

"It's not fair everything in this room is one-sided," I said bitten, "You get to know about my life and I know nothing about yours."

The colour of autumn auburn blended summer cooling turquoise, "We're here to talk about *you*, Em, not me."

"Don't tell me you haven't loved and lost, Susan?" I prize in, "Everyone has."

"And you, yours?" she sneakily adopts, "Loving and losing?"

She asks it like I have an immediate answer for it all. Well I bleeding well hadn't.

"That's why I'm here, isn't it," thinking neatly that I've tied it up with that sentence, I shift in the chair feeling more patient-like and a mood comes down; my mood. "My loves and lost," I grumble inaudibly, "here for you to see."

~

Caroline and Emma insisted the rumours be true but had to prove it to me. All I can remember that day was telling some 'rock-guy' to get fucked and then being gloriously fucked myself, so I was not about to let Jack's searching fingers inside my *Wednesday* panties stop teasing the moistness coming from inside me to have a symptomatic chat about test papers.

"Told you," my blonde friend says, "Look?"

Emma's dishy face moved sad as the three of us stood behind a boundary wall casing the back of the gym hall. It lead out on to three sizeable playing fields that produced some pretty decent hockey and rugby players, football not so much, and circling it all was foliage of a great kind; luxuriant shrubbery that stayed blossoming throughout the entire year. The landscapers were renowned talismans and many thought Carlton's luck in the university performance charts ran solely on them.

Wish I could continue to believe that were true as now having heard there *are* cheats floating about the halls fell shameful.

Our trio of maturing youth femmes peered round the wall at the same time; Emma's head on top mine, mine above Caroline's.

Three pairs of examining eyes watch soundlessly as we observe Jack and two other boys flicking through a pile of A4 laminate sheets.

Okay, not conclusive, but their body language appeared dodgy enough.

"What do you think?" I get asked in unison by each of my friends.

Was I unwilling to see the troubled picture after a slight distract 'told-you-so' from Emma's elbow nudging my side.

"Those two have got a test later this week," Caroline whispered, "They're in my physics class, John and Mark. Pair of-"

"How do you know they're the test papers?" I query fast.

Emma gloomily feeds me her eyes. "We just do, Em. We knew you wouldn't believe us so why don't you go over there and ask them?"

"What?"

"Well you're only going to grow more suspicious spying on him, aren't you?"

I nervously bite my lip.

"Love conquers everything," Emma shadily, as the three of us repositioned to stand with our backs against the wall. "He must be good in bed."

Good? He was God. The Great Wall of China couldn't match him for interest.

"Listen," I invested, "I'm gonna speak to him. I have to hear him admit it."

"Admit what? That he was just *sharing* notes with those two? Come on, Pearson, grow some tits will you and go and confront him."

Tits! I like the way Jack said tits. I liked the way Emma said it too. Fuck it. I was too scared.

I check each girl and see they are itching to have me go over there but I niftily avoid their prompting and start to make my way back to our dorm.

"I'll talk to him later," I said turning round and scurrying away before they could emphasise their phosphorescent disappointment.

Jack my wonderful Jack, cheating on test papers? What else would he be doing if he were capable of doing that?

~

Nothing out of place; a therapist's office as it was, always showing the same things every week, every hour, every minute. The only things that changed were your improved, or disapproved behaviour, and the reaction of 'yours truly' being told all. Oh, and a change of clothes. You shouldn't be seen in the same garb each week except for the likes of me though. I had to be the same. Susan adorned attire once wore by I. Tailored cuts from named designers with bright colours foraying, lining the body to enmesh curves in all the right places. Each week she wore different. I on the other hand looked the same in my grey sweats with a bone-white T-shirt sticking out underneath. If I hadn't kept my trim size I would have looked no better than an elephant among sand dunes. No matter the garb, dreary colours looked good on a slim frame so you can imagine Susan's effloresced gear clothing her make up. I'm thinking, five-foot-nine, under ten stone, her auburn hair worn down today so that everything matched superlatively. The navy blouse, white lined skirt, push-up bra. You could tell she thought very carefully about her appearance in front of others. As though this is what we can expect given second chances, the ability to be a woman again, desired, in charge, clean, homely. Most of us could be. I felt bad for the ones who wouldn't.

I learned Jack didn't much care for crisp tailoring. It usually went out the window as he would leave me minus any clothes in an exhaustive heap after creating sex. My designer labels meant diddly-squat then. His hands tearing at my panties or a smelly foot marauding up my shirt like his toes were able to undo my bra, which soon came negligible anyway as he liked me when I didn't wear one, and seeing his sperm stain my jeans was a big headache as the colour wash never lasted long.

Loves and lost, they made you, they broke you. They gave you strength and weakened your senses. You woke with desires and waned when left wanting. Sex wasn't everything but it helped when other things weren't going too well.

~

"I can't believe this shit, I got a fucking *D!*"

"Hey, come on, take it easy."

I chucked him my marked test papers while he lay on top my bed without a care in the world.

Dote complain, "Hey, Em!"

"'Hey Em' what, have you seen this crap, I worked bloody hard for this?"

"I know you did," spoken like making a cup of tea and aims for my midst with a greedy rough hand.

Grabbing my denim waistline he brings me in to a *frisson* take of my middle.

"Listen," he starts smooth, "you can do better next time, don't worry about it, it's just a glitch."

"A glitch?"

Grinning, that slight crooked grin, he reaches up and joyfully punches my chin.

"It isn't funny, Jack!"

"No," he croons, climbing off the bed and controls me backward in to the wardrobe. It doesn't work, I'm not won over; I'm fuming.

"You're not taking this seriously."

"Hey, come on," male simplicity at its worst timing, "one measly test."

Still fuming after that apathy response, I punch him right in the chest and he dips back from my strong blow, a pluck winded I guess but it doesn't stop him from skilfully caging me up against the teak wood. His attempts to regale leave me splenetic.

"Move?! I want to go and see Hadfield."

"No you don't." A leave of breath, he shoves a playful knee in to my groin preening me from escape flirting his face inches from my own.

"Jack?"

"Emery, Emery, Emery," he sings childlike while dancing that goddamn knee semi-hard against my crotch. "You don't want to see Hadfield you want me to fuck you."

"No, you fuck off, Jack!"

"*Em?*" song sung.

"I bleeding well mean it!"

I plan nice.

He doesn't.

With a pause of his dancing knee, he watched mine eyes shone fury before jabbing that limb firm in to my abdomen. I lose a shot of air as he holds the knee there stopping me from moving. Okay, I punched him, he knees me, maybe fair to some, but I didn't think so. Yet why did I casually watch while waiting for my slow intake of breath from his gasping in to my mouth mere millimetres away, why did I let that be?

"Alright," I sash, "I won't go and see Hadfield."

I don't know why but something drives him to knee me harder, a little harder this time and I cough some and bend over before he straightens me up, cups my disturbed face in his hands and messieurs me a smile. I snatch tiny breaths from his approaching mouth. I wanted to recapture my full breathing and he could read this, knew it was my primary, so decided to bury his head under my chin, mowing his shaven jaw round each side of my neck, making me weak, attentive to him, zealous of his actions, and to cater my febrile.

Slow he brings his knee down grating my thigh and plants his right fist between my legs. Immediately I grab hold of his face and he stares in to my eyes. Whatever was going on sensitised my arousal and I pissed feminine gunk from my hole. I was open, aware, and he felt everything.

There were no instructions, no guides, no words to write down and deliver a performance, yet my eyes said something, spirited an emotion, because Jack hit me hard enough in the stomach springing me double then threw me on to the bed.

My test papers scattered as I curled in to a ball and Jack got on top of me rolling me round to face him. I clutched my midriff while he held my knees.

I was okay. He understood I was okay and cautiously pulled me to lie flat on my back before mashing his face in to my jeans front.

~

"You've never said if you were ever married?" I put to her.

A saucy smile breaks. "Would you think me more interesting if I revealed that to you?"

"And make *you* more interesting or me?"

"You're interesting, Em, I think you know that."

"So are you."

She bats her lightly made-up eyelids and says slim, "But you more."

Yeah, I'd heard. I heard through the channels that three other therapists were interested in taking my case: *Three.* That was some bidding. Don't worry, it makes me seem special but I can tell you right now that I'm not. I was no more special than any other person receiving therapy. As far as I understood that morbid trio wanted to explore me, turn me over, and make me something of a freak-show for their unfettered project. I could fill their pages with mind-fucks and leave no stone unturned then they'd write a book, make me out to be some kind of something, express gladdening's or un-gladden, and have a rapacious audience eating the stuff up. I sat no different from most women occupying the damn planet. Read, write, decently cook, wanted a good man, a family, and a safe home. Most women wanted that, I strayed no different, so why did I feel different, and like probably most of the women aforementioned, why do any of us settle for what we never bargained for?

"I never married," she eyes the needle.

Now an un-plucked brow I raise. Tweezers weren't allowed but a visit to the scheduled bi-monthly beautician could be arranged. It was free of course but I never bothered. I got used to my outgrown hairs and thought they made me look younger.

"Why didn't you?" interestingly put.

Seeking to drag this out longer were I. Come on, Susan, take me on a small part of your revolutionary journey. I'm sure it's as creative as you think mine is.

Swivelling in her authority chair she answers, "I just never did."

"Well," fussing to keep it motoring along, "there must have been a reason?"

She muses.

Alright I had a final session next week, maybe more, so do something to please me for a change, will you.

She hears my thoughts.

"I never met the right guy," she explained.

"Or girl?"

A soft smile creates. "You seem a little hooked on the gay line?"

I can tell you I wasn't.

"The gay line," I raided, "No, not me, it's just that in places like this women in your position always seem to enjoy it when other women find them sexually attractive."

Attentive eyes appear accusatory, "Other women?"

"You know," I look to strengthen my fort, "The ones in need of your...so-called help."

She acts as if I've cut her. "You can't really believe you never needed any help, Emery?"

"Help for what?" I challenge, sensing her growing excitement, then rush to say, "For loving someone, needing things, and wanting to be just held sometimes?"

She marks my revelation with an invisible ticked box. Her mental notes must have been extraordinary.

"Must turn you on all these people needing you?"

"No, it doesn't," she responds cool, "It's my job to actually help those who ask for it."

But I knife, "I thought it was compulsory having to do all this?"

"It is for some."

"Oh," my somewhat disappointed, "I thought every head-case had to come and chat with you in order to could get out of here."

"Not everyone's a 'head-case' as you so fondly put it. Some people just need a session or two to make sense of what they did."

"Guess I'm not so special then?"

"I wasn't saying that. Everyone is special in their own unique way."

Makes sense, so: "And my unique way?"

"What you did was unique, Em. Not everybody can do what you did."

And what had I done? Studied, worked, loved, made a home, studied more, worked harder, loved more, and made that home. What had I done? Be born female.

Chapter Five

"You were a twinkle in your father's eye when he taught me to enjoy books."

Books, gah! My mother handing me another of what she thought would be an exciting read of this author named S.E. Hinton. I thought it would go nicely sat on top the pile of *Jackie* magazines already gathering thick dust on top my wardrobe.

"It helps with your grammar and being able to express yourself to others."

Sounded a bit deep to me, bloody hell, I was eight and didn't think I could relate to these two bad looking boys on the front cover of this thin book.

So I object, "Looks rough, mum."

"It will help you understand boys, Emery. Your brother could use with a little understanding."

Err, sorry, I was *eight*.

"You two could get along a bit better and stop pestering one another. I don't want to raise a house full of brats."

She's got to be kidding, right. What two biker jacket wearing lads had to do with my relations with my brother Lucas was a mystery to me. How on earth was this supposed to help me understand my older sibling did not make any sense, but if mum said reading the book would, I had to believe her. She never lied to me, not that I could ever swear to that fact but I don't remember her lying to anyone. I just remember her being honest all the time. And when my friends' mums would lie I found it really uncomfortable. My mum always told the truth and I felt I had too as well.

"It's Lucas who comes in to *my* room and fights with *me*."

"I don't care who fights with whom, Emery, I've told him the same thing and given him one of your Jackie annuals so he's going to read it just like you're going to read that book."

She snatches the pillow that I'm lazily flopped over and fondly bashes me on the head.

"Now are you going to fight with me?" her ask while getting me in a playful headlock but I'm too busy trying to escape and laughing my head off.

Soon, I give up.

"Okay, mum, okay!"

Climbing off my bed she tickles me silly. Defeat felt right with her.

"It's not always good to fight, Emery," she states, fixing neat her clothes, "You shouldn't fight if you don't have to and it isn't very ladylike."

"Ladylike?" my eight-year-old mind tries to grasp, "What's that mean mum?"

Taking hold the bedroom door handle she reaches for simple lines to help me understand. Her tight fitting, '70's jumper and hipster jeans make me admire her, and love it that she's my mum.

"When you grow up you'll be a lady and you don't want to be fighting with anyone. Trust me. It'll get you nowhere in life."

Left more confused, I let her words go as she leaves me to myself. I take the Hinton book in hand. Rumble Fish; It's short, the writing looks easy enough and I'm strangely drawn to the big guy with his fist on his hip painting the front cover. I open the first page and begin to read.

~

Lucas is attempting to be more accommodating of my younger self I can tell. His reading of my *Jackie* annual must have helped or maybe it was mum's fine words that tried to make him change toward me. Our scraps weren't evil they were harmless grapples but he always won and I never much liked that. I never picked on my smaller sister so why should he pick on me? Boys were yuck.

"Mum said you shouldn't go near there!"

Lucas's voice boomed from the top of the spinney as I climbed down the grassy hill to feast my eyes on the frogs in the brook. Mum let us play out late as it was summer and many kids from the estate enjoyed creating their adventures in the nature-rich wonderland. Several robust car tyres, tied with fisherman's rope, hung from super thick tree branches and we'd swing from them all day long. At times we dared each other to swing across the brook and leap safely to the other side. Avoid falling in and getting mud-wet was our *World of Sport*.

I glance back at my brother with a scolding look.

"I just want to see the frogs!"

"Frogs, yeesh, they're slimy."

"No they ain't," with my continued scramble down, "they're interesting."

I end at the bottom and watch the brook's never ending flow, the coloured pebbles and boulders like flickering stars underneath gliding water. Peering as far as my eyes could see I wondered where it came to stop. I never ever made it to the end stream but knew it had to lead to something more magical.

My heightened thoughts were interrupted, "Emery, get back here!"

"No!"

I couldn't get wet, mum would know I'd been at the brook and she would not have approved. I usually did as I was told but it was summertime and I had to see the frogs. I just liked seeing them.

By the time my feet met the sludgy edge and my fingers were combing rushing waters, Lucas stood behind me gazing over my shoulder.

"What are you doing?"

"Look?" I point and we both see a good sized frog pop its eyes above the flow.

"Uuurgh, it's flipping horrible!"

"No it isn't!"

He makes this look like he doesn't get it then grabs me and pretends to push me in beside my watery pal but I brace myself and shove him off.

"Lucas!"

He laughs.

Sisterly telling off, "You idiot!"

"No I'm not."

"Yes you are!"

I'm upset. He sees I'm upset; effects of the *Jackie* annual maybe?

The frog bounces off after noticing our childish play and thinks, 'I'm outa here fast', but suddenly Lucas is drawn to its escape and goes after it.

I don't want him to, "Lucas, no!"

"It's alright!"

Watching with horror, I, as my brother brilliantly tip-toes over huge bouldering stones touching the top of the brook's sinuous spectacle with adroit boy instincts and tries to grab the slippery green reptile. I'm speechless as Lucas slips and falls in to the water then pops back up shaking the wet from his hair.

"Lucas, don't!"

He makes another boy-look at me and continues after the frog as it darts back to the brook's edge seeking to stay free along the bank. No chance. I watch my brother chase it with agility I had not seen before and capture the frog in his hands.

"Lucas!"

Steaming, I watch him struggle steady, hands cupping a large frog and with a more dexterous display gone afore, return to me along the bank proudly holding out his hands.

"Lucas."

"Shut up, Emery!"

I'm told off. He tells me off but it is more than that. I don't feel hurt but feel astonished instead.

My sodden brother does not care his wet clothes and hair will make mum go ballistic for she will know we have been by the brook as he slowly opens his hands and the frog's head pops up between his thumb. I am aghast.

"Lucas..."

He gestures me to take a look so I do.

And I'm touched.

And I'm fond of him.

My brother, the frog catcher, "Told you they were slimy."

I thought he didn't like them, I thought he found them messy, I thought...

Stroking the squishy head of the ugly-beautiful reptile was my highlight that entire summer. And seeing the way Lucas thought so kind of me that day made it extra special.

Boys were not all yuck after all.

~

Although Toby and Sean definitely were!

Those two seemed motherless and after one hurtful day at secondary school in my third year, my younger sister

Jamie said words to me I would always remember: You can't let them win, you have to control them.

Should I?

Seeing that many teenage girls at Montery Secondary were of the 'giggly' set; always flicking back their hair and seeming easier to wound than what was considered normal, like overemphasising slight shoulder pushes, shriek awful cries when a whisper would do, tumble helplessly if a finger-poke hit their chest, and file looks abashed when boys cracked really stupid jokes. Ugh!

My mates though were a fair set. Lyndsey, slightly chubby, could float well in netball, and gifted stamina that outdid mine yet I had the athletic look. Kaz was tall, not really spindly but well-built and could handle herself if a boy dared mess with her. And of course there was Jacklyn, who all the boys secretly fancied yet she wasn't interested in any of them. All four of us, thirteen-years-old, were a budding bunch who held our own. Still, there lingered Toby and Sean who got their kicks looking to upset us and sometimes they managed it, other times we shook them off or embarrassed the hell out of them. Boys blushing were a sight to behold especially when it came to those two.

I hadn't played it safe one home-time while awaiting Jacklyn and Lyndsey who received thirty minutes detention because they overreacted throwing a friend of the aforementioned duo, Mark Gibson, across a desk during Music. The ensuing melee saw the teacher, Mr Hill, part the three pupils and instruct my two friends to wait for him outside the Headmaster's office, hence their following detainment. I never got the chance to tell them I would head home so decided to wait at the rear of school and we'd all trek back together.

Too young, my naivety were shown by having to cross the boys' schoolyard to find a quiet spot left me at the hands of Sean, Toby, *and* Mark. The three boys were looking to exchange words with me concerning my mates' unruly behaviour during identifying the gentle sounds of an oboe amongst the other loud brass musical instruments.

Listen, it wasn't me for godssake, I tried telling them, I had nothing to do with humiliating their third-year friend Mark, but sure as shit they didn't give one as Toby and Sean grabbed each of my arms fixing me like plaster to the wall. Yeah, I knew I was going to get it but they really didn't need to go as far as they did. We were third and fourth years and I understood you could be influenced by stuff you saw on TV, still, that didn't mean you had to try and act it out yourself because it was never really the same. It was worse. People in TV-land acted, and Sean standing by my right before immersing a fist inside my stomach, I knew this wasn't acting. It gave licence for Toby and Mark to deliver the same and I could not prevent a bleeding thing as they took it in delirious turns to hit me again. I tried to cover up but Toby and Mark shackled my arms and Sean punched me in the face. Talk about overkill. With that I sunk like an anchor to the ocean floor and that's when my mates showed up. I didn't see Jacklyn or Lyndsey out-hassling the sadistic three but I later heard the boys took a day off because they were damned by the R.S.V.P. nose-bleeds my mates gave them in reply to their beating up of me. After the episode I tried to make sure I was not alone around those lads but had the super Jacklyn and Lyndsey watching my back. Sometimes it worked and sometimes it didn't, however the following year when Jack Charles intervened, I never got hurt either by Sean, Toby, or Mark again.

~

Despite their messing up the three boys, I thought Jacklyn and Lyndsey were really cool and really 'ladylike'. With flowering appearances they could handle themselves and still command a proper lady's presence. I wanted to be like them. Unafraid, tough, and yet still be a lady. Mum would approve, I know, and I couldn't lie to her she were able to tell so I kept shtum about any tussles at school; my black-eye that day the result of a hard fought netball match. I couldn't let them win, spoke Jamie, I needed to control them, and my sister's words would come to mean so much.

~

Lucas got wind of things and wanted to smash all three lads but I convinced him to stay off and let me handle it. In the end I handled nothing as it was usually Kaz, Lyndsey, Jacklyn and me, who did.

Our girl-quartet was like a light sweeping round school. We held out more of a spark through channelling high academic scores and good character reports. Nothing skewed us and nothing got in our way we couldn't manage which spread a telling of stories teenager-embellished that we became giants for the impressionable youngers. From afar the four of us sensed murmurings admired as we were also of blossoming nubility. Jacklyn had it in abundance though never flaunted it. Others mothed to her and some were insanely jealous. Dislike snapped at her heels, but she showed no Achilles with an open apathy I wish I had. Kaz and Lyndsey graced ease with confidence and if honesty were truly open, the younger ones wanted to be just like my three; so did I. Thinking I measured a table of stats beneath my mates, it took one afternoon of frolicking about during a game of Rounder's that my three friends laid bare it were *I* they covertly liked and adored and respected. Among the display of whacking the ball and making full runs round the posts, it was casually mentioned I unknowingly owned a level of control they each sought. And because I had no idea what they were talking about, I forgot all about it until my first meeting with Susan. Every adult exhibited control, just that some knew how to administer it and others didn't.

~

The '80's popstar posters on my wall I started to take down. Their music I still listened to, however there was something in me amiss. Turning fifteen and seeing Jamie become thirteen, I felt a duty to teach her all I knew about secondary education and the highs and lows experienced. My sister was a best mate and she could have my posters now. I didn't need them. I needed something else.

Words were becoming proviso and so were my feelings. Something was happening to me at night and it was beginning to dominate my thoughts.

I had not dated anyone. I had no boyfriend. My mates and my family took up much of my time, but sod it, there was a part of me missing. Before another dawn broke, I reached up to touch that something missed but touched nothing and could not find what I was looking for so I touched something entirely different instead.

As far as I could tell, my breasts were the same size as Jacklyn's, yet I wore a bra and she didn't. Mum gave me one at fourteen saying they would droop and leave stretch-marks if I didn't start holding them up. I owned three pairs and contemplated suggesting Jacklyn have one but decided not to. Elders, boys and girls alike, always ogled my friend's form and I thought she was an idol. The long viewed historic books in the library of marbled and porcelain statuettes left powerful images, as did my mate's budding frame, and all the while my thinking I could never leave such a mark, I was unwillingly doing so.

~

"You going camping with the school this year?" my dad's ask with a lovable glance from over the sofa.

I'd just put down my schoolbag and was shuffling around to take a look at our latest homework.

"You didn't go last year," he noted, "Thought you might want to think about going this spring."

Look, I'd enjoyed it when I was twelve and thirteen but soon got tired of it. Mm, I was no more keen on seeing semi-naked fellow pupils prancing about and teachers aiming to cook pork sausages over an open fire; Nah, no more my thing.

So I lovingly inform, "Me and Kaz were thinking about going to a sports convention in Birmingham, dad," without saying of sorts I had grown out of camping. He liked us kids going camping. He thought it made us youngsters be better adults. Not sure how he figured that. "It's more interesting," I say, "and there are older kids there."

His heart lurched, "Older kids?"

Practically jumping out the sofa he scrambles over the arm of it and reaches me inside three unbalanced steps gracing a look of absolute horror. It was a sports convention and my lot liked sports; come on, it wasn't a pornographic attraction.

He mutters, "Who with?"

"Dad, there's nothing to worry about, it's just Kaz and me, we'll be fine, it's on a Saturday and we can catch the last train back."

Fingers-crossed my information helps him settle.

"You haven't given me much time, Emery."

"It's next month, it's no big deal."

"Are any teachers going?"

"No, dad," my growing limp, "it's not a school thing, just us two. Please say I can go?"

Dad-eyes certified bad territory and I understood his worry. Girls alone, boys would be there, adults parading and advertisers cruising. This was life. This was the Eighties. No more was it *his* time.

"Wouldn't camping be better?" he seeks desperately.

Oh God, no, I squirm, my mind tracing back to adolescent behaviour. Watching little weenies as the boys went skinny dipping with us girls poking fun at such a fruitless portray of the next generation's discoveries was extraordinarily boring. Older and exciting people were a train ride away and I wanted to see their sweaty bodies and massaging hands knead and console sore muscles.

"Dad, I don't want to go this year, I'm fed up with it. I want to go to this sports thing with Kaz."

His eyes appear to loosen but I couldn't reveal my real desires for wanting to avoid camping nor why I really wished to be at the convention.

The wandering hands inside camp tents was a mucky affair and could get strangely twisted with the self-discovering open to being exposed to anyone surreptitiously wandering about. At least the sports convention meant I could exorcise some of my demons with a short work-out.

"You really don't want to go?"

Mopey, I sort through a couple of notebooks I need for homework and pick up my schoolbag.

"I'm not going camping, dad, and if I can't go to the sports convention then that's okay as well."

In a huff my turn to leave forces him to take a hold of my arm. I did not want his concerns or his prying.

"Something happen at camp?"

"No, dad, I'm fine, everything's okay."

"But...you'd tell me if something's upset you, right?"

"Really, dad, there's nothing wrong, I'm just bored with camping and prefer to go to this sports thing instead."

Fathering, he makes my eyes and smiles semi-comforted. God, we could be a soppy pair at times.

"Go on, get upstairs," he smiles, "Do your homework and you can go to that sports thingy like you said."

With a teenage 'whoopee!' and careful to avoid dropping my school luggage, I hug him big and kiss his cheek before bounding excitedly up to my room.

~

Jamie mentioned some girls in her year were becoming bothersome and slowly admitted she didn't want things to get worse despite believing she could fight each of the menacing four one by one, but together, that was out of the question. She feared they would gang up on her and I did my best to comfort letting her know that mum was a rabid dog when it came to confronting bullies.

Mum tenderly stood up to dad when he wanted to watch golf and she wanted to see the music festival highlights. Her being a woman saw nothing she could not meet exact as a man. Don't get me wrong, it was never aggressive or nasty like, it was firm and conducive and she always expressed herself well. So, no, you couldn't push her around.

Nobody should be pushing around my sister either, spoiling her right to be a free-living schoolgirl or have her educational days be an un-lanced boil. Bullies were the Black Plague and needed lancing by having their heads removed with the guillotine. Unladylike ponderings, my mum would have reprimanded, so I had to be careful. Firm and conducive I couldn't do. Not like mum did anyway.

Seeing the anxiety in my sister's eyes I suddenly embraced her in a warmth laying, older sibling protection. Then I remembered my three good mates. Kaz especially, after her winning move over me at the sports convention, I duly thought it required to be passed on to those in need of confidence.

It was that memorialised Saturday afternoon at Birmingham's NEC where we crossed over to the wrestling stall and watched these videos playing on this stylish VCR, that when the instructor pressed *'pause'*, you could see precisely what he was aiming to reveal. Some of the moves were hypnotic so his offer to show a brief lesson - to which Kaz promptly volunteered - was spellbinding. I thought Jacklyn should have been here as she was intrinsically good at fighting but this wrestling stuff offered a special discipline, and seeing Kaz don with this fit guy was unintentionally erotic. Many of the spectators were mesmerised as he showed my mate several holds and moves and how to affect a winning pin. Listening to Kaz's heavy bouts of breath and shine of sweat on her forehead told me she was working bloody hard and after a good ten minutes he offered someone else a go.

Of course I jumped before anyone was pushed and what he showed left gasps and deep breathing of my own. Then Kaz and I were thrown together to see who would come out on top and without wanting to concede the better person won, Kaz in fact did.

I remember frantically hauling her around but she easily countered my moves, happy to sling me about and make the winning pin. Why the hell couldn't we learn this stuff in school? I began to think it belonged right up there alongside Maths and English as it left me with a discipline I would share enthusiastically with my sister.

~

"Have you seen Jamie, Emery?"

"Isn't she in the back?"

Watching mum crane her head out the kitchen window she appears rightly concerned.

"No, she's not there, she must still be heading home from school, go and look for her will you."

Evade of say anything anxious I head out to search for my sister. I knew about tough times at school and didn't want to panic mum.

It isn't long before I find Jamie down an alley, crying profusely, sitting against graffiti laden concrete walls. Shit, I get over to her fast.

"Jamie, what is it, what's wrong?"

There's tizzy in my voice and I try to stoke in calm. My being upset would make Jamie more so.

I sit beside her and make out everything is okay as I am here and she will come to no harm. My poor little sister is weeping some and she finally lifts her head to cover me. Sad little light brown eyes nail my hazel ones and I instantly notice we are our mother's borne.

She is the tail end of us, "Emery?"

"Hey, come on now," I mildly coat, "you're safe, you can tell me what's up?"

Trepidation swarms as I wait to hear the four bully girls have beaten up my sister but I am left astrophysical by my younger sibling's account.

During hockey they had made a series of questionable swings with their sticks leaving my sister's shins a bit sore, so after showering and heading home across the sport's field, the four banes legged it after Jamie to administer a bit more soreness but she astutely stood her ground and offered the biggest one out; the group's bashaw leader who looked somewhat bemused by the challenge.

Jamie was clever. No eye-gouging, no hair pulling, no kicking, no biting, just everything else till the first one gives. And amid jokes with feathery teasing, the group leader went ahead thinking it was going to be damn easy, however her twisted wrist, bruised elbow, and dislocated shoulder said otherwise.

Fuck.

My little sister was crying because she had seriously injured the girl and couldn't get over what she had done.

~

Naturally I lay off the wrestling techniques and shied away from sports for a while. I concentrated on lessons and getting good marks as I saw my brother heading off to college seeming to have an exhilarating time.

He would arrive home with a bunch of stories that were thrilling and filled with enthusiasm I had not noted previously. He was maturing, dressing sharp, and packing out like those action-series actors on TV. He was becoming a perfect gentleman.

Liking what I was seeing, I welcomed his gesturing and explanations of events at some of the more intriguing college classes. There was much to discover and I knew I had to go too.

"Mum, if I do well at college can I go to university?"

Her eyes are resplendent.

She folds up the dishcloth and promptly slaps it down on the kitchen sink's edge.

It's the start of summer '85 and my finals are coming up at school. The year's gone well and even I'm impressed with myself regularly assisting my mother doing her motherly things.

She keens, "You'll be the first in the family if you do go."

I see her delight in being proud but I wasn't looking to make her proud or be boastful, I simply wanted to go as I'd been injected with an incentive to find out further. After such magical times with my school friends, I was disappointed they were showing interests in getting married and starting a family. I wanted more.

"You do well at college, Emery, I'm sure universities will be eager to have you."

My green light!

Go, study, show willing, and learn. Grow greater, farther, and mature. My new world waits.

"I'll be living in the dorms, you know," I hoop mum, like I am there already so she needs to start preparing to get used to missing me.

"Emery, you haven't got through college yet," quickly putting me in my place, "We'll think about the dorms after, okay."

I shake my head though I know I will be going. Nothing is going to stop me after seeing my brother grow the way he did and I thought stopping his education at college level was crazy. There were vast amounts to discover and he must have been insane to leave it all behind in his approaching last year.

Of my inquisitive self I dig Lucas later that night after he lets me in to his room. I can see that I'm asking too many questions while laid next to him on his bed but I didn't care and kept on going.

"What about technology studies, exploring tech-drawing and designing buildings and stuff, what do they call it, architecture something?"

"Becoming an architect," he says, growing tired of me, "And anyway, that's usually for boys."

"Oh gross, girls can do it too."

"Girls can't do everything boys can."

I'm ready, "Oh really?"

"Yes, really, my dear little, sis," said rolling across to me, and he thumps my upper arm a bit too hard for my liking.

Impetuous I hit him back and he gives me this, 'hold-on-a-sec-look', and decides to hit me again prompting us to embroil in this rough-and-tumble match that sees him clearly outdoing me. College strength in a robust young male out-winning the slender needlework schoolgirl, and as one who does not enjoy losing, my short-term wrestling moves kick-in because I remembered everything and furnished myself round the back of my brother and delivered this disabling choke-hold.

I don't realise my own un-channelled strength until Lucas is desperately clawing at me and his sudden angered pinch in to my right side is crippling indeed, so I finally release him.

"You cheat!" I holler.

But he is literally beside himself, "Shit, fucking hell, Emery!"

He gags and splutters and hits me annoyingly on the leg then scatters off the bed. I make to go after him but he flexes out a hand maddeningly demanding I stay put.

I do.

I can see he isn't happy.

"Jesus Christ, sis, don't you ever do that again!"

"Do what, you hit me!"

"I was flipping playing, you idiot, not bloody beating the frigging crap out of you!"

Shit, I recede. I fucking recede and feel every pore breathe apologies in abundance.

Lucas, I'm sorry.

"Don't you ever do that to anyone," his cough, "do you hear me?" another cough.

"But Lucas, I never meant-"

"Just say you *won't*, Emery?!"

Rubbing his neck I absorb his sorrow at my manhandling of him and are left devastated. Christ, I just wanted to hide.

"I didn't mean it," my cry, rushing toward the bedroom door, "I'm sorry, alright!"

Upon hauling it open, Lucas comes up fast, spins me round and takes a firm grip of my arms. I never expected this and wanted to break free and flee to my room but our sibling eyes hold in a conveyance from him he's gravely concerned and I identify it with my easing shame. How could I have done that to my brother even though it was my first - and last ever - win against him during playful combat?

"Bloody hell, Emery," galling *and* thoughtful, "You can really hurt someone doing that shit."

"Lucas, I'm sorry! Please don't tell mum and dad."

"Tell mum and dad?" He feeds me these quizzical eyes while releasing his grip. "Are you silly, I wouldn't tell them about that, just don't do it again, you nearly fucking knocked me out."

Not snitching to mum and dad I'm eternally grateful so blind him with a heart-stopping hug.

"Hey, get offa me!" Toying, he forces me loose and holds me at arms-length. "Beat it, go on get outa here! We'll talk more tomorrow about college."

He potters me a morose smile then gentlemanly opens the door and usher's me out.

Turning round I meet the door close in my face and say again through it, "Hey, I'm really sorry, alright."

He opens it several inches and tells me affectionately, "Piss off."

Chapter Six

Usually we can say what we mean to most people. Few make us insecure or unable to ask for what we want, and yet, truth be revealed, we can't ask, or be even seen to ask for what is deeply buried inside our souls. Well, most of it tends to be tabu and knowing truly it is too troubling to dare venture in, who were we really?

Forever are my thoughts about honesty without flaw. Who's to speak openly and not suffer scarification for daring to go against the grain? I mean, once outside, spilt from all the other ingredients, you got mopped up and were never allowed to re-join, so, how come?

Unanswerable questions, dear Emery, unanswerable, some dear learned would say. Probably why many of us are in here in the first place, no opportunity to be real, a different mix diluted among the regular set. When you were different you were different, even as you tried not to be, you were. It would always show itself, mum said.

~

Already *different* from my old school friends I headed to Somerfield College clasping a cool, stylish sports bag packed with paraphernalia to get me through that first day. Classes sorted, I possessed all the books relevant for each subject seeing me prepared and raring to go.

I mustn't show confidence as it would turn others off and I did not want a bad start to my new educational life. I was already missing my school mates and had to be assertive about making new ones. It would be a blessing if I could meet another trio as rewarding as Jacklyn, Kaz and Lyndsey. Understanding I shouldn't try to emulate my school years, I secretly wished that I could.

Heading to the reception desk already sensing a few of the other newbies and veterans eyeing me salaciously for I oozed assuredness with my strong shoulder bag, model figure, and dare I say, okay looks. My jeans fit well allowing room for my legs to breathe, and the simple black jumper over my cream-coloured cotton shirt showed even simpler appeal.

I was no big-head but I admit it felt good being watched by this curious older-set.

Innocently I receive a hard bump as a chief bunch of students make my crossing and one of them turns round to courteously offer an apology.

"Hey, you went to Montery Secondary, didn't you?"

Breaking my stride I lay open wide eyes upon another mature, male-actor-type. It's him.

"Err, yeah, I did," all coy and suddenly sixteen-years young nearly seventeen-years wise.

There is no break in his happy stroll as he smiles briefly and says, "Good to see you. It's great here, you'll enjoy it. I'll see you around, okay."

Jack Charles was gracing the same college corridors as me. Well I never, I truly never.

~

"Not being free to be who you are could make anyone a head-case."

Susan's psyche-eyes propel outside of her face. I've done and got her frazzled once more. It's as though I have dismissed everything good she ever brought to our off-balanced table.

Yeah, I seem okay with that.

"You're blaming being prevented from being who you are on what happened?"

"Well, it plays a part doesn't it?" asking my therapist such obvious questions, "Having to act about everything all the time, it's got to start hurting?"

Susan does her heedful shift then selects a pose of that neatly attired honed frame of hers. Deep stuff's coming.

"How do you think you were acting, Em?"

The navy blouse clings nicely to her torso and I'm thinking of ripping it off her just to glimpse that shapely form. Yeah, I'm beginning to think weird, and I'd let her beat me up, alright.

"It's like being married to the wrong bloke, I suppose," explaining my patient-log, "Faking love your whole life, knowing you've wasted it marrying the wrong guy. Imagine how that must feel?"

"But did you?" she questions healthily, "Did you stay with the wrong guy?"

"No," I brush off easy, "I knew I met the right one...just that there were...surprises along the way."

She rubs a pensive palm over her thigh, "Like?"

"Stuff like you never expect," I make out, "or feel you should have to do because of..."

A smile fills her face; a lovely smile.

"That can be said for all of us, Em, don't you think?"

She moves slew-like to the left arm of the chair and throws her right leg up to dangle across the left thigh. Don't know what to read in to it but I open up some.

"Surely you made the wrong choices too," I lay out my sleek Indian rug to her, "Like being sat here instead of a privately owned office for the paying few who could afford your services. Doing this could have been wrong, no?"

The smile stays.

There's no way she would let that leave me not while we commanded each other's presence.

"I want to be here, Em," coriander stated. "Private practices are as rewarding and we all want what's best for our patients."

"I don't believe that for a second," my come back to her, for distrust in her words was emphatic, "Private idiots play out their pathetic drug-fuelled weekends, affairs of the financial heart or some boring hedonistic emotionally detached story about nothing." I lean forward and catch the neat fold of her blouse over the skirt's belt line. It's precision alright. "You don't want to listen to that heartless garbage day in and day out, you lot come here to get all the gloss, glory, and mental craziness. That's why so many of you do this type of work. It's exciting and filled with people conundrums you just can't help getting wet."

Oh no. I say something unintended and close my eyes at this growing weakness I feel. Shit, that was really foolish.

"We don't *get off* on the stories you tell us, Em. It's not our job to be aroused, we're here to help you figure out why you did what you did and help you understand not to let it happen again."

"Happen again? You can't be sure anything won't happen again."

"The therapy can at least *try* to help us stop those things happening again."

"So what, so that I can be let out of this place I have to explain to you what makes me tick, what hacks me off, and why I did what I did?"

Stop! You're getting upset. It's just the fold of her blouse over her skirt line, nothing more. She's a flipping dame for godssake, not a guy, and not someone you want to do that to. She wasn't Jack.

~

Looking over my weekly schedule I notice I would not be willing to make any 'socials' in my first few weeks at Somerfield. It would be spent getting my head down and off to a sprint start. Beginning slow wouldn't be good for I knew I could get side-tracked with the flurry of activity inside the college. There were political groups, academia ones, girl-only and boy-only meetings, and a nihilistic set for becoming the next generation of successes. An unhealthy introduction to the ways of alcohol and drugs awaited the vulnerable, because when you thought about it, combining the two would not a great mix make.

While staring at the meetings board a hushed voice encroached.

"Thinking about going to any of them?"

What a lass. She came straight from the Edwardian college building in a time when Edwardian females wore the insistent docile look. A pretty little damsel she was with her hair wore up like a princess and donning a frilly-edged jumper that would have made her a bulls-eye in any given working-class neighbourhood. Definitely grammar-school naïve as an unpleasant world waits to devour her wiles.

Stealthily I check her more and say, "Yeah, I might," her wandering eyes cross over me tying up any curiosity and I ask, "You?"

Shrugging her racy-core, she answers, "Maybe."

I feed her my chummy inviting smile. "What do you fancy?"

Her quick scan of the notice board, I am absolutely convinced she just speed-read every damn meetings poster, she turns and faces me. I'm a couple inches taller than her and I sense she likes that. Make-up free, her Edwardian-style reaches out genial.

"The new-thinking group," she gushes.

Wow, how did I know she'd choose that? Poor blot could be read a mile away.

"Nah, not me," I turn my face up. "I'm going to go to judo."

Her eyes light like fire-rules. She clearly hasn't met a female who can make such a masculine-free choice.

She flushes over, "Really?"

"Yeah, why not?" me blithely: "See if it's any interesting."

"Judo?" she blinks.

I leave her another smile before turning to walk off and she leaps alongside to question me.

"Yeah, but judo?" said gobsmacked, "Girls doing judo?"

"You fancy rugby instead?" I bounce back.

Appearing more shocked she embraces her disbelief at my wording.

"Oh, you're just pulling my leg," with a giggle.

I could see we were chalk and cheese. Opposites gave you a broader understanding of life, mum once said. Staying among the same mode of thinkers kept you narrow-minded and ignorant of others. Told you my mum could be magical. So I share my magic.

"You ever think about what you'd do if you were attacked from behind?"

Left more disbelieving at my fine example, her Edwardian head could never contemplate such a thing. Really!

Don't know what came over me but I grab her frilly jumper and toss her neatly over my hip carefully controlling her to the granite hard ground. I didn't want to see a scrape made on her fragile being.

With her on her back and looking up at me in absolute horror, I realise I made a big mistake until she plaits me this confederate look. The large smile which follows is a thing to behest as I figure I acted inanely and embarrassingly reach to pull her up.

"Wow!" She's aflame, and this heat bellows out from under her, "That was amazing!"

Grinning, we ambitiously introduce ourselves and sure as hell my new friend Carla attends judo and I go to new-thinking group.

~

"Do you think you can talk about it?"

Of course I could. I would too if it were maybe someone else sat before me. Women were the least to understand other women. Come on, they prejudged, gossiped, blamed other women for their men cheating, hid gross jealousies of the better presented, and hated growing old. We were our own worst enemies.

I try to stay fresh as Susan enters, "About what makes you, Emery...sometimes tick?"

She wasn't able to grasp it, I believe. It's all talk in these places to be arrowed with a merit or two, to get oneself a ticked box that allowed greater autonomy here and there, even perhaps awarded the indulgence of watching a major sports event on TV. It looked good for these mind-professionals and yet knowing they had not truly rooted out mental fuck-ups, for fuck-ups stayed fucked-up. Medical reference interpretations could never be accurate across the board. It was all bullshit as far as I was concerned, and you - the patient - simply had to go along. Most of us would fit nicely in to any category given star-aligning and upbringing, and our tastes would not vary so much if you looked real hard: Because if you looked real hard, only a greater being were capable of such grandiose understanding.

"You didn't answer me," I replace polite, "When I asked why you never married, you didn't answer. I've got a funny feeling you know why, and it's probably similar to what I would say for what makes me tick."

Sliding back in her leather chair I am again making her acquaintance.

My page I turn.

"We all have something that makes us tick!" my fun-start, "and for most of us it's the usual shit but for some..." I see a quick narrow of her beautiful eyes as her mind opens. "Like you, Susan," I ponder proud, "You never married because your sexual interests aren't the usual shit."

Oh yeah, I know it's not as simple as that but somewhere in between, I know it is.

"You have a theory, Emery?" she said, corking a smirk.

Yeah, I've got a theory, thinking to myself, I've got one on everything, and I'm quickly moving to annoyed.

"Marriage would get in the way of all this, wouldn't it?" I declare to her un-mirrored. "I mean, where would you be able to command such authority in any old job with a married life clamping at your heels? This is what you married, this is your sexuality, all this...this...being in other people's heads and fishing around, cos if *married* meant all this to you - you would have done it long ago."

~

The first time he touched my lips I stepped out from the new-thinking meeting during late October of '85. He purposely waits as everyone is leaving the cramped room while mincing stealth chattering's with their fellow students. Many are focused by his whim and articulation and you can see some just want to be his friend.

I step out aside Carla and she's prepared to jump all over me with the *feminine-movements* night's discussion but notices Jack hastily disengage an older girl student and head straight toward us.

As first time newbies he wanted to see what we thought of it all.

"It was interesting," I break before Carla. "I like the stuff you're thinking of exploring about growing female empowerment. It's new, I like that."

My friend shuffles her Edwardian persona and coyly allows us room. For her, it's awkward.

Appearing chummy he wets his lips then links Carla's look. "How about you, what did you think?"

Like her very first meet of the opposite sex she batters her eyelids and I could have burst out laughing but I get her un-assuredness. It was like having a baby sister all over again.

"It was good," she fixes. "I think you're going somewhere with this, so yes, it was really good."

At her he smiles an uneven smile and I want him to give me that smile too.

"Hey, you girls want to go for a quick drink? The student bar's still open promise we won't keep you up late."

Immediately Carla shakes her head dismissing any haste of needing to get further acquainted. I, needless to say, wanted to get down there fast and delve in to more new-thinking. It was Jack and three other bright-fixed students who'd come up with this meet and it was starting to gather huge interest, both good and bad.

"Oh, we'd love to but Carla and I have an early class tomorrow, so...best not."

He drops us both this huge grin and turns specifically to me, thumbing my chin and brushing a forefinger across my lips.

"Okay then," he sings, and after heading off, "Some other time," before spinning back round to add, "Glad you're both coming to our meetings."

Needless to say Carla is stunned by Jack's leaving motion and I think she's about to faint.

"He touched you!" she shrieks quietly, "Oh my God, he *touched* you!"

To hide the glowing red warming my cheeks, I take her hand and playfully yank her by my side but she reacts as though she's threatening to commit a judo throw so we mess about a bit and she ends up grabbing my arm pulling me along to shake off my embarrassment.

Yes, he touched me and I didn't mind him touching me.

~

I've been punched a few times during my up-and-down life so I knew what it felt like, and after witnessing Susan's reaction to my words, was equal to her being punched. Some say you weren't alive if you hadn't been punched. Layman's psycho-analysis for every other life not being perfect from the get-go but ending up a total misery on someone else's plate.

"You're stating a non-fact, Em. It isn't the same for us all, whatever we choose to do as adults."

"For us all, we're here aren't we? The restless and abandoned because we, us here, decided to do things differently. Well I did things differently and look where I winded up. I guess when you choose to be different you end up in places like this."

"You make it sound like a conspiracy," she swats down.

"Isn't it?" I rise, not about to be held inward. "You step out of the norm you become a target for the authorities. They have to bring you back under their control, don't they? And this is one holy way of doing it."

She orally prods me like I've slashed her wrists, "I can't believe you think you should have got away with what you did. You can't believe you didn't need any help and shouldn't have to face up to it?"

"You say I have to deal with it," pulling back the knife free of her flesh, "I say to you, deal with what? I cannot stop being this woman that I am. Why should I try and be like everyone else, I'm me...I'm just not you."

She rolls out this body movement that makes me want to climb all over her. "I'm not asking you to be me, Emery. I'm trying to help you understand having done what you did doesn't stop you being who you are but to stay within society's law, even *your own* law, not to do it again. You're a smart person you must know it was wrong."

She calls me a smart person not smart woman and I wonder why. Perhaps by being a woman I should never have done what I did. How could a woman do such a thing? Had I been a man it may not have been so frowned upon. Either way it did not matter. I'd done it and I knew it was wrong.

~

The very first time he lit a hellfire beneath me I could have swallowed every drug on the planet. The sheer brazenness of it all made me think of my mother and father capable of unleashing a mortal spider-web as they crafted their bedroom in to a complex thread of silk. Did they know about this? Did they try it? Were they aware of what a cunt could do?

He's circumcised but not Jewish. He smells like a woman would smell, clean, deodorised, almost powdery with that strong scented soap he uses. My mind wafts around his smell. I cannot accept his body is so clean.

He could pay more attending to his digs though. The bedsit was liveable availing him to cook these fast nourishing meals and I liked him lots for that. A large bathroom was shared by two other females residing in the semi-detached house so the smell of sex always lingered in Jack's room. Well, we didn't bother rushing to bathe afterward.

He taught me not to be ashamed of the smell of sex. Menstruation a guilt trip you couldn't shake clear, no matter how much *he* didn't care, *you* still did. Bleeding and sex never favoured me until I was introduced to it subtly and unashamedly.

The first time I stood over him and he masturbated was a scene forever indelible. His poor cock, I thought he was killing the bloody thing the way his hand worked it so hard, elongating and swelling that damn organ. It was an ugly part of him I hate to say, but he used it with professionalism as a heart-surgeon a scalpel. He had this way, this movement this waltz. He needed no showing, no guidelines, no investigating, he just got on with it and could do nothing wrong. The measure of the man left me fighting for breath, quite actionable at times, and I fell deeper in to him. He fell deeper in to me with my discovering his hands could not only dwell and swell his cock, but possessed a gift that could dwell and swell my clitoris. And only I could monumentally achieve that heightened greatness.

So I gag and almost choke after his hands pry open my legs as he works wonders between my crotch, surfacing a mind-blowing high only to play with me and tease my cunt that I think he is looking to finish me off, I mean literally kill me. No, he's just starting and everything I remember from my teenage years mixes with my new growing college ones. Back then I needed something different, something to challenge me, and after taking down my popstar posters, I went searching from that moment to find it, and whatever it may be, goddamn it, this young man began to reveal it.

~

"What makes someone smart?" I ask my therapist, "Academia or social wares, or a ranking in class? I mean, you have to think you're smarter than me, right?"

"It has nothing to do with class, Emery. Anyone can be smart from whatever background."

"That's right, but still not given the same opportunities. I know you think most of us in here are dumb? Why else would you be here digging around inside our brains, trying to tell *us* about ourselves, that makes us dumber, right?"

"I'm not picking a fight with you about who's dumber or smarter, Emery. That isn't why you're here or me."

"But I'm your partner," I declare, "married remember? We're *all* in here your partner and married to *you*...this is your marriage and you can't accept it."

An analytical smile turns up at the corner of Susan's mouth. "If I choose to accept what you're saying," she searches, "then can you tell me what *you* feel you were married to?"

I slink back in the chair leaving the sight of her blouse over her skirt in my mind. Married to? I take it in for a short break during my mini tirade and realise most thing's should stay closed. But can they? I've opened up in her a special something and need to feed it free, so I have to offer something back. And I do.

"I was married to him," I un-rind easy, "Not on paper but I was married to him. Our lives were a marriage because we were there, together, all the time, eating everything up...everything that was exciting to us."

Her arithmetic measure of my words like a speeding train hurtling toward us promising to send us both flying through the air; I know she wants to be flown in the air. My train stops and hers kept going. "And what did you find...exciting, Em?"

"Everything you don't."

Yes, I suspect she's a right proper woman, standard position, on a bed, maybe push it as far as a bathroom someplace, eats three times a day, and reads the Sunday papers. Fuck! That's why she's married to this place.

"Being real," I start to lace up, "Being true, not lying, not trying to fit in and make everybody happy. We were married in our heads because we were each other's lives. No job could create what we had. No one could tell us how to live. It was simple but it was more than that, it was..."

I've lost my flow and Susan full-stops it for me.

"Fulfilling?" quaintly answered.

Yeah, alright, fucking fulfilling! So you are smarter than me, eh, and I thought these 'sessions' weren't about that?

Blinking liar! I am *so* your marriage.

Chapter Seven

His spurted cum in my hand's a jellied mess and I don't fancy wiping it in on the bed sheets, so for some bizarre reason I wipe it on his cheek.

"You bitch!"

What was a bitch, oh yeah a female dog, did I have four legs? Why the hell did men call women bitches?

"Not very nice is it," I say to his frantically wiping away the gunk.

He looks like he's been smashed with a hammer and I relishingly smirk.

Sudden, he tries to give it back to me so I bury my face away under the pillows to avoid that crap anywhere near, but alas, Jack is pretty nifty and manages to do the sly, punching my belly leaving me curled up and exposing my head he rubs that male mess in to my face.

Before I can load any defence he viciously snatches my wrists and spins me on to my back, drops a measured knee on my abdomen then fixes his self on top. I was a little winded and had no chance but to see him further his advantage, making his body high upon my chest willing me to fight back but I could do no such thing. We were in complimenting white vests and he wore boxers - me, slinky briefs. Our braised flesh like a grit challenge so it was easy for him to lug me about after slyly taking advantage.

"How'd you like it?"

"Get off me, Jack!"

"No, Emery, tell me how'd you like it?"

I stop wriggling because that just knackers me anyway as he weighs some, so I relax and meet his sparkling eyes. That mop of hair falls forward framing his look to one of a heavily disciplined child.

"So how'd you like it, Em, hm, not nice, eh?"

"Get off me!"

"No!"

I completely fall still and reissue any lost air then get this feeling of being bullish, being *him* for once, and tell it like it is. I think he'll be a teeny bit hurt but wonder how he'll be in the long term.

"You think that shit's okay," I rasped, nailing on to his eyes, "Think it's nice, all flipping over you, well it isn't!"

"What do you mean?"

He held a good smile then loses it.

"It's bad enough spewing all over the place you think I want it in my mouth?"

"It's just sperm," he says shocked.

"Just sperm, then you fucking taste it and you swallow it, big man."

Like a balloon popping he jolts back and stares at me. I knew he'd be hurt but not by that much.

Damn, I should use my head more yet I felt guilty not being truthful to him. Could anything he lay open rip me apart so?

"I thought you were alright with it," he thinks.

Alright with that, come on, what woman is really alright with that? Blow-jobs maybe, but having that shit in your mouth or swallowing it, you must be shitting kidding.

Some idiot made a scroll women ought to accept that but I didn't. Yes, he ate my cunt and that was acceptable but he didn't swallow anything either and yet he thought I should eat his gunk. No fucking way. Just - no! There was more to everything we did and I didn't need that.

"Sorry," easing his body off of me, "You should have said something."

"Well I just did."

I get up slow holding my hit stomach and he circles round to my back curving his legs to cup outside mine. Using his right arm he snakes it beneath my chin while his left felt its way across my middle holding me tenderly.

Leaning over my shoulder I get the gunk smell of his face against my cheek warming my senses. The rest of his body scent scales down to my lungs and he squeezes me hard like he knows I have to release that breath to allow him to squeeze me again.

Enclosed am I inside his structure, a glass sheet 'tween steel girders, touching my every crevice, fixing neat to my whole. Once more I am his and his left hand feels the bountiful wetness seeping through my slinky briefs.

~

Conflict a daily occurrence in here as you strived to keep above water and play it cool without drawing attention. Stick your head above the parapet and they sliced it off. Daily squabbles were a constant so these scheduled sessions tucked away with Susan a marriage this was. Step out of line you were put back in, look to make above your station and be shot down. You'd think after the Second World War we'd be more united as a country and a people, but we weren't. Challenges had to be met, and many were, but usually with conditions attached. One had better rights whether due to race or creed, you thought you were being accepted yet you knew it was one big show. You couldn't make the system accept you but you could take out of it what you could. Make the most of anything good in your life because it never seemed to last.

Being one of Susan's partners in marriage during a stay inside here would not last. Most of us reached divorce status and usually never pretty ones either.

I do wonder why Jack and I never officially married. Despite all the trimmings of marriage, why not simply do it? I had no real answer.

Her automated words then hit. "The way you two were, Em, it couldn't have been sustained, could it? It simply couldn't go on."

"How do you know?" thrown back, "You're married to this place not the actual world. You're trying to find your sense of real by working here and doing what you do but it's not enough is it. What do you do when you get home? I mean, how do you find your place? There's no partner, no real family there or work colleagues popping round, just you. So...what do you do with everything that we tell you, you have to do more than just write notes and speak in to a tape-recorder, don't you?"

In meditation she flicks back to earlier. Why do I tease her so and leave myself wide open as well.

"You think we really get off on the patients stories?"

I pinch inside, got to keep this going a bit.

"Rebels, deviants, the mad, the bad..."

"All fascinating," she cuts me off, "and clearly to you too."

"Me?"

A creep peeling of her lipstick lips invites. "Over six billion of us and none of us are the same, including the rebels, the mad, the bad, we all do things differently."

"So how do you do it differently," I descend, "Do you get wet or do you just jot down your notes and can't wait to fuck someone else's head in the morning?"

No, I think I wounded her. Damn! I did not want to go so far. I didn't want Susan to think I appeared ungrateful for all the time she'd given me. I just wanted her to be honest, like me. Tell the God's honest truth for once but I feel she could never do that.

"Emery, I'm sorry you think I..." trailing off like that tells me I hurt her, *"fuck* people's heads."

I apologise. I was out of order but I was being real too. Aren't we meant to be real and speak it as we see it? Now I no longer wanted to reveal more. My time with her was running out and I was messing it up. You fool, *"Reach out and touch...*

~

...somebody's hand..." the soul song played low in the background with lyrics profoundly sentimental you had to be moved by them.

I didn't take Edwardian Carla one for the old *Trojan Record Label*, let alone smooth 'rhythm 'n' blues'. She let me borrow her soul LP as I headed round to Jack's shared house because one of the girls was having a birthday party and my thinking a little bit of soul would come in handy late in to the evening. Mum and dad always smooch danced to a bit of soul after one of their late night socials arriving home and putting on an LP. They let us kids, who didn't get that slow-dancing thing at all, watch the first song float in to bedtime before being seagull-flocked upstairs leaving our parents looking like idiots as far as we could tell.

But now...now I got it.

Now I understood the significance of such smooching and dancing and being drawn to get serenaded. It was desire. It meant he wanted to be near you. It meant he could sweep you off and carry you someplace where you felt immense joy even if it was a simple living-room in a mate's house. He could take you further than that room; in your mind he took you far away where it all made perfect sense and that dream of him making everything right would become reality. How could a woman not want to be serenaded? Who could say *no* to such sublime moments? It was romance in its purest form.

Carla didn't want to come as she felt she wouldn't have mingled with the house fellows somewhat so I left her heading home from college. She was becoming this spunky little thing and her confidence from learning judo showed. I often wondered what she told her parents when she would get back late. That extra activity was probably moulded in to 'special mathematics'. I'd loved to have met her parents and introduce her to mine but we thought we were above all that and didn't think it quite proper for eighteen-year-old friends. We were growing up, being adult, and discovering many wonders along the way that introducing our parents seemed like an insult *they* wouldn't have known nothing yet had experienced the exact same things we were now beholden to.

Some of Jack's pal's I liked making their acquaintance and others I didn't. His two housemates were in to smoking dope but not cigarettes and I could never get my head round that. Watching them practically flat-out on the settee inside the living room after an *ABBA* song faded in to the atmosphere, I thought they were missing out on physical contact. You know, feeling the hard and soft parts of another human being.

Okay, so they *were* feeling the hard and soft parts of someone else for the stinky-sock foot which lay neatly on one girl's face looked like it happily belonged. They weren't aware of the toxic feet rested on them while I changed over the mixed-pop music LP to Carla's 80's soul.

Soon Jack had me so close I heard his heart beat. His bosom my cushion for a restful head where I knew nothing need go further. Our heads stayed clear of any influence apart from a couple of beers because the natural high we began to feel in each other was more than enough. I thought Carla needed to meet *her* Jack. I thought all the girls needed a Jack because then they would treat one another better. I saw the divide that was creeping in among women of all rankings. Men were getting in the way, breaking up friendships, controlling unsuspecting women to follow them and leave their families to settle down in to isolation. Rarely was it love. You know, real love for another. I saw the way women let men boss them around and control things that in the end made so many feel obsolete then they wondered why the relationship wasn't working. Would it happen to us all? Deep down did we want that significant other to take command and we just follow? Weren't those types, sheep? Were all women pretending to be sheep or in fact naturally so?

I remain close to Jack's body and seal my arms round the small of his back. We continued to smooch away the night. He learns exactly my movements or maybe it is me who learns his, either way, it prints precise. I feel I am him, he feels he is me. Being inside a womb, yes, that's what it was like; inside my mother's womb.

"*...let's make this world a better place, if we can...*"

~

"If I had fucked with your head, Em," Susan, cooling, "I think you'd tell me." She steals the upper hand. "You like throwing things back, don't you, so I'm intrigued why you like to play around with the idea we therapists get excited over our clients sessions."

I bay in response, "Really," because *now* I'm having a go, "You wouldn't tell me even if you did get excited over something shocking, and I don't believe you've never got turned on over something someone tells you. Even a fly on the wall in here would sometimes get turned on."

Oh wow, she laughs lovely and I had to smile at her. We've graced back to our beginning and I'm feeling good.

"Is everything about getting turned on with you," the smile coruscates, "Does it all have to end up around sex?"

If she had her Jack, then yes. I wonder if she's secretly recording our conversations because I'd want to share them with my fellow professionals. Come on, this thirty-six-year-old under legislation of the authorities who in their minds has shown little regret for her actions and tries to shake it all down to being at one with her spiritedness. Still attractive, yes, and alone in here with my thoughts, though on allotted times allowed to open them up and have them chewed over, so if I pick my sayings carefully I'll be free. It's what we all want, right.

"I thought everything came down to sex," carpeted for her. "You're married to this job so your sexual feelings have to be in here too. They go hand in hand, don't they?"

Chivalrously asks does Susan, "For you?"

I shrug my shoulders and know she has taken a can-opener to my background. He was my saviour at secondary from Sean and Toby, my surprise boyfriend during further education, so heading to university after he went there first meant I trailed after my sex, hadn't it. I give her the can-opener back. "You mean my following him to uni?"

She's going to make something out of this so I need to be ready.

"It began in your teenage years, right," she plays her position, "And you went after him to university to continue what you started, yes?"

Hold on, that wasn't all of it.

"Oh, but I *wanted* to go to university," she sits corrected. "I saw my brother at college become a gentleman and I wanted to be that too, a lady."

"A lady?" the tip of a fresh smile revelatory, "And being a lady to you, is?"

I answer, "Being my brother but female."

I think I'm clever but I know it's a weak reply. A female version of my brother could never be probable unless he held dark secrets like mine. I mean, most men do. Their testosterone levels were out of the annals from freak shows. They butchered, slaughtered, raped and pillaged, no woman anywhere in historical records bore capable of such atrocities on an even scale. But I once thought I could have touched it, in a much minor way mind you. My thoughts studied the rushing waters which were made still when I slunk beneath to witness all the black and felt myself forever drowning. I was afraid. I had been afraid for some time. I choked out my brother, I taught my sister to dislocate another girl's shoulder, I tossed Carla over my back the first time I met her, so shit, yeah, I could have gone that way.

"You want to be an old-fashioned or a modern-type lady?" She strokes her crossed thigh. Why the hell did her actions bother me thus? I wasn't gay yet her little gestures were engrossing. Her being this polite studied fem who gave a toss about others was both enchanting and requital, like one of those haughty nineteenth-century novels the bourgeois ladies wrote because they could: Bored wives of their male counterparts, who were often, it turned out, sleeping with *other* men. Bet those ladies back then faked their shocks.

No, no, I did not want to sleep with Susan, I already said I wasn't gay. No, I wanted to do something *else* to her.

"Don't remember the old ladies wearing britches," my comment, recalling bits of history during lectures; unless mounted on a horse it was duly frowned upon and I suppose rightly so. Those times were different and today we women are, so, on a horse or otherwise, we could choose to wear britches.

"Not heard that expression for a while," my therapist a slight nonplussed.

"My frankness shocks you?"

"I'm not shocked by anything you say, Em. I told you I'm here to help you get the help you need."

"And I remember telling you I didn't need any?"

Nodding, she says, "I understand you feel your actions were alright and that you believe what you did was acceptable, but the powers that be don't think so, and I have to say, quite frankly, Em, you still surprise me with your insistency that you still do."

Lifting my head I level hazel eyes at her. Turquoise-blues reflected nicely against auburn hair. A distinctly unique match-up only few women in the world could have made so wonderfully stunning.

"I was within my rights," I stated plainly. "I did nothing wrong but I'm told I have to say I did wrong in order for you to get me out of here."

Soulful, "Emery," more soulful, "You're going back on all what we've discussed and everything you admitted and agreed to."

"I'm telling you the truth," I add, and imagine leaning across the desk separating us to brush aside her clean and conditioned flowing hair to whisper something in her ear. "I told you I was sorry and what I did was wrong in the eyes of the law and I accept all that. But what can you give me in return surely must be that I *still* think what I did was right and that I did it in a way I saw as just, not drawn out and cruel. None of that means that what I did was *still* wrong. I know that I shouldn't have done it, I know that now."

Okay, I think I'm getting somewhere.

I acknowledge what I did. I acknowledge the consequences and answering to the letter of the law and the appropriate persons involved. I acknowledge it all. So why couldn't the relevant authorities acknowledge me?

Chapter Eight

"I did it."

Not wanting to think about what he did as my head was in a frigging turmoil after he'd fingered me to the point I almost cried. I needed far more than the single minute he gave me to enjoy that life-evolving orgasm and feel the gluey deluge between my legs smoothed over my thighs by his virtuoso hands.

He crafted his masterpiece with my vaginal spew covering the four corners of my body-canvass. He never said any dirty words today as though he understood his 'Did it' confession would feed a crossing of bad language and so refrained from any use during our sexual play. I manage to utter, 'Did what?' before his ruse round to my back cranking both my arms to hold me in a full-nelson and at the same time herding his penis brilliantly beside my arse.

Christ, he was bone hard it felt like a fucking super-sized dowel and I wondered where he was about to put it. I clenched my fists strengthening my frame to indicate I am about to get out of this restrictive cradle but no sign lay outward that he would do what he was about to.

"I cheated on those test papers."

My large gulp and attempt to turn myself round to find out more, he startles me with a massive shift of both our naked bodies on top my dorm bed, lifting and shoving me down, flattening my face in to the pillow. I think he's fucking kidding right, but no, the full-nelson is fully applied and I can't get free. He lifts my head up and hurtles me unequivocally over the pillow, and yes, I'm able to breathe though I cannot move.

"Jack?"

No more syllables were allowed to come out as I felt him inside me.

Jesus, it hurt, it fucking hurt, and I cried out.

He never sought permission for that and I never gave permission either and I seared inside.

His fingers crawled up to grab my hair and yank my head back and I spluttered somewhat, keeping my eyes closed with the blast furnace in my bottom hitting me with an energy of hysteria.

He did not dance, he did not motion backward or forward, he remained where he was and I thought I'd dissolved.

From afore my swollen clitoris stayed swelled and increased its size for I could not stop myself exploding again.

He grabbed a chunk of my hair so hard I felt my neck stretch long as he gravitated my head forward placing it hanging over the pillow. I lost some air and stiffened my torso, the pole of his fucking prick piling deep from in me made all my seasonal elements crunch in to one. I had passed through the moon and stars and touched the sun, and his reason for being a test-paper cheat with this cowardly display leaving me a *towering inferno* was beastly Neanderthal.

I wanted to kill his cock.

My fingers gripped the bed's under-sheet so tight I felt the mattress springs against my nails.

Fucking bastard!

With more spluttering, my clitoris pulsates and he lets go the bloody full-nelson. He remains on top but with a more controlled pressure, my knowing he's there, and his attention to me were deeper sought.

I cannot believe what just happened. I don't know how I should be.

Resting a hand in my hair he strokes gentle my head. I need water because my fire is dying slow.

"Emery, are you alright?"

His hands mastered my clit, his penis danced for my vagina, his mouth made glory of my lips and here I lay teary-eyed after coming through anal penetration.

Christ, what was that?

"Emery?"

My mind awakens to his voice: That sleek, masculine voice. I did not know what to make of him right now. I did not really understand anything. I wasn't a kid I was twenty-one and liked our being together. Yeah, I really liked us being together as it was shaping the meaning of mine everything.

"I'm alright," I manage to say quiet through faint sobbing. "I'm okay."

He slides a concerned hand underneath my abdomen and holds it there.

"Emery, look, I-"

I break his stride. "Jack?" He kisses my head and my neck. "Don't you ever fucking do that again?!"

~

"Perhaps we should have got married," regrettably slipped, "then maybe I wouldn't be here."

"Married or not," the felicitous Susan springs back, "More than likely, Em, you'd still have been sent here."

Cold hard facts, I suppose. Having that official piece of paper might at least have made things easier on me. If we held the title of man-and-wife we could have claimed greater clemency on the grounds of humanity by showing commitment to one another for our respective families, and include too, those who made the law of the land. Two singles residing and setting up home raised stifled scoffs off the moral police and sometimes left financial securities requesting proven credit from our elders for looking to better our younger selves.

After Jack got kicked out of university I finished that year with friends Caroline and Emma constantly breaking in to moulds of sweating flesh and rubbing vaginas that I couldn't wait to leave Carlton. Not them being overt lovers or anything just that I continually burst in on them making impassioned sex. My social life waned because Jack wasn't able to visit anymore and I spent a lot of time hanging out in my dorm. I know it had to piss off Caroline and Emma as they'd always respected mine and Jack's private moments.

"I could have done anything with all his stuff," I say suddenly, too aloud were my thoughts, "Made a pyre and burned it all."

Susan sits up and places her right forefinger and thumb neatly chinned. "And then what, Emery," she queried, cultivated, "not save anything for keepsake?"

Souvenirs, tokens, it depended on how you read them. Feeding hectically good and bad memories could lend to the emotionally wrecked majority suicidal, or the angering minority dumbfounded. Either way it was taken left conflicts needing remedies. Medicines weren't always a satisfactory answer to this myriad of problems we give ourselves. I saw the pill-popping antics of many students so stayed well clear of that dependant side-effects shit. Consciously I chose not to do drugs and never felt the need to. Jack was my chosen drug of choice and I think Susan got that.

"People let on about special trinkets," I pin up for her, "or one of those faces inside a pendant you carry round with you. Some people need all that, I never did."

"You really kept nothing?"

"You sound like I'm insane for not doing so."

Another shift inside her chair, "Okay," her smile lingers, "you're saying memories are enough?"

"If you've loved big, memories are always enough."

"What if someone wanted to share them with you?"

She has to keep asking, eh. Sorry, but all my images and stories conveyed suffice.

So I lain out for her, "Look, I can share talking about things. It's never bothered me."

"Did you talk to your mum and dad about it?"

I pause and absorb a breath before answering, "I always talked to my mum and dad. I just never cared to share details of my nights of passion with them. Did you?"

Again she folds her right hair-free leg over the left thigh. Smooth as silk I glimpse her tan. Was Susan about to reveal her parents explained the *birds-and-bees?* No wonder she's so uptight; parents discussing God's gifts was one thing but exact descriptions about masturbation and highly-prized sex another. I believe that's why she chose to feel us lot out in here. We were the ones who left the beaten path and scoured a foot-trail taking us to new unexplored depths, yet little did we know these unmasking's were nothing new but a nuance in finding the same old openings and closings. Take the introduction of gas-masks for instance. The First World War had much to answer for the fetishes that emerged from such a destructive time. I mean, who would have ever grasped the concept that gas-masks would be an aphrodisiac?

The sex educate reapplied.

"Different generations have different concepts about things like that," Susan stretched, "I don't think my parents would have accepted today's sex-education policy any more than my children would if I were to have any."

She's so box-formed. "Well, your parents," I start to say, "wouldn't have any worries, because today there just *aren't* any."

Her enquiry flies modest, "You were never taught them?"

"Taught?" I nearly laugh. "A few diagrams on the reproductive system, yes, but not how to use them correctly or the importance of first asking then being given permission to explore."

She palpates, I think.

"Sometimes discovering things for your self can be better that way."

"Doesn't appear so," I said, derisory, "Most people can't even say vagina and penis without sniggering."

~

The lecture in Biology was a genetic bore. I sat in a middle-seat half way up the hall and watched Mr Jenkins point his metre long rod at the projector pictures illuminating most of the back wall. No technical drawings of private parts yet, just organs and blood terminals, capillaries and veins. The deeper stuff about *apex beat* and the *heart in sternal depression* to come later and I sat there wondering why on earth I had picked the subject. No *Florence Nightingale* instincts were in me and it wasn't due to Jack. No, Biology filled something: I just didn't bloody know what.

The students mainly floated boys as they were seeking to go in to medicine or some type of gynaecology. Again why is it usually the men who liked poking round a woman's vagina? That idea through the ages of men being in complete control of women still reflected today as they were the ones in dominance poking round the sciences involving sex and reproduction. I never saw a promoted woman take away the Nobel or Pulitzer Prize for stuff reigniting sexual evolving or tissue enhancing.

Coming over sleepy, my eyes take to wandering when Mr Jenkins, our super slender, youthful in appearance professor, announces the workings of the *myocardium* are to be next addressed, and to my sheer serendipity I pick up on two students, marooned closely, sat three rows below me and several feet to my right. I wonder what Caroline and Emma would make of my witnessing the girl's hand gently caressing the small of the boy's back. Her fingers pinched him occasionally before taking an interfering amble round to the front of his pants. No not right now she wasn't. Oh yes she was.

Mr Jenkins lit up the lecture with his brash new opening yet I only checked him out briefly as my eyes hurried back to the cheeky boy and girl clandestinely feeling each other up then her hand disappeared down his trouser zip. From the timed rhythm of her delicate movements it was quite clear she was full on in her hand-job techniques as the boy sat casually taking down notes. Rules unwritten laid out a time and place for such well-loved moments but I tried not to judge. That's probably what was incorrect in all of us. We judged when we should be looking inward at ourselves.

~

"You enjoy all of your frankness, don't you, Em?"

Susan stays playful as I rather, "I try to be open with you."

"Open? I get the impression you wish everyday people were more like you. Let things out, get it off your chest, say what they mean."

"You disagree?"

Modern, she sits up and takes her tanned foot down then a fingers brush through her auburn tresses is passed out; an indicator for a show of frustration. That's what I'm reading anyway.

"It's very hard for some," she begins, "Not all of us can be open about every facet of our lives. If we were then most of us would be walking around like zombies doped up on some type of medication to make sense of it all, and so many of us wouldn't be able to cope with the honesty. We simply couldn't handle it. It would be too great a burden to bear on a daily basis."

"And why is that?" my looking to modify, "We've never been allowed to be honest on a daily basis anyway. We're taught to lie and to cheat, to be somebody else, to hide things and play the real *us* down. That's the systems fault not ours?"

She measures that measure of a refined learned with her bigger picture of everything earthed. I listen.

"Emery, don't you see if all of us could be who we are there'd be absolute chaos? We need some sort of system to try and reign in those who would otherwise act out anarchically. We can't have that. We can't have the strong taking over the weak."

"Are you serious?" I flung back. "Susan, we already have that, we're already living it. We have chaos we have anarchy, it's just that the minority uses it to control the majority. You don't see it because you're part of that controlling minority and I'm part of the majority needing to be reigned in."

In my chair I slump a little, my displeasure evident and of course I regret it. Here once again I regret riling her and yet that is why we are both here. To get riled, to be riled, to let it all out, to un-charter, but being female I have regrets. I cannot see this end.

"You still think it comes down to your sexuality?" her ask of my sullen self, "Because of society's...disjointed view of the sexes?"

Men never waived power nor were willing to share it, and that 'disjointed' opinion they carry throughout their lives of the weaker sex would never waive either. After nearly a year with this wonderful woman I could not believe our talks came down to semantics. And after what I'd done, and what I could do, it all fell down to simple semantics? Male and female imbalances during relationships were the one-box-ticked for every troubled life.

Fuck!

Chapter Nine

Jack's expulsion meant he wasn't allowed on campus so we made arrangements to meet up outside university in the town centre but it was never quite the same. After doing this automatically for a few weeks, I settled down and got my head round to studying and visited my parents fortnightly just to see them. Even in adult years I never thought I'd miss out on having my mum hug and kiss me telling me she loved me. Why some thought that maturing display of mothering affection yucky seemed silly because for me, it was a welcome emotion I think more of us needed, even in to our twenties.

Late in the autumn of '93, some type of international rugby tournament was being shown across the country. I was in the backyard helping mum hang out laundry when dad came rushing out the back door and affectionately tackled me resulting in my losing the bag of clothes pegs. More embarrassingly after my fifty-year-old father wrestled me to the grass, I got up irate and chucked the grounded pegs at him. Laughing like a teenager he was, mum told him not to be so silly and continued hanging out washing like playtime was over. He went back in the house leaving my bemused self still floored and I realised my never noticing, or liking, his goofy foolishness before, and mum's apathy toward it all was simply put down to being the blooming Pearson's. Yeah, I missed my family. And I was missing Jack.

~

"If he and I lived on equal terms things might have been a bit different," the words come out unplanned yet Susan computes quickly.

"And you could claim that for everybody, couldn't you?"

I navigate. Kings and Queens, husbands and wives, boyfriends and girlfriends, yes, you could.

I leaned back lazily and stray tired eyes to the floor. I could no more change my feelings or the outcome of what I'd done. But if I sit here and lie by telling them everything they want to hear I should be okay, shouldn't I?

"Relationships come and go, Emery," Susan succour, "Many choose to start over, some of us can't, and others just wallow in unhappiness."

I know that's an underhanded dig at me. Come on, I'm thirty-six, still look okay, a whole life ahead of me yet I'm stuck in the past. Why wasn't I moving on, Susan's thinking? An eager line-up of worldly men spread waiting to date me, I know, but none of them were Jack and I didn't expect them to be. No matter my expectations, no one could ever be Jack.

"Emery..." she starts to say then dies off. I match up her sea coloured tropic blues and hold on to them. That start of her tone in saying my name melts inside me. I'm up for shedding anything. "Does your missing him hinge on everything you've held dear stop you leaving things behind to start over?"

I want to start over of course I do. I'm just not sure I'm up to facing what I did to everyone else. I don't want to argue about it, I don't want pushing in to a corner. I don't want to have to keep explaining away all that I did. I constantly go on about making new and moving on, just that I don't think some people will let me. No, I think I'll be forever punished.

"My love I hold dear," I tell her. "My feelings about it all scare me but I'm not worried about facing anything."

She looks for more, "Then what, Emery?"

Susan, you can't have loved like I have loved, you can't have felt what I felt. You can't believe what I believe because you wouldn't ask me that. It was unexplainable. I couldn't explain. So what the hell do I say? Say anything, something. Okay, and if I do, will it be the truth?

Every day the sun rose and fell slow from the sky. In reality it went nowhere, our planet was the one running rings round it and so another deception played out was lifted from superstitious mutterings. A truth unveiled, so...

"I'm afraid," I utter, "I'm afraid to be me...and...I'm afraid of finding him again."

~

Surely one this talented must see that education regarding sex and relations was a non-starter here. Our teachings didn't exactly endorse the bigger picture about social relationships like the Europeans during your school years, and maybe if we did, perhaps if we had, we wouldn't feel so repressed all the while. I say that yet when I take the time to think about it, I don't think it's a big deal for the likes of the Emma's and Caroline's among us, they just didn't give a shit.

"Hey, Em, we're having a do in the small hall on Friday night and it's on the uni's boundary so Jack can come. We know you're missing him something terrible and we just know it'll cheer you up lots so we've already invited him."

Okay then, I had no choice in the matter but my friends were only thinking of me. It also meant they could probably have a sordid night together while I danced with Jack. We hadn't smooched for some time and I have to say in my gut I was bursting with anticipation. Maybe Caroline and Emma could get another room and leave me and Jack the dorm.

Deciding not to call him or anything as I wanted the night to be like a wedding; he would not view his bride, nor I; my bridegroom. The arrival of him exciting enough as the university teemed with unpleasant gossip after the test-paper cheating was uncovered. It left a sour taste in many mouths and I had not gone undetected for finger-pointing and fabrication.

Caroline and Emma stayed by my side while others were disgusted and some even disputed my own test results. I didn't care as I knew I did not cheat. My parents would have been let down and I couldn't do that to them. Being brought up on fairness in our household was something Lucas, Jamie, and me were very proud of and we showed our appreciation by exemplifying fairness in our own lives. My brother at twenty-four was on his way to becoming an Officer in the Royal Air Force and Jamie, now twenty, completed two successful years at nursing college looking to become State Registered. At twenty-two I hadn't made up my mind yet though hoped it veered on Jack being there with me.

Lacing up low-heeled boots after pulling on a black polo-neck to fit comfortably with my blue-jeans, the dorm door knocked. Hastening to answer, I reached for the knob and to my surprise, Benjamin Knowles entered without an invite.

The highly studious young chap from the neighbouring room quickly shut the door and braced himself against it.

The party was underway and I needed to be there and thought Benjamin looked hopeful to get invited along.

"Hey, Emery," slightly panting, "You going to the do?"

He knew I was and perhaps wanted me to hold his hand. Well I wouldn't.

"Yeah," I say fast, "and I've gotta get going."

"Is Jack gonna be there?"

I play like I don't know. Maybe Benjamin would snitch to the Dean if he knew and get Jack kicked off campus even though the small social hall teetered on the university's boundary.

"I'm not sure," thinking I gave away nothing. "It's Caroline and Emma's get-together for some friends out of town."

Fixing my shoulder-length hair in an untidy bun, he monitor's my movements then I step to get past but he steps in my way and I now know something's up.

"You'd think if you cheated on those tests," he equipped me, "you wouldn't want to be here," adding, "And if you did cheat on those tests...you *shouldn't* be here either?"

Immediately I grow annoyed and tell him to sling his hook but he just stares at me like he failed the whole year.

"Move will you, Knowles, I have to go!"

But he remains where he is and I see him change, from nothing he just changes.

"You think you're so special, don't you, Pearson?"

Christ, this was the nerd Benjamin Knowles from next door who continuously had his nose in a book and displayed no close friends. And here he is in my dorm with this challenging face that says he has a few choice words to hand out to me. Okay, I'm not perturbed yet but growing more disgruntled.

"We all work hard and you just show up, wag your arse, push your tits out and cheat your way through uni. Girls like you make me sick!"

Now I never suspected he had a screw loose but they always say watch out for the quiet ones. It was an open secret about sexual assaults on campus but I never felt the threat. I was confident, maybe blind to it all, and Jack's prowess had me believing I could handle anyone.

"Knowles, get out of the way, okay?"

He watches me like I'm Christmas Dinner or something and I get he's juggling an attempt to make a move on me. I just didn't know what or expect anything meticulous.

"Think your noisy shagging doesn't get heard all the way down the hall?"

Okay, I'm in trouble.

"Think all your showy canoodling with Charlie-boy goes unnoticed?"

Damn, I had no clue my antics could make this guy so screwed. No way would I have thought Knowles a peeping-tom, or worse.

"Get out of my room, now!"

I point to the door for him to shift his arse but my determination to show bravado is fast laid to waste as he completely takes me by surprise by crouching low and rams his head in to my stomach.

After dropping to the floor breathless I feel him reaching all over my body and I can't get him off.

I deserted my preparedness, I dismissed his attack, I believed he was nothing, and now I was frightened.

I tried to grab and push him away but he skilfully held me down and viciously kneed my gut. The blow subdued me and I felt him climb on top struggling to pull off my jumper.

Shit! Benjamin fucking Knowles! No way!

He wrenches the polo-neck over my face and I feel a devastating fist crunch directly below my sternum then he hits me in the nose. Boy, I'm done, that's it. He's beat the crap out of me and now he's...

~

I childishly play with my grey sweatshirt and adjust the white T-shirt beneath. Yes, I'm evading why I am afraid and why I need not expose *everything*. I remember people talking about me, discussing who I was to my physical presence upon entering a room. Really, why was I there? Convincing myself going to university after college seemed a natural course to take and yet I hadn't made up my mind what I wanted to do with my life. Where was that career? I enjoyed learning. I liked exams, course work, and tests. A profitable career looked like the next step but I wasn't so sure anymore.

"You can still attain anything you want, Emery," Susan says bright-eyed, "You're at an age to be able to do whatever you feel like, nothing's out of bounds. You just have to go find it."

Young of an age, maybe, but not like the young I used to be; vibrant, bold, vivacious, uprooting and moving, challenging and changing. Now I sit staid, bored, plodding away days, same routine after routine, I have become as everyone else.

"Why do you think you've shut yourself away today?" she said considered, "Of all the days to pick, are you worried about next week?"

Mm, they tick their box and shuffle their papers and I am free. Or am I? Sure you are, free to re-join, to mix with the steady flow of workers, teenagers, parents and children. They all merge in to one big boring universe. What else is there to truly stimulate ourselves, to desire, to grow, and forever unravel new? If I was afraid of that unknown, then there was something wrong. I wasn't claiming to be better than anyone. I only knew what Jack and I had were good and not cloaked in fakery. I loved him, he loved me, and I'm talking about real love, not him bringing in the finances or paving the way home, but a love of him, his infectious laugh, his mop of curls, and his brooding moments. I loved *him*. We could be anywhere on earth, the tropics, the ices, homed or homeless, I would always love him.

"The outside's a lot different," I mumble sadly like an unwanted orphan. "Stuff changes quickly. Nothing seems to last anymore like it used to."

"You make of those changes what you want to get out of them," Susan poses, "It doesn't have to be turned upside down for you to feel accepted."

"I don't want to turn anything upside down," my sadness propels, "I just want to start over and be me. I don't think people will leave me alone and let me be."

A heart-warming smile, "Not everyone's going to feel the same about you, Em. There are bound to be those who hold grudges. You won't be welcomed back by everyone."

"Like in here?"

"Why in here?" she dazzles, lifting her left leg above the right knee again, one of her many characteristics that took away the edge and you shift focus from trained thoughts to her glowing limb. Female friendship was underrated. A vast appreciation of another female minus crude tales was overlooked. Jealousy clouded it. I knew Susan wasn't jealous of me nor I her and instead of me fishing for compliments from one I admired so, I couldn't let it drop knowing that her thoughts about me were really important. I wanted to leave this place feeling good no matter the challenges waiting.

"Did a lot of things happen to you, Em?"

Like butterflies to florets I had been received fair by the majority, but my attraction to others did not go down well after I refused certain flesh held manoeuvrings. I would never look to replace Jack let alone find a temporary situation to divert my feelings. I wasn't that type of person, I couldn't fake play. Jack made me, *me*, and I wouldn't alter it.

"All your history reports say you kept to yourself and you didn't want to mingle. Some saw you as a bit of a snob and that doesn't go down well in places like this."

"I was never Miss Superior," I inform quick, "and there were those who were only too happy to let me know it."

"Trying to keep you inferior?"

Susan blinks and I see she imagines me getting worked over or worse. Yeah, she's thinking, how can anybody want to hurt Emery? I never showed cunning, or braggadocio nor threat to another. So why would anyone want to hurt me right?

~

Days later I heard Benjamin Knowles was attacked at a train station. He'd been pulled off the platform and dragged in to bushes behind chicken-wire fencing and got the living daylights kicked out of him. He was unable to finish the year or take any exams due to a broken leg, ribs, and shattered jawbone. I knew it could not have been Jamie because the wrestling moves I once shown her proved detrimental when she applied them so I know she would not have taken revenge. Lucas would have let the law do its job, saying two wrongs didn't make a right as his officer training was going well and couldn't jeopardise his Air Force career. He did get leave to come and see me that weekend when I went home to wrap in the comfort of my family. In times like that your family were the only match for complete cherishing.

Emma and Caroline were both great. After walking in on Knowles kicking a half-naked me in the stomach, they duly hurled him off and threw him out in to the corridor. I couldn't cry, I couldn't do anything as I lay busy pushing away the pain when Caroline sprinted after him and I was later told she threw him down the stairs. Though a built lass I didn't want her or anyone else harmed. For me it was over; no reporting it, no Dean, no campus security, no police, and yes, I had taken a bit of a doing over, however I managed to stop Knowles's sexual assault when he flew in to a rage, got up, and kicked me. If Emma and Caroline hadn't arrived on the wrathful scene I'm not sure what would have happened next.

My bloody nose and bruised torso had Jack holding me for what seemed a never-ending time. He didn't care about facing charges if the campus security found him, he only wanted to hold on to me and not let go. Being clutched I buried my face in his chest while sobbing like a new-born baby. I don't recall having cried like that since my days start. At the same time I heard Emma and Caroline crying. Afterward, Jack began crying too.

~

"Some people don't like the way I look," put freely, "I can't help looking the way I do."

Another smile is lit and I wonder if she has any fillings.

"Your attraction can make others envious," Susan's statement below par. "You must have wondered if you'd be a target at some point."

Entry to college, first day at uni, bad days at school, etc.! My parents never warned I'd be in cross-hairs because of good attributes. Dad did try to talk about boys, mum did try and steer me toward studies. It was their way I suppose of saying we know you're handsome and need to play it down. Even showing brains you need to keep it under-played, and I did. I never acted big-headed or showed pomp. Females had it tough without hating each other for being blessed in some areas yet we still chose to make one another's lives miserable. What number sin was envy again?

I tended disquiet, "Make life easier by disfiguring myself, that's good advice."

"Don't be silly, Em, I'm saying attractive women are often targets for anyone's insecurities."

"Then they're the problem not me."

"And people of sound mind know that. You can't help your looks and you should never play it down to please others. And anyway, something tells me you never did."

She uncrosses that leg of hers and places her elbows crisply on to the beech-wood desk. Prodigiously they complement each other along with her crowning voice.

"Emery, you've never let anyone stop you doing what you wanted to, and you still haven't. You're headstrong, and I'm sure you can take care of yourself in most situations. I think your vulnerability at times is all show. You're a tough-cookie, inside and out, and I think you're ready for any challenges...even next week's."

My smiling brings her along with it. The warmth from the sunshine basks inside the office favourably encompassing us in core heat. Already up for feeling the bark of trees neath my fingers with the kicking of autumn leaves at my feet, those were the positives. Now push away the negatives.

"So then I tick all your 'yes' boxes?"

Her tropic-eyes float inside white water.

"You're not afraid, Emery," she spoke clear, "You know you don't deserve to be here and you should focus on getting out: Permanently."

Her lain down ultimatum; I was okay with her so I had to be okay with everybody else. And why shouldn't I be? I posed no warn, displayed no wrongs, overall I stayed relaxed with no ills to my fellow troubled so it was time to move on. Hold it a sec, how this world of *others* saw me would be a different case altogether: Analysis of making one's own bed and lying in it.

I worryingly placed, "You're in the minority I suppose, because a lot of people think I should stay here and never be let out."

Her coolant sense fills me. "You've accepted what happened, Emery, haven't you? You've atoned for it."

I don't think this a confessional. "My reasons for doing what I did I am still not sorry for. I'll always believe it was right even though a lot of people saw it as wrong."

Uncovering another vowed smile she seems to weep. "Accept your time here, Em. Show you made mistakes, that you're sorry and have regrets. Don't mess up your chances of getting out. You don't need to be talking to me for another year."

Staying and talking to Susan for another year was a viable option I did not mind. I wouldn't have to face my fears of being real. At some point though, it was inevitable.

In a few words things could change for the better. Susan and I had a funny knack when it came to little being said but leaving much felt applied. We came meeting at the same path therefore could begin to stroll down it.

My first joined steps with her were about to take place. I would not fight, nor seek to wander, she could take my hand and lead me, if at first tentatively, to face who I was.

Chapter Ten

It rained thunderous for over an hour and I couldn't see clearly because my hair splayed stuck to my face during our protracted morning walk. Neither of us checked the weather reports assuming the day would be a nice crisp winter's start mixing sunshine with natures unfolding.

The Lake District needed to be seen to be appreciated.

Geographical logs spoke of Earth's beauty along the equatorial lines with their continental rainforests, however I believed our own Lake District was a match for any of The World's greatest landmarks.

We were staying the weekend at Jack's parents' house; a fully-detached home thrown among a thousand others that invaded the rural surrounds. The old timber beams laced every room in the two-hundred-year-old property and the sitting-room's open-fire greeted us each morning feeding us its cheerful glow. How could anyone not be happy growing up here?

Mary and Jake Charles were the spitting image of those old-farmer types indulging their appeal like they'd been borne from fauna's extremities. Waxed rainproof jackets and hats to match and rubber boots that'd seen every inch of The Lakes throughout their thirty-year marriage, these two came scripted from a futuristic Dickensian novel. Perfectly placed, perfectly paired, they were just perfect.

An older born son saw his likeness in Jack simply mesmeric. If not for the stouter appearance and longer straggly hair, I'd have thought I kept bumping in to Jack in all corners of the Charles' abode. Joshua had flair and coolness just like his younger brother, however his actions over Jack, by almost three-years, having should have stayed home to become a productive townsfolk, irked him so. I saw instantly why Jack probably left though still loved his country-style family. It can be too much when older siblings tried moulding their younger's to copy in lifestyles, and most of us know that nudges in an unwanted direction pushed you further the opposite way.

Unfamiliar to sudden weather change up in The Lakes, our long walk crashed to a halt and we had to seek shelter. No visible buildings were in the vicinity so Jack and I ran in to thick woodland and uncovered a through-bridge carved under hillside made safe with interwoven masonry-work and wooden transoms. Two signs indicating the train station lay three miles to our left, and for the four-thousand inhabited town head right.

I laughed out loud seeing Jack's unhappy face realising the depth of tread we needed to overcome in order to reach the radiant open-fire of his family home.

My cheeky grin made him hobble over to me and grab me roughly round the waste and spin my back in to his kernel torso. His filled-out woollen top guzzled my body as he squeezed me tight and said I love you.

I stopped moving. I know he'd said it before but this time it was the *way* he said it. Turning round to face him my emotions momentarily cloistered as he instinctively lifted his hands gripping hold my wet, thick, borrowed jumper from his old wardrobe, and practically hoisted me off my feet.

Wait, Jack, I manage to utter before he kisses me and asks me to say nothing, please say nothing, but I do, hurriedly pulling free of his mouth I take his face in my cold hands and he gives me this shy smile. I wanted to bite his puppy-brows. His green eyes come alive with the trees behind him and I tell him simply: Hey it's okay, it's okay, I love him too. Tilting his face down I kiss his forehead and as a huge smile sweeps across his cheeks, he hurls me up by the jumper front and carries me to the wall and slings my body in to it. I feel nothing untoward as he matins me with hard kisses to my neck and chin. Bra-less, under several layers of vest, T-shirt and woollens, I feel his hands make way with a thrashing levelling of my breasts, muscling them hard. The handiwork could have mistaken for mashing misshapen clay but I allow him be free to ravage my torso; the urgency from him laying claim to my reply to his love you, it sealed in us a doctrine we were of each other, and could never be set apart.

~

Mary dolloped a fat black-pudding sealed in pastry and onions to wolf down, and after filling out her husband and brood, I offered polite to help her wash-up.

"I insist you don't, child, you're a guest and I'll have none of it."

But I'd persisted and stood my ground alongside her in the Klondike kitchen that could have used a few up-to-date white-goods. There was nothing wrong with that old wood-burning triple-stove cooker though. A relic it may be but worth a fortune in todays' market. Whatever she placed in that oven it cooked perfectly. She was a damn fine cook and there wasn't a cookbook in sight. A proud moment indeed!

"All learnt from memory and watching my old mother pull it off blind," brashly was I apprised. "She didn't need cookbooks either."

So, would I?

Mary loved her son. I could feel it erupt from every maternal gland as I made her sit down and took off her rubber boots after she'd hauled out the garbage bags to the bins in the front yard.

An open-fire crackled and churned inside the stone-floor kitchen.

Leaning back in a grand looking armchair, the mature woman laid on me fixed eyes from a Celtic Warrior ancestry. I had better do nothing to hurt her son.

"What are you doing?" she mutters fidgeted.

"You're on these all day long," I linger, pulling off her thick winter socks, "You should put your feet up and relax for half an hour."

"What is this, I've no time for play, girl!"

"Please, Mrs Charles," urged I, "only ten minutes," beginning to massage her swollen right foot. "Then you can ask me anything you want."

I pressed her motherly button and that fixed look is unerringly shifted away. My offered up grin sees her relax somewhat and I play with her worn foot. I hadn't done this to my mum and thought maybe I should.

"Are you serious about my son?"

Continuing to palm her instep I take a moment to absorb her question so she sees I take her reverentially.

"Yes, I'm serious about Jack."

"Do you love him?"

It's straight to the point with this one.

Holding her wrinkled eyes I tell her yes.

"You won't break his heart, will you?"

A look stupefied.

"You know, my child, if you want to leave him you'll do it right, won't you?"

"Leave him?"

"You young ones nowadays don't tend to stay together, do yus? It's easy to move on to someone else, isn't it?"

"I'm staying with Jack," said assuredly, but the mother doesn't flinch.

"Nobody stays together anymore. You young ones are too carefree and can jump from partner to partner. Easy!"

I give her a Pearson truth.

"Well I'm not one of those girls," saying hopeful, "I don't believe in taking relationships lightly."

"Relationships?!" she almost leaps out of the chair making me halt my massage techniques. "I'm talking about loving someone, setting up home, having children and bringing up a family. Relationships!" a drop of spittle hits my cheek and I see her inferno, "That's for those young ducklings thinking they're blinking swans!"

Thrown back by her passion she hits me a stern look then garners her foot with silent instructions for me to bleeding well carry on.

I'm almost afraid to take back the old limb and roll on my massaging.

She scolds jovial, "That was feeling pretty good, my girl," watching my hands tentatively reach round her Achilles for a good grip.

After a minute kneading and pressing her foot, she plays crinkly fingers on the arm-rests of the chair. I figured it's a good moment to show my determined effort was no floozy with her boy by simply looking to fill my time during university years.

"I wouldn't hurt, Jack," to her said soft, "I love him, Mrs Charles, I really do."

She squints at me like a beetle hastily entered her nostril.

"Love, my child," she leans nearer, "What would you know about love?"

I knew right now that he made me gravitate toward him, that he could hold my attention and make me laugh and make me wonder about things. I knew he was smart in his own unique way, not needing to prove manly traits with qualifications achieved from an anachronistic system. I knew the way he held me and made love to me that it would take an unattainable individual to surpass, and even if found, it could not be equalled. I would go insofar as saying I would die for him. That was love wasn't it? Well it was my love but I never did tell her so.

~

The big brother was more of a challenge. At times it felt he deliberately avoided me whenever we bumped in to each other and I found it disconcerting the way he clearly steered conversation from anything to do positive concerning me and Jack to something about families and Lake District life.

Oh, I got him alright.

Jack's departure six years previous to live with his aunt meant to be a brief life-turn-round, however he fell in to a style that afforded him to see things differently. He not only turned his life round - it stayed turned. His political leanings, his views of the opposite sex, his new outlook on the way he wanted his life to go, he would not return to The Lakes for a life like his family wished of him. No, seems he was content to stay with me and I understood big brother furtively did not approve. I mean, I get it Joshua's looking out for his little bro but Jack was now a young man and could make up his own mind. He didn't need me telling him anything. I couldn't cajole him to stay down England's belly and remain forever with me, nor if his sudden wish was to stay up here after our week's lay. I couldn't alter that and wouldn't try to either. If he preferred open lands with the beauty of nature swaddling his every breath, I would not try turning him to come back to the City and start up home with me. The only question was if Jack asked me to stay with him. Thinking of such I don't think *I* was prepared for the flip-sided answer. Still, I got the feel Joshua would not have liked it. I don't think he thought much of me until one evening the three of us hit the festivity celebrations to the approaching Christmas of 1990.

It seemed every bar and restaurant was booked in advance for each heady local and breaking tourists. You could hardly locate foot space in many of the public-houses let alone reach the bar for a round of drinks. Jack, Joshua, and me, were looking to hit some sort of common ground as I promised myself it was his family time and I would do my best. Jack let me know his brother had shown awkward and he'd tried his utmost to keep things running smooth. I told him not to worry as I knew what was shoved up Joshua's arse but I had no beef with him and would show none.

We successfully propelled a route to the lounge area inside this ambient plush looking place with guest-rooms upstairs if any patrons got unmanageable to head safely home. Heaving with country beauties and sturdy male folk with a mix of Germans and Swiss and soft Southerners, Joshua and I were returning from purchasing a tray full of booze to start off the Christmas season when I noticed Jack had attracted unwelcome attention from a pretty-handful looking blonde.

Placing the tray down she already made herself comfortable in my seat and Joshua clearly had no intention of given me his. Jack gestured for a quick swap but I told him not to as this blonde was spoiling for an argument. Her daggered blue eyes shot in to me I was found unfavourable in these parts as I had stolen one of their best nubile males.

She'd obviously remembered Jack fondly and hectically reminded him of their old school time crush long in the past though thought she would try to rekindle it.

Unfriendly words were exchanged however I played cool and Jack continued to try to give me his chair. Then feelings got Hades-ridden when she cheekily reached for my drink on the tray and I snatched hold of her hand.

Semi-drunk, semi-dangerous, semi-coherent, among a flurry of vile swear words; the blonde lass went for me in a flash of muscle-memory reaching out to claw my bare face. Well, unlucky for her, my muscle-memory kicked in too and I showed those old wrestling-come-judo moves, quickly dismantling her attack before Jack or Joshua could do a blinking thing, and stitched a frenzy of gawping patrons at my expertly delivered body-toss of her, and controlled the stunned girl looping her arms behind her back on to the fag-ends, booze-spilled floor.

This unwelcome outsider was un-thanked for her efforts by the pub-lounge's owners; a burly retired rugby player and his three equally burly sons and curt missus, for my physical manhandling of their fully-humiliated regular would not be overlooked as they bundled me outside and told Jack and Joshua, in semi-polite terms, they could go too.

Maybe if I'd let her scratch my face we could have stayed and had a wonderful time but I wasn't up for getting scarred to save my pride trying to pry wandering hands away from Jack.

His apologies profuse whilst trying to effuse calm, I wrenched free from the strong grip he held on me and I bumped in to Joshua stood close by. The seriously firm but equally dramatic grasp of my hand by the older brother's, he immediately let go and told me I did well, those moves were impressive, and I showed restraint in an escalating bad situation. That was the most he'd ever said to me while I stayed at Jack's family home.

~

Of that adrenaline rushed incident it led to an adrenaline rushed night of tenacious-come-amour sex.

Joshua parted our company upon entering the house and before either parent could request if we'd spent a good-evening out - though surprised at our early return - Jack and I disappeared to his old room, which thankfully carpeted a thick rug taking up most of the floor space.

In my annoyance I tripped heavily over the protruding woven edge and hit the side of the bed unintentionally kicking Jack's legs because he kept clung to the side of me. Our heated discussion made more aflame as I turned round expressing disapproval of his late intervention with the blonde.

Yes I was pissed, yes I wanted to go back and slap the girl's face and feed those country morons a piece of my mind, instead I chose to slap Jack, and he slapped me back.

They were real slaps too. I'd hurt him and he knew he had hurt me.

Pausing, I watched his chest heave up and down and I don't know why but I reactively punched him with everything I owned right in his stomach and he doubled over coughing up his guts.

He fell on the bed and in my empathy I jumped to cover him feeling that built frame of his light up inside me as I crawled over him to soothe some of his pain when he gallantly, or not, however one wanted to see it, shoved me off of him and I crumpled against the side of the bed.

Fuming, I got back up and hurled both pillows at him whacking him in the head each time and he grabbed them and hurled them back at me.

You fuck! I remembered shouting, to which he lunged across and got my angered self, tangled round his arms, legs, and torso. Panting under a Kraken-like grapple we fell on the bed and he desperately made attempts to get control but I wouldn't let him. Inside our cauldron of rasping and swearing I showed him just how good my physical being was and I kicked him off of me in his semi-winded state and slapped his face hard before he fell from the bed.

That loud thud had to have been heard by his family despite the solid flooring and timber beams separating the rooms, but I didn't care if they came rushing in looking to see what all the fuss was about. This was *our* fuss, and the family, as far as I was concerned, had no say. Yes, it was their house, yes, I was their guest and I respected their boundaries, now, I wanted them to respect mine. Even if they felt it necessary to never allow my leave, this night with Jack belonged to us and I was going to lay in to him and they were not going to stop me.

~

The mood over breakfast wasn't great nor was it caustic either. It measured somewhere in between and I understood the uncertainty surrounding casual conversation while chewing salty bacon and the best spicy scrambled-eggs ever.

My embarrassment, greater than anyone else's, I evaded the disguised looks careening at, across, and all around me. Jack displayed a small bruise to his left cheek and I wished I hadn't left a mark: Evidence from our fight-night cringe-worthy. Maybe if he'd stuck to a sport he could have withstood my slap and not bruise so easily; actually himself no wimp either because I couldn't complain after he'd got me through the legs and lifted me up to body slam me on top the bed. Wimp my arse, tough bastard loved it!

The authoritarian mum told the men to leave while she asked me to help her wash-up. I'd thought of offering anyway but would have met shame if she'd told me offhandedly, no. I'd near beat her son up and he'd retaliated so there was no argument there. I was out of order for doing it in their home and I knew it too.

"Young girl, did you have a wonderful time last night?"

I almost dropped a plate.

"I see you and my Jack can talk things through, alright." She reaches eyes across that drench me. "That is good to see," added, handing me another plate to dry before I'd finished this one.

So I'm careful not to drop both. "I apologise for my behaviour, Mary, I shouldn't have let things get out of hand."

"Well," she studies, "Joshua says you didn't. You kept your ground and showed something special there be in you."

I shrug off the half compliment. "There's nothing special about me. I only did what any other woman would have done. I'm just sorry I messed up the night for everyone."

"Now there you goes," she says, "apologies for everything, apologies to everybody," and hands me the last plate as I put the dried two in the rack. "You're a young woman and shouldn't apologise for being you."

I view her indebted.

"Because you're a wee lass therefore expected to behave like one...ask yourself...what is a wee lass supposed to behave like?"

I try not to think that I am reading her incorrectly but I can't help feeling that what she is saying is going to impact me greatly.

"Another little fledgling comes up," she says, "and tries to trouble you and your man and he's expected to watch you both fight over him or is he expected to do the honourable thing and tell the little troublemaker to sling her hook? Which is it?"

She leaves me in a quandary and I don't know the answer to give but I don't need to as she has one for me.

"Young, Emery, my dear…it's *both*," she says, in that lazy Lakes drawl. The placidity of her home in these placid surrounds comes through in her matriarch elegance, "No one should tell a young lass how to behave in emotional circumstances and no one should expect she behave on their terms either." Mary Charles was opening up her support-book. "We females are told to control ourselves, to not lash out and let things be, but we can't always. You've shown a side to yus, girl, one I may not approve but I'm not one to instruct you on how you should feel. What comes naturally will always stay with you, my sweet, but remember…it may not be right which always comes natural."

Chapter Eleven

The Mother-Charles left me clear-sighted about emotions over Jack being alongside a determined ego she could see, and speak up for, as she travelled precisely how I felt about her son. This Lake family were no slouches and Joshua kissing my cheek prior to mine and Jack's offing back further south, told me without words to stay ballsy and confident. The added wink said he were sure I could take care of myself, and Jack too. I wanted to reassure him that I could.

His father dropped us off at the train station while insist Jack accept the five-thousand pounds being shoved in to his pocket inside a brown envelope. Their beautiful home already brought and paid for a decade ago left joint triple incomes ready to assist others if necessary and I wouldn't say no to an injection of cash from anywhere. I lumbered part-time in one of the student bars as Caroline and Emma told me it would restore my faith after the attack by Knowles but it also helped with books, bills, and travel fare to visit my family before finals.

I graduated with relative ease and still had no idea of what I wanted to accomplish. I only felt real about the relationship I'd developed with Jack and accept sadly my uni friends were going their own way. Over time I lost contact with Carla from college as my time was spent feeling out who I was during university and we only spoke on the phone occasionally. She was moving in to high-finance and I wished her all the luck because she deserved it. I was heading with no real path laid out but I wanted the very best for all my comrades who had shown passion and understanding of my sometimes selfish comings. I was lucky to know the people I had known and that included Jack's hearty trio.

His mother wrote me a letter of congratulations when I graduated. Reading between the lines she was enforcing her throne that I be the debonair girl and still hold on to my valour. 'No matter that which may be thrown your way, stand up and be yourself, signed, Mary'.

~

Mum patted down my graduation gown before the customary photos were taken of me, me and dad, me and Lucas, me and mum, and me and Jack.

He quickly disappeared leaving our family make-up chatting away while he caught up with Emma and Caroline amongst their graduate group.

"You still haven't made up your mind, have you?" mum glances in Jack's direction.

I appease her little. "Everything's opening up for me, mum, I just don't know if I'm gonna go somewhere for a few months first."

She palm brushes my wavy gown. "Your father and I want you to do well," gushingly noted. "We don't want you wasting all the time you've spent here, all that studying, writing, and exam passing. You've worked too hard, Emery."

I looked over at Jack and he's made his way across to my dad engaged in man-chat. I'm glad my dad liked him, it meant a lot. Mum liked him too but I could tell she worried about my feelings for a man over my future. Jack was my future and she had to understand he came included in whatever I chose to do.

"You're sure he can take care of you?"

Oh, mum, don't worry.

"Yeah," I said believable, "He's got a good job and a mortgage and we'll be moving in soon. He just has to finalise some things then we'll be off but you know I'll keep in touch. I'm not gonna abandon you, mum, never."

Poor old girl, she remains deep rooted in doom and I can only give her a grand hug before I feel my sister leap on to my back like a school kid looking for a piggy-back ride.

More joy restored.

We all thought Jamie couldn't make it because she was in surgery at Warwick Hospital working as an anaesthetist but she managed to get here in the end. It was good having the whole family here.

"You bloody did it, Em!" she cries in my ear, "Next it'll be marriage and a pack of kids! Flipping hell, well done!"

Ecstatic for her and for me, I tried bringing mum in to the vibrant conversation but she'd turned away and I saw her wipe at a tear. Jamie hadn't noticed as she was in a rush dragging me over to engage Jack and our dad, and when we literally crashed in to one another, Jack embraced me and my dad embraced Jamie.

Among our excited mingling bodies, I strained to look over at my mum as she relocated my brother attired in his sturdy professional Air Force get-up. The pair snuggled close to one another and he kissed the top of her head. Family came to mean everything and until you were grown and making your own way without the guide of those more wise, it left me feeling bare from the spiritual pouch of my mother.

~

New feelings stowed.

"When all's said and done, Em," Susan lays dear, "you'll be the one who has to face everything and handle all kinds of situations, no matter how difficult they are...and...in your own way too."

Difficult situations were everyday part of life. Nothing, not cooking, settling back to a routine, making new friends, adjusting to technology whether for better or worse, finding a job, keeping it, and making both families proud of me, none simple, all tough obstacles needing to overcome.

Perhaps it was easier to stay for another three-hundred-and-sixty-five days in this place before facing up to my responsibilities. Was easier, wasn't it? I swallow another year of what I thought to be emptiness, of sharing wash-rooms with so many, eating three-meals-a-day with dozens of others who either displayed good or bad table manners, and living with the constant threat of an argument escalating in to worse. Tempers frayed at the drop of a hat and you either rolled with it or challenged it. Challenging being the least best option. Come on, Emery, you yourself said things could only get better, stop procrastinating, meet the outside, face the families, go to a church even, ask the Almighty to cleanse and forgive you. That held a massive relief did it not? God forgiving over all earthly people was equally paramount because they could touch, feel you, reject your apologies or accept them. To carry forgiven I was sure to hear whispers behind my back as I'd begin to, once more, find my place in society. Was I even a flex in control that I was willing to confront all that? Would my bitterness shape too strong and hold me back from taking harsh opinions of myself? I couldn't lash out, I couldn't lose it, and if I was to make it out of here after next week, the verbal lashings and debasing would accompany me too. Was I ready to take it on the chin or would I revert to an earlier type?

Susan could lash me anytime, that wasn't a problem. Of course my bias toward her couldn't be dismissed but all the other people out there I might have problems with, not so sure. Those who didn't know me yelling crap in my face or some other unpleasant act being committed, I didn't know if I would keep my head or lose it. I had some hard choices to face. From the same spoon I'd take positives with the shit negatives, and in equal measure too, and my bitter pill to swallow would be another life lesson.

~

"So you're off?" said in unison, Emma and Caroline, as all three of us finished packing our suitcases ready for final valedictions.

I stopped a sec and addressed my university pals with optimistic eyes.

"There's so much to be done," reaching to embrace Emma first then Caroline.

"Where are you going again?" enquires the blazing redhead, smoothly rubbing my right arm.

"Further south," I answer, "Things are apparently beginning to boom."

A brooding start to the new Nineties was slowly moving aside making room for burgeoning ideas. As a postgraduate I thought moving southward would help decide where my long term career plans were headed.

Emma introduces, "Yes!" with all the joy of a new parent, "And we're going *all* the way down, baby, to London!"

She dives back on my freshly made-up bed and flaps her arms hailing Caroline to come join her. One looking to become an architect, the other a professor of antiquities, I'd never heard of such a thing. Both excelled while they were here and they would excel anywhere.

"You two'll do well," I feed them as they stretched back lacing fingers tidily behind their heads.

"Why don't you come, Em?" suggests Emma. "I mean it, come with us to London."

I shrug off the motion and Caroline dives across the bed, grabbing hold of me, yanking me between their resettling bodies. I try to sit up but Emma affectionately pins me down and Caroline pokes me in the side. The dig gives me the giggles and Emma makes a point to poke me too.

"Okay, stop, okay, shit!"

In typical Emma-Caroline mode they decide to delectably beat me up and I do my best to ward them off when all three of us end up tangled and laughing like banshees. Our playtime comes to a gradual stop and I'm stuck between each girl while catching my breath as Caroline wholesomely places a palm on my stomach, and Emma affectionately puts a hand on my left cheek. I, in turn, clasp both my hands over theirs. They are warm and soft under my touch, and as I look in to their eyes I feel the emotional bereft begin.

"We're going to miss you, you know," Emma smooches.

I nod. It says I'll miss them too.

"I wasn't kidding, Em," she repeats, "come with us to London. Bring Jack, who knows, you both might find your careers and enlighten your love for one another."

Enlighten our love, it was enlightened already.

"Yeah, Emery," adds Caroline, gently pinching my naval area, "There's so much to learn, so much to do down London, it's more open-minded down there, not like the stuffy conservatism up here."

"You're kidding, right," I hit them both, "Up here isn't stuffy, it's getting just as liberal too."

"But not with the same speed," lays Emma, rolling on to her back snuggling close to me. "There are bright lights, bars and eateries, entertainment not like up here but with a bigger variety and open to all sorts of people."

I smile coy.

"I get you two are open to anything, but my future's with Jack."

"Christ, Em, bring him along too, he's just about as maverick as they come! And they like maverick down London."

Caroline swirls on to her back and neatly adjusts close so I'm feeling like a human-strapped jacket. No matter though, their wonderful pressurising would not work.

"Just think of all the political bullshit he could get involved in, and you too. Shit, you're both rebels and you know it and I know you'd love London."

It sounded like a drug. The big capital and all its hedonism, nihilism, and politicism, it would be perfect for Jack, right.

"We've made plans, Emma," I say, keeping my eyes firmly on the ceiling picturing a fairy-book ending to it all: My prince and his princess having everything.

"Not all plans have to keep," Caroline scribbles, "You can break them you know. Not everything's written in stone, you don't have to stay tied down."

"I won't be tied down."

"Yes you will," reaffirms Emma, her tone almost afraid for me, "There are lots of people you could meet, lots of jobs to try out, lots of opportunities, different stuff you could do."

Lord, I sense something else going on here, some type of panic for me and it involves Jack being in my life. Emma and Caroline were lovers of a different sort, not only being two women but two women who saw things differently, openly, and farther. I got that feeling from our very first meet and I saw it grow and fix strong and it had to be marvelled at. Like a blonde never failing to look good in black, Emma and Caroline, two striking women, congressing two striking personalities, whilst dishing out truth and compassion to a dear friend.

They got me thinking for a minute.

"You think Jack'll hurt me somehow?"

Both girls switch on to their sides and feast me liking to haste away any upset.

"Ems," feeling Caroline's concerns swell, "look, he cheated and got thrown out of here and you were attacked by that shithead but it could have been another shithead and where was Jack, he wasn't here, was he, he left and you were by yourself. You could have got hurt by someone else holding a stupid grudge because of those test-papers!"

I grew uncomfortable.

"Is it because he's a guy?"

Emma snaps blunt, "You think we give a snip if you like cock over pussy, come on, you saw yourself how you'd got quiet after he'd been kicked out. It affected you and it shouldn't have in the way that it did. It wasn't healthy, Em. He cheated, you stayed. Where was the guilt in that?"

But I remember it tore Jack up something awful and he was twisted double over it. He didn't take it lightly and he missed me too.

Sitting up I reflected upon my friends then they sat up beside me.

"I know you guys mean well," I start, like having had my first kiss, "But hey, not everything goes to plan. You've got your ideas set on London and I wish you all the best in the world but I wish you'd be okay for me and don't worry, I'll be fine. We'll be like any other couple making our way in life."

"Beginnings like that aren't okay, Em," stirringly entered by a trusted Emma. "He's shown he has the upper hand in your relationship and that ain't good."

"He hasn't," I counter somewhat dejected, "I mean, we're both equal, I've shown him that and he's shown me."

"What, by your crashing bedroom antics?"

"Are we scoring points here?!"

"No!" Caroline insisted, taking an affectionate grip of my leg. "A lot of people liked you, Emery, a whole bunch did, and they could never get near you because of Jack."

"Wait a second," I lit back offended, "I didn't have a 'do-not-approach' sign in front of me."

"You never needed to," flecks Emma, "It oozed from Jack without him even being present."

Again I check both with a look of trepidation. Not knowing of their ever feeling like this I am left more uncomforted, however it is quickly donned over with the grandest hug from each girl.

"We want you to be okay, Em, we really do. We hope you know what you're doing and that you'll be happy."

"And," finishes Caroline, "you know we'll always love you, Emery, no matter what."

~

I deep down believed Emma and Caroline would stay true to their word if I were ever to meet them again. They sent me cards every Christmas with little notes attached about their lives going good and they always wished me the best of luck. Knowing the security personnel read everything that came in here first, I threw away their cards and notes after reading. I couldn't risk other people in here knowing of any close friends favouring me that much, especially as I didn't want the favours inside here to slouch any closer. Many let it be known that I could get anything I wanted, smokes, pot, chocolate, phone-cards, all I had to do was be open to getting myself one of the power-women. I mean, that's what they were called for some obscure reason, 'power-women'. For me, Susan had all the power and those inside here merely craved it. Who in the world would not want power that gave you freedom and authority to judge over others? Susan doled it out; the guards doled it out, so naturally that left the detained to dole it out on one another. Life was one big hard lesson and we were all forever learning. For my second day in here I got my head smashed against a shower wall for refusing to buy dope off one of the power-women's cohorts. Don't be stupid, I didn't retaliate, not right away anyway.

~

"We can close it down for today if you feel like?"

No, I didn't want it closed down, not yet. Susan allowed me extra time to get my stuff out but I wasn't getting it out. Not all that I felt I needed to.

My studying eyes take a stroll to her hand-held stress-ball sat on the desk. "Maybe I will accept this after all," spoken quiet, as I reach for her 'private Jupiter' upon the beech-wood.

A file rich moment she lets me play with the previously offered present then casually leans her elbows on to the desk's leather padded writing surface. I stop playing 'planets' and watch her eat in to my poring eyes.

Observing she states, "Clearly avoiding the subject again," with a furrow of tweezed brows, "I can't help you, Em, if you won't talk to me."

Hey, I had talked to her. Okay, maybe not everything, but surely suffice.

"We can let next week role itself out," her soft words sarcastically disguised, "Let it come natural with no plan in advance that might actually *help* your case."

A slight pilloried from her, hm, okay, go in blind, I could handle it. Rehearse little shit and they'd be able to tell I wasn't serious about my rehabilitation or expressed remorse, which of course I had in bucket loads, and at the time you could clearly see I meant it. I wasn't some eminent gloater bragging about unrequited love and the effect it had on you. Neither was I telling the world this is what you do when love conquers everything. No, no, no affirmation. I was explaining that Emery Pearson did it her way. This is the outcome she saw and chose to take that road however un-beguiled.

Love *could* conquer everything, though not everyone's love measured the same.

Susan breaks our unhappy quiet. "It feels like you've grown tired of being here and you're just going through the motions. We don't appear to be making any progress today. You're bored, clammed up. You've shut down when you really need to be opening up."

"Are you telling me what I should be doing now?"

"We're not going to argue, Emery. I have to make a final report and let the people in charge know you should be given credence and won't ever come back here. Done, *finito*, end of story! Adieu! You want to be gone, yes?"

Wow, her face shades darker. I've unrest my treasured timepiece and want to price her back together again. Sorry, Susan, I will come back to you.

"I'm pissing you off, aren't I?"

Splendid she gruffs, "You're not giving me anything I can use today to finally seal that deal. Come on, Emery, don't be difficult, they'll see all this. They want humble, respect, lessons learnt and all that. Surely you must know to express it for them."

Right, I understand the seriousness of my situation and must be reeled back to embrace my mind-fuck. I could change for them I could change for anybody. I could do what the maestro Susan wanted me to as her body flung itself back in to the spinal shape of her chair making this wonderful gasp escape her coloured lips. It came across amazing. Suddenly she whips her hair up and fastens it fast, her auburn locks shaping a scruffily tied bun. The sun arching through the windows captures her defined jawline which peels in to a long ballet dancer's neck. Glorious! Simply glorious!

145

My unhurried-placed, I ask, "What do you need me to do?" so I could hear her gasp again with a lean forward this time to fold her arms on top the desk. It was a sound I often liked hearing, like one were making surreal sex so that it knackered you to the point of being incapable of taking a breath. You know, when it gets knocked out of you during foreplay or you're coming to a marker like your head is about to explode. Yeah, that utterance, that sound, that stolen air, it has a quality uniquely sexual all its own.

Chapter Twelve

I can't remember details of what happened however I was left with bruised ribs, split lips, and both eyes blackened. That beating peaked. I received rough treatment from all corners for I was deemed to be a bit special.

I'd entered someone's 'allotted' space during the one-hour yard time before we were hoarded back to a diversity of brick-built cells. There were dorms, quartets, doubles, and the most prized being a single-cell usually given to real hard-arses or those deemed too vulnerable to share. Clearly I was afforded one after my callous beating and saw it as a reprieve from the power-chasers who constantly had me in the corner of their eyes.

"Who the hell do you think you are, Pearce?!"

I mean, that's what they called me in here, Pearce, you know, short for Pearson I presumed, but I also believed they wanted to burst my 'arrogant' bubble. The murmurs struck after my first breakfast in here that they'd branded me a snob because of my refusal to buy dope. They hated the fact I didn't smoke cigarettes either.

"Who the fuck're you, eh, some uppity-class cunt who doesn't wipe her own arse!"

My graduation from university labelled me, 'bourgeoisie' and 'stuck-up quean', of which I was neither but it didn't matter a toss. You were what they wanted to think, and if it meant you were going to take a pounding because of so, then that would be the case.

Initially I'm crest-off cool which I think infuriates them more. "Listen," my easy, "I don't want any trouble, okay. I don't smoke fags, I don't do dope, I do drink occasionally-"

Whump!

My style of dry-humour unappreciated and one of the power-three hit me in the belly with everything she had. I listened to them laugh at my doubling over and choking from the effect. I knew right then in my invaded quartet-cell, these three non-idyllic women would grab every opportunity to hurt me as I sensed plenty of enjoyment in their watching me react from that thump.

So not long after, less than a week passed, a couple of neutral others informed me I needed to grow eyes at the back of my head cos word went round I was going to get a heavy seeing to. Not just 'seeing to' but a 'heavy' seeing to. Now in here you didn't tell as it meant signing your own death-warrant so I tried to stay in view of the guards every second that I could.

"We know you're pissing yourself, Pearce," a voice rasped behind my ear, "Hanging round the brass-shit so they can see your chicken-arse! Well they won't be watching your scared arse all the time, will they?"

I had my warning.

I couldn't exactly stick a weapon under my pillow because, against three, they'd use it on me, not that I would have anyways but I tried letting things be, be. No matter my old judo-wrestling I couldn't take on three power-women at once and neither did I want to. I thought of Jamie challenging the biggest of that girl-gang but in here was different. You had to take on and win all three and I knew it would have been insane but not at all impossible. Trying to stay focused while expecting my bashing to come at some point I just wanted to get it over with; the wait for it being far worse as few other detainees met my acquaintance for fear of being targeted too and that was okay, I got it. I didn't want to bring anyone else my pain and besides, I could get on with doing my time and avoid bringing other people's crap in to my life. So some chose to see me as a snob, others liked exchanging a sentence or two, and that was that.

The system gave me my privileges. One letter a week I could write, and domestic duties were rewarded with time-collections that were totalled at the end of every month and you improved your chances of phone-card allowances and snack-extras from the treat-shop. My first visit from my mum was due at the end of my second month inside so she kept in touch penning me letters weekly. Jamie would still burst out crying when she thought of me and Lucas remained steadfast in his Officer Training, practically refusing to even believe my incarceration at times. Dad wanted to be the first to visit but I knew it would be too much for him so I asked just to see mum instead. Something told me she would better handle what had become of me because her non-judgement throughout each and every hearing that passed before my sentencing, she maintained a level of support and understanding I had to admit even shocked me. I recall kind words relayed impassioned by the Judge toward my mum before he sent me down. Twelve year stretch and I would probably do most of them, if I kept my head down and did my time clean. So that's what I was looking to do. But with three wolves hunting to tear me up at every turn, I was going to have a bloody hard time trying to stay clear of trouble.

~

I entered a book-reading class to keep me occupied and my mind off the impending three when I found among the dozen or so of us attending, only four from the dozen could actually manage to get through the first few pages of Wuthering Heights. The majority came there to avoid chores or break up the mundane day-to-day routine.

My eyes were opened at the flipping lack of suitable adult activities leaving many of these women in dire need for help to literate adequately. I could see why the main crowd thought I was a snob for the fact that the very first time in my entire life I discovered there were grown-ups who could not read or write well. My mum was left astounded by what I'd told her. She couldn't believe it either. Further discoveries I made when told a lot of these women were here for selling their bodies in order to buy drugs or pay bills. That kind of stuff was hitting me between the eyes and I realised what good fortune I'd been bestowed. Pried open were my wares to the severe imbalance in the treatment of men and women throughout their lifetime. The women moaned that if their men didn't pick up the slack, they 'upped and fucked off', how the ladies put it, and they were left to somehow make things work. The rent paid, the kids sorted, the clothes on one's back, all needs to be met by an unfortunate somebody.

"So you just had the one guy?" I'm asked one morning by a slightly older girl looking to interest me in a novel about romance for the next select-read.

She sounded a lot like Carla and I was glad it was not her.

"Yeah," I nod satisfied, replacing the Heights book back on the shelf.

The outside-teacher tells us detained to choose a new book as she'll be preparing next week's lesson then merrily exits the well-stocked library. Those not great at reading hastened to head off elsewhere leaving me and two others browsing for our next read.

"So why'd you do it if you only had the one guy?"

I was such a matter of interest.

Why did I do it?

I stop mid-reach for a book on the Crimean War and stay her eyes. Not sure if this was a wind-up or she wanted some home truths.

"I don't know," attempting to cater, "I fell in love once and that was it."

"It can't be," she throws back, like I must be deranged, "Girl like you and you only had the *one* love?"

I shrug. "Never felt the need to sleep around."

"Is that what you think we all do?" Shit, I hit a wrong nerve. "Sleep around? You think we're all slags in here, is that it?"

"Look, no, I-"

The library door swings open and the power-three enter to the complete surprise of us reader-three still looking to narrow down our book choice.

No words are necessary as the two remaining book-readers shuffle their way out leaving me and the jackal trio alone. The panic-button was by the door so I couldn't get to it, and indeed if I had, other thoughts laid that I would be sorry ever more had I pressed it. These unsigned rules were a mockery of all things to let be. The system that crushed these women was able to save them but an unsworn tablet of un-virtues prevented this from happening: The guards against us - and us - against the guards. You felt you'd lose at every turn. So I could try and make the panic-button but where would it leave me with the other women in here? A break of their *own* rules was seen as heresy.

Two of the rabid dogs started their approach and a third, the leader, picked out this thick geographical book and flicked loosely through the chiselled pages.

"Hey, Pearce," the dominant flashes confidence and barbarity at the same time while the other two make either side of me, "read much?"

A clever distraction for she hurls the damn thing at my head and I duck to escape allowing the other two to grab my arms and tussle me with grim determination greasing my back flat against the wall. I remember being in this position before at school though back then I was saved, I wasn't hurt too badly, and teenage boys did not hit as hard as these power-women did.

I tried utmost to brace myself and absorb it all but after the very first blow knocked the wind right out of me, I suffered every vicious shot to my gut for the next couple of minutes as she let go a twine of profanity in between her sinking punches. Receiving pain in here no matter of a slap-and-tickle delivered quick as assaults came with their very own personal storybook. *Sleeping Beauty* or *Cinderella* fables left hanging at the entrance to this hell, and new reading material sought in the vein of a damn fine battering. Feeling like my soul had been removed from the planet leaving my physical self a heaped mess on the floor; the power-three mentioned something about not hitting my face because it would draw too much unwanted attention. Oh, I thought it was due to the fact they just enjoyed punching me in the stomach.

~

After word spread the powers had shown me a 'timid' time, the next series of reading classes grew bloody significantly as I took up, along with the other two-aids who'd flaked away during my assault, helping teach some of the mindless brutes a thing or two about literacy. The outside-teacher left us in charge of one class as we opted for our own book choice and got a gaggle of new and curious women to attend. For ever I could not seem to work out why so many wanted to make our classes; the professional teacher wasn't in any way a *70's-Farrah-Fawcett,* nor were we three-aids specialist converters, but there lay a bond, a trust the other women galvanised, and their belief that we three book-readers could help them improve their lives with better grammar and spelling, maybe even a miracle to include a book borrowed from the library might also get read, those miniscule bonuses were welcome.

"You ladies are proving to be a hit with this," the outsider framed all three of her 'assistants'. "The guards say the atmosphere on your wing is less tense."

My fellow teaching two loved all the attention and mushroomed with credits piling up each week. Phone-cards, sweet treats, and more merits, added to a growing reputation of teaching the unteachable was breaking ground insofar as some uptight guards grew resentment, and the steadfast calamitous who hated system change, flaring their nostrils at us catalysts.

"Keep all this up," a senior officer noted, "and it'll help push your release dates a lot closer."

My gushing two, with added glee, scrunched up their shoulders and I could see everything come crashing down if the malevolence feeding its way to the other wings came full circle to bite us from behind. Oh, we never boasted, were never bumptious, but regime change where others thought it helped the system more and not the detainees would never get acceptance. What I couldn't figure was the fact we were helping illiterate and poorly read women to improve those areas yet we three were seen as colluding with the enemy.

"Maybe if we'd done music lessons," my untrained colleague commented, "and sung carols at Christmas, it would appear less of a threat."

Being different in here was a handicap and I could see why prison was supposedly a further imbalance for impoverished women. They were mostly from social economic backgrounds claiming destitution or hardship and I guess were expected to stay so. Learning to improve their reading and writing a curse to their equally impoverished detained. Envy was which sin again?

~

I spent another yard time in another book and got a football purposely kicked in to my face.

"Hey, bookworm?" some crony yelled from nowhere, "Let's see what you got in the goalie front!"

Urbanely, I shook my head no and rolled the ball back then refocused on my book when the groans and mumbles surfaced around me.

"Hey up, Pearce!"

I try not to make eye contact but quickly glance up and acknowledge my view over.

There are maybe twenty women on a netball size court, some half wearing their grey sweats, others just sweating through them, however all were peering at me like they wanted to come over and fuck me really hard. It was well known that I didn't do women but I never belittled them either. I honestly did not give a shit whether gay, straight, or the banded about new-bisexual, I wanted to stay alone and saw no problem with it.

Others didn't, "Single-man lover, hey!"

I tried to get back in my book.

"Hey, Pearce, all that one-man-loving shit, you might try sharing your experiences and show the rest of us why you don't feel the need to exercise?"

Come on now, I was blessed with good genes, my mum nor dad were overweight and my siblings stayed the same, and maybe my sports-loving upbringing left me in good stead. We were a slender family, nothing magical going on. No diets, no charms, no spellbinding mystery, just fortunate being born a Pearson.

"It might improve your standing if you weren't such a stuck-up cunt, you know."

I never used the word vulgarly. Jack once told me a cunt was a beautiful thing and I admired that. I would never use the word to insult.

"What's the matter, Pearce?" another voice hollered. "In your fucked up relationship you never used the fucking word?!"

They could never besmirch Jack's use of it. They would never understand he swore with elegance and emphasis, not demean other women daily by using the terms created to keep them subjugated. And neither would I.

The field of footballers floated with raucous laughter as I got up and headed for a quieter location. Upon my turning round I was introduced to a small corsair group who gathered directly behind me and it seems looking to add to my discomfort. Feeling the snarl in their cheerless eyes I evaded their greeting and stepped round to locate that lone spot. These wild women could not comfort me, yet at the same time I felt some of them genuinely wished they could.

~

The power-three thought my attitude ranked and they let me absorb another 'timid' beating. This time they motioned two others from the earlier football game to join in and I got hammered across my body leaving my ribs frigging sore and my stomach a mess. The usual verbal's were dished out to include a demeaning of my morbid affair as I soaked up the punishment and on that occasion, I felt the threat of a sexual assault come near. They didn't touch me in any way though. The threat had been there the way two of the women pinned my arms back and one curled her forearm around my throat while two others took turns to fucking wallop my torso.

Despite fresh word going round the wing that I got taught another of life-inside's-lessons, no one really knew how much I bleeding well hurt until I showered some days later. The severe bruising oil-painted my frame and the women understood why I couldn't take up class that week. It filtered back to my fellow two teacher's-aids, and our outsider, the real reason for my missed participation which helped fuel divide that the power-three were too amplified when dealing with me. Don't think the triple-set appreciated the criticism much because at breakfast, sympathies for myself allowed some, brave enough women, to let me know my part in the lessons were important to them and they wished the power-triangle would just leave me alone.

~

Upon my half enthused return to the classroom, the women swelled to near double in attendance and we were struggling to get through our revised programme in order to accommodate all so we doubled up our suggest and were granted two classes to be taught weekly. Even then both sets of women had pushed to all corners of the library and making it difficult to reach the bookshelves. Novels over three hundred pages had to be shared between two as the reading budget was constantly getting squeezed and biting in to other resources so we began to offer a more writing-based structure to the classes. Notebooks being far cheaper, the women could return to their cells happily scribbling down their inner-most thoughts with vastly improved spelling. That course of action on our part also turned out to be a little disconcerting as many of the detained thought that sharing their night time ponderings had to be shared with myself and my two unqualified aids over breakfast, plus once again, channelling heightened attention our way. It led to a surge in receiving shoulder barges so malevolent they left somatic contusions and we tried to instruct the women to do their part and submit queries or read a poem during the ascribed class times *only*. Some felt we were being miserly and a few did not return to the lessons. Trust me; it was a move which meant we were looking to avoid confrontation for all parties.

~

At times unpleasant jealousies reared among certain participants attending the classes who would embarrass the writings of their fellow detained by mockingly reading aloud private thoughts, that quite honestly, should have remained, bloody private.

"The *Emering's* teacher flew out her arms like butterflies and wafted a deodorised scent equivalent to a perfume fashion show. Her light brown eyes sparkled at the whim of any movement marvelling from the rear of the classroom. All the women fixated on this approaching body pacing up and down between us for when she femininely leant across and perused one's writing's, the bosom for ever a pillow be laid upon."

Of course those who thought it fun to poke humiliation on someone's personal words burst out in hysterics but a growing number, the vast majority now, hated the childish antics of the tormentors.

I felt terribly sad for an older woman named Charlotte who had clandestinely penned the paragraph. She never came back to our class. I fully understood her sincerity, I would hide away too if my heartfelt words written about Jack were read to everyone on our wing. No, I wouldn't leave myself open to easy harm. Any thoughts of him stayed locked up in my mind. However it was an open secret the way some women felt about me but I never flaunted. I wasn't Miss Universe nor did I pertain to be. Neither was I above the others yet clearly some fantasists thought I was.

"The class went really well today, Emery," our teacher shoved at me as we tidied up the emptying room. "You've got a special something for the women in here, I can tell. It pleases you to be so helpful, doesn't it?"

My nonchalant shrug is smiled over, "Just trying to help others with their reading and writing."

"Reading and writing!" she cries, "You've come a lot further than that, you, Thompson, *and* Harriot." Her glance back ensures the other two teacher-aids hear everything. "I think you ought to be rewarded after all you've accomplished," addressed so loud my two colleagues stop putting books away. "You undervalue what you've done here, Emery," another plotted say with her eyes transmitting admiration. "In less than two years you've brought these under-achieving women from a basic knowledge to an advanced level. Believe me that could not have been done in any school."

Okay, some high praise was good but I was beginning to feel giddy that something else was coming.

"You three," our outsider joyously announces, "have been put through to take the test for your teacher-trained part-one pass. I've no doubt you'll do well and it will leave you all in good stead for the future. Imagine when you get out of here you'll carry that certificate with you."

It was recognition alright and Thompson and Harriot were overjoyed. I was okay but not jumping with gaiety as another award for me in here felt like a draw back. No praise please, I'm fine you appreciating my efforts, just don't make a song-and-dance about it.

"Hey, listen, I'm alright," my Pearson makes out, thanks-but-no-thanks. "Give something to the women they've done all the hard work."

The outsider with alacritous concern takes a hold of my arm and shifts her body to stare in to my eyes. Look, I didn't need to be everybody's pinnacle.

"Emery," a suave forty-something begins, "every time someone heaps praise on you-you throw it back in their face. Why can't you just say 'thanks,' and be done for?"

I smell deliciously cooked incarceration food, mash potatoes, mince-pie and peas, float inside the room, a brief distraction from her words that mean much, however for me were to be left aside. I am a tad grateful, truly I am. I know she's an excellent teacher herself but things should be left at that.

"Honestly, Miss Trimble," my eyes smiling at their in-hock best, "do something to reward the women, I've had my fair share of tests."

Her disappointment in me is obvious however I won't be her trophy. No way. Not in this place.

~

So with our grouped-quartet teaching efforts we were turning women round for the better. Miss Trimble shared in her glory with the Head-Governor our growing success and un-rushed praise started to grow.

Like I knew, any outward reward seen in here equivalent to being a grass: especially if it earned you good credits and the strong possibility of time off your sentence.

"You're keeping your head down, Pearson, staying clean."

I was introduced to Governor Barron my first day. After everyone's induction we were introduced to her one at a time. Four of us came out the security van together and marched in to be strip-searched, calculated, and numbered. I'll never forget the outward impression of this relic of a building. It succulently met the penal system's leanings: Dark and foreboding thick walls, and wrought-iron from an Elizabeth-Regina-time with the mood to match. I did not want my family to come and visit me here. Was there anything I could do to get shipped out

159

somewhere less martyring? Nobody was asking for Butlins, but come on. And they wondered why rehabilitation rarely worked.

"You're a good woman, Pearson, really good words about you, good thoughts, yes, good."

Barron was well scripted to this place. If there need be an artwork polarising this institution it was a statue of her: You could smell her love for committing ill's wronged to get banged-up and taught a harsh lesson. Rehabilitate? Pah! Incarcerate, incarcerate, incarcerate!

"You've shown aptitude and altruism," laud said, "and I think that goes a long way in here," more warmer presented while flicking though papers on her desk that must be about me. "I have to say I am quietly impressed."

Mm, after her show of indifference, those wishing to better their self academically could be congratulated, if very reluctantly, and I did my best to put the needs of others first as I could see many needed it. Caroline and Emma's words about an equal society were digging in. They forever championed the lesser and begged for additions from the giver. I now saw why they argued fiercely for things to be put right. My understanding knew it would take a mountain of movement to really put things right, especially for the majority to have better lives. Didn't it make absolute sense? Surely there'd be far less problems in our society if we were all afforded the basics without having to battle each step of the way for them. From what I'd gathered being in here, most of the women would not have done what they'd done if things had been different. That weaker-sex adage filtered through to everything, especially as most of their crimes came from *being* the weaker sex: *Weaker?* Fucking any guy for money to feed the family or a drug habit, stealing paltry gear for God knows what, and passionate shit over some significant other, weaker? Yeah, but we could all relate somewhere in that bunch of acquired failings couldn't we, and yet still, I was left finding that if they had not been women, would they have got banged-up so hastily? I was starting to feel more and more that's why I had been tossed inside and figuratively got the key thrown away. I dismantled every rule bespoken of me.

"With the way you're going, Pearson," a piped up Governor sang, "you might be eligible for an early parole hearing."

Eh, what?

"You've clearly displayed a willingness to help others and that sticks favourably with the likes of me and my team. We've seen change for the better all round and you've a growing reputation. You are well-liked by the women and I think that's very good indeed."

Oh, shit, find that thrown away key!

Suddenly I know it all sounds too good to be true and I know there is a 'but' in there somewhere.

"But..."

Fuck!

What is it?

"...You haven't *exactly* shown your crime to be...regrettable."

Eh?

Now wait a sec, to lay a more preferable open-institution I had to show regrets? God, I was so sorry, but regrets? Of course I had regrets. Anyone would with my unfortunate outcome. I'm locked-up in here for Pete's sake, there had to be regrets, there *are* regrets, aren't there?

So tell me more.

"If you could possibly..." neutralisng paperwork she accurately places it aside then interweaves her fingers before issuing dictatorship-eyes in to my prison-owned, "...be open to, say...several months of...some type of therapy, say...you know...accept responsibility and show awareness you've measured yourself to be a healed child in the eyes of God, well...it could go a very long way for you."

Jesus, what!

Free of charge, it's made clear, I get it!

Or do I?

By taking out months of chat my sorry arse could be up for early release? You frigging bet I'm in.

She stands with her air of spiritual superiority and slips my paperwork in to a drawer full of files next to her emblem soaked antique desk. I do not mistake a move from her rattled old bones.

"Think about it, Pearson," she reaches her conclusion, "Several months in therapy...and you could be free."

I had *nothing* to think about. Like wanting to breathe, seeing my family at home, cook my own dinners, and remain forever Jack's, I really, seriously, had nothing to think about.

Chapter Thirteen

Some women had tried it before. There were success stories you can imagine and ones where no amount of talking could sway any bad behaviour for good. The more challenging women in here - the 'lifers' - had little desire for it, unless they wanted aid to change for the better, and because I had been slayed with twelve years though may be out in five - five being far better than twelve - I was willing to give it a go. With nothing to lose, but hell, everything to gain, I remained up for it and not due to an early release date alone, I would actually see if this stuff worked. What could a stranger find out about me? What could I possibly reveal to a total stranger?

Of the many who used dual-personality conditions to get lesser or acquitted rulings was something psychology majors argued over in uni. For me, I didn't believe in it, and I was mortified that mind-professionals did. I mean, why is someone always deemed 'insane' when they kill, especially when they happen to be of the wealthy kind? Why didn't they just walk down the street and throw all their money away to everybody? That for me was insane!

This defiled excuse of a strange occurrence happening when you took a life during some temporary madness was unbelievable. Sure a person snapped, there's a moment of anger, the will to harm, to take every and anything away, but to give it that label of 'brief insanity' each time and watch murderers of others walk free; nah, never got it.

~

"Mum, I could be out early if I agree to some therapy treatment."

She's ecstatic at the possibility. My first three years inside were tough on her as they had been tough on me. Each time we saw one another she left in tears and I could do nothing to ease her suffering.

I asked Jamie to write letters from then on after seeing her during several visits became too heart destroying. I wanted her to concentrate on getting the midwifery certificate as anaesthesia had come uninteresting. That was Jamie, following her big sis with getting cold feet after a while and moving on to pastures new. Whatever she lassoed she kept hold of, and that meant *not* lassoing my troubled situation. She had to stay free from all this, for my sake and her own, and I had to let her stay free.

"Your father wants to come up next visit," mum informs me. "It's been a while and he wants to see you, Emery."

I shiver at the thought.

"Mum, he can't handle me in here. He's a nervous wreck when he leaves."

"He knows," she flits back, "and he doesn't care. He just wants to see you, he loves you and misses you and he wants to be able to see you sometimes."

I asked that he not attend either. Writing letters was fine because his visits were a sobering experience. I let my family down badly and wished they'd pay me no visits at all but get on with their lives. I would understand if they chose to do that, however the opposite was happening. Their concerns for me were devastating.

"Just say you'll see him if he comes, Emery. Please don't push him away, oh God, he loves you!"

And I loved him too. So no, I would not push him away and never would. He was welcome to come and see me I simply wished that he wouldn't. With his worrying, never mind aging health deteriorating, I prayed for him to stay away and be strong.

"Of course I'll see him, mum, you know that." Unsteadily I begin to cry and other detainees in the visiting room catch this. I didn't care.

"Emery, I never meant to upset you, I'm sorry."

Mum reaches to hold my hand and a guard comes over with a gesture that we release, however he sees my tears and figures on letting us be.

My mother squeezes my hand so hard it hurts then she kisses it. She does not want to let go but the guard returns and this time we keep free.

"I've left a package for you to collect when you're ready," she lights up, as I wipe at my tears. "I know they have to go through your stuff before giving it to you, but there's everything you need. Oh, and Lucas gave me a book, now he's military obsessed, and it's about mental training in all these different combat forms but he thinks it will help while you're in here."

I offered up a smile whilst thinking of Lucas smartening his shirt-collar to appear stunningly bona fide in his Officer uniform and realised then perhaps if I'd taken the military route under the guide of my brother, I was pretty sure I would not have ended up here.

Mum let me know he was going from strength to strength and that he thought of his lil sis every day and would try and make next Christmas to pay me a visit.

"He doesn't have to," I tell mum, "He's got so much going on he doesn't need to break stride to come and see me."

"He wants to," she says undeterred, "He misses you too and wants to see that you're doing okay."

"You can tell him I'm fine, mum."

"Emery," she puts down religiously robust, "*you* can tell him *yourself.*"

I sigh heavy and lead off another best smile. It is all I can do as the beeper for visiting-hour stings. Unwilling, we both rise and mum steps round the small table to give me the most fabulist embrace I had had in a really long while.

"We all love you, Emery," she says, "and we think of you every single day, do you hear me?"

I heard my mother. I smelt her hair and her perfume and she smelled me. No matter all my wrongs our bond could never be undone, and feeling such turmoil drilling around inside me, it took the very same guard again to approach us and say, it's time ladies.

~

I was handed three personal letters that week from dad, Jamie, and Lucas. They were all long, detailing events in their lives which were euphoric. I knew dad would have a better grasp of things after mum's visit knowing he'd be made welcome on his next schedule time with me. From the absolute beginning I kept all my family's letters yet it took one miserly cell-mate to steal them away after she received upsetting news that a distant family member crossed-over to the other side and decided to snuck in my bunk drawer to read through my mail. However I caught her red-handed.

"You nosey git, give them back to me!"

She's taller, broader, fearsome, but we never had quarrels. She stayed out of my business, and I hers, so there was never any reason for our butting heads: Except that day.

Whipping round to avoid my outstretched hand, she tears up some of my mail and I begin to lose it.

"What the fuck are you doing, they're my letters!"

"You're so secretive, Pearson, you got too much to hide!"

I step back and give her a warning look. Hand them back or we are done.

"Teacher's pet, governor's arse licker, women's tease," she's spitting all this fury glancing over my mail then spurts out family names. She's pushing it!

"'Love you lots, Emery, love from us all, Em, can't wait to see you, Emery'!"

Her chest rises up and she inflates with rage. My family paying attention to me, despite my lock-up, was not anything to bother her yet today it gravely did. I was sorry she lost a family member, anyone would cast sympathy but it had nothing to do with me. I wasn't a miracle worker as she continued to swell, and I'm swelling too, though not with rage but tears. I want my letters back without more of them getting torn up.

"Fucking spoilt bitch, Pearce! Everyone spoils you!"

Not wanting to pounce all over her to retrieve my letters because it will cause unforgivable damage, I just wanted them back without further burden.

"Okay, Sicily!" That's what everybody called her, some old Mediterranean connection from afar. "Hey, just put them down will you, you don't have to rip them."

She stops and grosses bizarrely, changing in the moment to heap a pile of utter misery on me and starts to tear my letters in half. I have so many she manages one huge tear then I'm all over her wrestling to save the untorn rest.

Our vociferous struggle fuses a burst entrance from two guards who grapple us both and she's screaming vulgarities about me and my relations. A guard holds each of us and I guess because I'm tearful he lets me go seeing as the ripped paper mess belonged to me. Dropping to my knees I gather up the undisturbed mail and torn pieces trying to thread things together.

Eviscerated felt I!

The guard's voice boomed, "Hey, Pearson?"

I couldn't talk as I was roaring my eyes out.

"Pearson?"

He reaches down and snatches hold of my arm, "Oi, Pearce?"

Through a cloud of stormy tears I see he's carefree and doesn't give a shit. Sicily is still spitting filth as the other guard drags her out of our cell. My tears briefly stay as the first guard pulls me up and contumely bashes me in to the wall.

"You stay cool, Pearson, alright, keep this to yourself, we'll deal with her, she's had a bereavement for chrissakes and we don't need you making trouble."

Me make trouble? Another brand of joker in here!

Behind distressed eyes I nod okay at him then garner the spilling of my family. My fast scan; there are some thirty or more letters that will need sellotaping together and probably another couple dozen that were in small pieces. I thought it a hallucination. How could someone be so cruel to destroy such treasured possessions of another? I couldn't believe what Sicily had done. I would never speak to her again no matter what. She wasn't a friend she wasn't an enemy. She was nothing. I was upset she'd lost a relative but she had no defence as far as I was concerned for what she did. I was hurting some and did not think I could get over that day.

~

Needless to say most of the women sided with Sicily due to her current mental state. Others thought her selfish actions unforgivable. She was allocated a single-cell after that as I strongly believe we would have banged heads following the dramatic episode. Christ, I kept questioning why she'd done it and always fell back on the explanation she was jealous of my mum's visits and the copious letters afforded me. She had family who could write I'm sure but it seemed no one ever bothered. Being well aware some women in here bore dreadful grudges I get that, but if you never did a damn thing to anyone in the first place, why the hell bore a grudge anyway? Society didn't pay in equal terms, ninety-nine-percent of us get screwed; the other one-percent seemed to thrive. Who do we honestly meet throughout our lives who appear well-grounded and content? Very fucking few!

I took time to peer inward. Truth be revealed, I was alright with what I found, though maybe some would say not.

Perhaps I was unaware-arrogant, even knight-errant, but I thought myself to be grounded and content, however traits like those aren't about happiness. They are one-sided and ignore the feelings of others. I hadn't done that, well I hoped I hadn't. I believed unerringly my feet were firmly on the ground, yet after all that had happened these last few years, I certainly was not content, and one without the other seemed unshapen.

A bad atmosphere percolated the wing since the Sicily outburst and I could be found piecing back the large jigsaw that had once been my family's letter-album. Miss Trimble noticed that week I'd lost enthusiastic momentum during both reading classes and decided to dig at my thoughts, though I remained quiet over the events. I occupied the quartet-cell most days as my two other prison-mates allowed me space to sellotape on the floor. Word soon spread I was busy trying to salvage all my letters and no sooner had I practically rebuilt my common-piece of family correspondence; I was shrewdly visited upon by the power-three.

They entered my cell in that ownership manner which said they'd all the time in the world and ensured no hapless guard was about to disturb anything as though they had already paid someone to turn a blind eye to their unrequested showing of my space. It wouldn't take much either: some smokes, dope, chocolate bar, or a percentage from a contraband drop to the prison later in the week. The jigsaw letters were almost complete when I got my left hand crushingly stood on by a size-eight foot eager to inflict damage. Grabbing hard the uninvited shin area I tried to push the leg off but my hair was seized and all three powers garrisoned dragging me off the floor before hassling me down on to a cell-mate's bottom bunk.

The usual festinate punches sunk in to my stomach and thudded against my ribs and I couldn't stop a thing as the leader climbed on top of me while the other two held me down and she happily smashed her head in to my face.

Feeling drugged and bleeding from the nose I struggled to focus only to see blurred faces growl and gnash teeth indicating the next series of fists about to crash in to me would continue until all my letters were destroyed.

In hopelessness I could neither move nor beg them to stop as the power-two controlled me by the throat and sat me up forcing me to watch their leader take the sellotaped letters, and all of my existing ones, to proceed steadily and rigorously tearing them apart.

I watched in vain as my family's communication with me got destroyed. These last few years those letters were all I had to recall moments of happiness whilst I remained stuck within these walls and facing the unpredictability of serving several more.

What was left resembled a pile of tiny torn strips kicked together to make a neat paper-shredded ant-hill, and all I could do was watch, spluttering and coughing from frequent punches still wantonly driven in to me.

The largest, most evil smirk I had the displeasure of witnessing, spread over the leader's face after she completed her destruction then slowly she approached me and sat herself tight across my legs. For once I wished I could fall asleep and wake up not remembering a thing but I'd witnessed my family's stories get buried before me and did not have the strength to even cry. The other power-two made certain my arms were well bracketed as their leader informed me that Sicily had slashed her wrists and I was to blame for sending her to a single-cell in her vulnerable condition. Really, my fault I attempted to get my own material she'd stolen seeking to abolish the lot? It didn't add up but did anything in here. Stop the excusing, I imagined saying, you three enjoyed besetting me whatever the given, so with my nose bleeding, my head held back, and both my arms nailed down inside a leering tribal pack, their leader took absolute delight in punching my guts till I lost conscious.

~

There were special words in there about Jack. Phrases, jokes, and sayings, that recalled treasured moments were penned in those letters. Written down, forever memorialised, past events from my family's interpretations that had meant everything to me.

They never appeared to judge what happened. They hadn't abandoned me or exclaim I should stay away from their friends. All the pain I'd caused I began to think my actions in the past were highly ill-judged. And the pain I received in here; a scroll from my detained fellows declaring - though not from all - I had it coming, and would endure everything they dished out. Constant talk about rehabilitation, readjusting, redemption, and I suppose a lot of other 'R's, one began to rear inside me and it was the ugliest of all: Revenge. God knows I ached something rotten with it after being roused awake by my two cell-mates who unwittingly found me and helped clean me up, but I could not take my eyes from the torn mess that had been a fragrant history for me. No graduate certificates, no academia of praise, nothing could replace the joy I felt when I got a heartfelt letter, and as I lay in bed that night trying to picture all the different styles of texts, some double-jointed, in parts single lettering, I'd laughed at Jamie's joking and raised brows with Lucas's accomplishments. Dad would throw in rugby scores when there were international tournaments, and mum stayed mum: What she cooked last Sunday, how the garden needed attending, the latest book she was reading, and I remember a hauntingly beautiful passage about the smell of my room when I left for university. My family's letters had held me together and now I found myself falling apart.

~

I never mentioned a word, not even a syllable about who'd done it but everyone knew. I applied focus in my teacher-assisting and tried to further open the women's minds by suggesting they check out the Crimean War or attempt finishing Wuthering Heights, and Miss Trimble ordered in copies of Rumble Fish after my request resulting in some women fiercely arguing the necessity of having good male role-models in a home. Many women recalled a book called *Kes* from their school days and that was gone over too. Suggestions and requests came from all walks of life as the broadening of tastes was met with enthusiasm and a natural haste to invite new unorthodox material provoked deep discussion. Soon the reading-writing classes merged with heated debate about socio-economics and the difficulties of centuries-old human stereotypes still permeating today creating obstacles for the masses. We made ask of Barron to increase the twice weekly classes to three but she shut down the idea fast. There was recreational time, visiting time, library time, all to be considered, and the already two reading classes was eating up a lot of guard time to ensure safety could be met on all levels. We stretched ourselves and were coming on good, so not to push it. When exams were taking place that too had allotted time and monies siphoned to grasp those certificates coming in thick and fast had to be taken in to consideration.

No third class, okay, my mind was filled with more than enough to be doing, yet I lay at night and let a tear fall as I looked over the growing new pile of my family's letters.

Chapter Fourteen

Dad visited every other month and sometimes he and mum came together. I got one or two letters weekly in addition and my pile was increasing though I never said a breath to them about the other mail being destroyed. They never queried if I kept or got rid of my mail. They left things up to me how I handled it. They wrote, they visited, and I saw in them how much I had let my parents down. Christ, I hadn't wanted this. I never knew things would turn out this way and I began to wish I'd never loved.

Seeing mum and dad holding hands and glancing at one another as though in the moment only the three of us mattered, I embossed every meet with smiles and secret wishes to be free. I'd start afresh, make them joyed, and even when a short outburst occurred in the visiting room, my parents rarely showed shock for they grew to understand the enormity of the task facing me. God, I loved them so and rebounded with characteristics of my being okay and coping well. I smelt the sweetness of my mother, and that strong, male aftershave of my father, and it expressed to me they would not drown in sorrow nor let their appearances or hygiene slip.

I was proud of them and them still proud of me. No matter the circumstances we all faced, we would stand by each other and my parents would stamp this in to me every time they came. I was not alone, a phone-call away, a letter, they would be there, and I, forever, inside their thoughts.

My family!

How did I mess it all up?

Why did I?

~

Inside class, true tales of real love were read out loud and thrown open to opinion from others. The women were brave when it came to revealing lost loves and wounds inflicted from past relationships I couldn't believe. From having petrol poured over your legs and set alight to the slash across the throat in a display you would never dare leave. Life's imbalances had to show God, or the Devil, whoever was running the bleeding planet, their plan wasn't working.

Witnessing such suffering, I mean, who the hell was capable of trying to understand an iota of it? The Devil could gloat and God would float. Only those two could handle the unbelievable savagery of man. I wondered how the emergency services felt when they saw this infernal damnation on a daily basis. How the fuck did they begin to cope? Not everything drummed down to facetious comments. It couldn't be that simple. Death, whether intentional or accidental, not all the time dismissed with flippancy. At some point it had to tear in to your soul and extinguish all you held dear. It had to.

~

The fragmented mail episode left me a long time with stomach illness. I felt mentally ruined and never realised how important penning a letter was from the person writing it to the one receiving. Like an umbilical cord's emotional attachment, it should not be broken.

As with that, my eyes were further opened when the women penned wretched details about awful childhoods to adulthoods as they lay bare their words which included some self-harming being one damning indictment.

I was left wondering who on earth managed to have a successful relationship that didn't hide defiled youth horrors in some way.

~

I'm asked curious, "Never an utterance, eh, Pearson?"

I look back over my shoulder and see Thomson collecting paperwork after the last woman leaves the library of our second weekly class.

"I mean," she continues, a glance upwards, "all the other women talk about their partners and their crimes and you just sit there not saying a single word."

From my literary pile I'm putting away this one book about 'father-daughter-rape' and I can't contemplate my dad thinking of me in that way.

"You don't talk about what you did, do you? You don't say anything to give anyone an insight in to you."

With the broadening of the women's intellect and smart use of words, interest in every other person here was a hot topic of chatter, me included.

"Why don't you talk about it, Pearson?" she fascinates, "You think you're any different cos of what you did? Jesus, you got twelve years for godssake."

Twelve!

Not many women were doing that sort of stretch. It was usually a lifer of some kind and I never believed I deserved to receive so long. Semantics, challenges, being a woman, and taking a dreadful decision made me all wrong. Yeah, I saw it that way now; after four blinking years.

"I'm like everybody else," I respond half-hearted, "Banged up because the system doesn't favour me."

"Oh don't give me all that bollocks!" Thomson rasped offended, "Thought you might have managed to squeeze it light cos you're uppity and all, top lawyer should have got you a much shorter sentence."

Here, still under puzzlement, they think I am not an ordinary gal who went to university and got a few extra qualifications to do something in life, but a love I felt led me to being here, and none, no one, not in this place, or outside, would ever understand that.

"What," I start, placing another book about abuse on its shelf, "you think we paid some lawyer to *get* me twelve?"

She freezes and lays supplicate eyes across me. Thomson was inside for running a brothel because her husband walked out and she was finding it hard to make the bills and feed a growing girl of six. Her sentence was nine years, and though she might serve five, she had shown increasing resentment toward the system for failing to pick up on her neglectful partner to punishing her instead. I kept my head of the idea the imbalances bestowed male and females being the reason why most of us were here. I wasn't saying we shouldn't pay for our crimes, just to look at the type of sentencing reflecting those crimes. A recent reduced manslaughter charge, dropped from murder, was given to a man who'd killed his partner during an argument because he claimed she nagged too much and was handed seven years. For our crimes, Thomson and I did feel hard done by.

She doesn't stop thinking about me.

"Then why'd you get so long? Why'd they throw the book at you, it doesn't make sense. Who'd you piss off?"

I shrug simple with no offer to indulge and perhaps that is why I am also here. I refused to indulge those who thought I should open up and let them inside my head and explain my actions, but of course I wouldn't. I wasn't helpless. I realise I could have helped myself but I was not in the habit of helping people like that: those mind-fuckers would have been happy to lobotomise me after sticking probes everywhere and applying electric shock treatment. That's ultimately what they wanted. I didn't want it and Jack would never have approved it either.

Thomson still hasn't left, "Shit, Pearson," she says upset, shelving another book, "You're a difficult one to work out! We're all laying it on the line and you keep silent about everything."

"Hey up," I reach round her, "no one…" one more book shelved; "no one has to speak out if they don't want to, these women choose to."

Facing me she clearly disagrees.

"No, no-you," her retort, "It's you, they do it for you. Can't you see that?"

Miss Trimble pokes her head in from the hall to check if we are done packing the books away. Thomson flashes we're finished and I hurry to shove my remaining paperbacks in to their slots.

"Great," Trimble says charmed, "the guard needs to lock up for lunch."

Thomson and I make eye contact and she has a sad look to her. I don't want to fish around why because I really did not want to find out. Her words that the women in our classes were doing it for me were unsettling enough.

~

I chased myself about and got down to business. Well, I mean business in here, writing back to my family, ensuring the women stayed focused on passing the latest tests, and assist with increasing their use of expression. A lot of stories told required lots of expression and the women's flourishing use of language applied with it.

My absence of revelation saw more resentment creep in but it also explained why Barron nudged me toward taking therapy. I hadn't broken down nor ever used drugs. I stayed inside and those who opened up to the world saw their attitudes change for the better. Our classes seemed to be a branch held out for anyone to join, and as places were full, a number had to wait till someone graduated. We ribbon-tied it with the term 'graduate' because others argued why had the term belonged to alumni only? So graduate it was. I mean, what was a single word between us detained? Not like we could etch it in the Magna Carta.

~

My face laid buried in another book this recreation-time and for some wind-up reason I got another ball slung in my direction. It clashed against the bench I was sitting on and because the badly aimed thing was on its last legs, when I handled it amidst polite intentions to hurl it back, the poor thing deflated.

I knew not to toss it then as that would have inflamed someone - for no apparent reason - so I rose from my seat and walked across to return it.

"You cunt, you burst it!"

"No, I didn't," said true, "It burst when it hit the side of the bench."

The heavily assembled sleeper-bench was put together from an old carpentry class and seen the test of time. Its life edging becoming a little sharp, the basketball-netball-whatever-ball, had seen better days over worn through stitching and erased logo. There was nothing to contest.

"No!" slammed again at my face, "*You* fucking did it!"

I paid no attention to this woman previous, I didn't know her and so it would remain. Not one for slanging matches during recreation-time, I offered looking to hand the ball over but nobody took it.

With the hair on the back of my neck standing up I decided to keep the useless thing in case the women thought I'd challenged them by making its return, therefore I spun round with intentions of getting back to my reading when I acutely, base-instinct, sensed someone's clothed malice run up behind me.

Oh, old school days, eh.

Never assenting to anything nor mean for anybody's misfortune, I wish I had not gone over there in the first place and remained where I sat. Regrets were becoming a familiarity.

A hideous blow fastidiously aimed to the back of my head, I ducked and repositioned fast, capturing my left arm across the woman's waist, and my right, diagonal over her shoulders, and instantaneously hoisted her a couple of feet in to the air and suplexed her fumbling form down on to the tarmac ground.

She yelped in pain rolling over upon my release and I jumped up staring in disbelief because I knew I had torn something.

My hazel eyes drowned in contrition for every witness there, and the women from our wing gathered round to register these long drawn tables getting turned.

I wasn't happy about it I was bloody annoyed. Wanting to wheel back time and stay nosed in my book, but hey, the cat was out the bag.

Lucas said I could really hurt someone.

Jamie overplayed her retaliation.

And I was in an institution that readily frowned upon such female actions.

Shame clouded that I hadn't controlled myself but what could I do with an animal on my back looking to break my head.

They gave me a fortnight down the block. Full solitary, no privileges, and a damning word spread throughout the wing that my sudden display of hidden talent had better be shared, just like my reading-writing classes, or else?

~

The third night in to my two-week's sojourn, a couple of erring guards thought it necessary to show me I couldn't capture a power-women title because I was, *'All sugar and spice and everything nice'*, and *they* didn't play that way. It was no good my telling them I did not want a thing to do with running the wing as I never cared for contraband dealings because it was a road to nowhere. They didn't listen and didn't care either way. Still, their beating up of me helped release some tension they carried round with them. Skilled in their well-worked torture techniques, hands wrapped inside tea-towels as they pummelled me from wall to wall, ensuring they left no bruised knuckles for themselves after hitting my guts and kidneys, and like the power-three, I could see these two guards got off on it and I remained crouched up on the floor for the rest of my time in there.

Little else improved with the reception I got when I returned to the wing for the women demanded to know why I'd kept such a skill under wraps. Why hadn't I defended myself more, why not challenge the power-three, why on earth be the victim when I could have crippled the terrible trio and be heralded a *decent* leader of the damned? I mean, no drugs, no violence, intimidation or bullying, but a prison wing built on better standards whilst those looking to improve their self-worth could? This slot would have been run like a well-oiled *Women's Institute*. However I never understood the craving for power in here. It only led to misery and a responsibility for others of which I wanted neither. No matter how much I explained I wanted to do my time with as little fuss as possible, the women would not let my telling skills lie.

~

Some couldn't understand that fighting multiple people was a fantasy for the film-maker and not real-life, and fighting over disputes was never encouraged. Yet I understood the women's point when alluding to the fact I got beat up and maybe could have stopped it from happening. Standing up to bullies was okay when rules applied but not all rules applied in here. I couldn't risk becoming a power-woman and having to watch my back every single day expecting the next threat to myself come seek. I could do nothing about the women of power wanting to regularly bash me and I would not go looking for it. I wasn't a fighter, no, I was better off a helper.

Nevertheless I could not escape surreptitious requests for *'learning those moves'* while overseeing paperwork during class. It filtered back to the wing-governor, a Jane Ruth, this sporty, retired Army Sergeant, that I showed willing to handle myself on the right occasion and perhaps could encourage some kind of self-defence stroke fighting-fit group. Physical-Education I could not teach, how the hell would I tell if someone's physical fitness was being pushed beyond their endurance limit or if a heart-attack was due any second? I made no want for that type of pressure and certainly no reason to help another dislocate someone else's shoulder.

"Kept all that clever shit to your lonesome, eh, Pearce?"

An old-lifer introduces herself across the table from me as we shovel a hearty porridge in to ourselves.

She continues, "Knew there was something 'bout you and that straight-up-walk of yours."

'Straight-up-walk' like I had been deliberately avoiding walking stooped.

"A lot of us forgot 'bout your snobbery when you helped the women with their reading and writing shit, and now you've gone back to your snob mode, well that doesn't bear well with some, Pearce."

I couldn't remember when last I was called Emery. I think it would be a shock if anyone were to use it now. It also felt very different when Jack said it, an appreciation of it, like a portrait *Van Gogh* would paint or a scenic plantation by *Monet*. I'd grown far from my first name and would wait patiently for it to be reinstalled when I were reunited with my family. *"Emery Pearson," The Judge exclaimed, "You have been found guilty-"*

"You need to come back down to earth," I'm told fast, "The women want something from you and you need to show you're prepared to give it."

I am offended.

"Give you what," I snapped, "A couple of judo throws, or arm locks, or learn to break someone's shoulder?" I edge my bowl away. "It's not up to me to teach you that stuff. I won't show you how to fight or do any of it, I'm not like that."

"Don't you fucking get it, Pearce?" her retort, practically reaching over the table and snatching my spooned hand. "That shit can give women confidence and self-esteem to feel better 'bout handling themselves when they're out there meeting some bloody nutcase. Something tells me you're not exactly afraid when you walk the fucking streets cos you don't look like a desperate cunt in need to sell your body just to get by!"

Well fuck me.

I make her wiser, older, wrinkled eyes and see she has been through the wringer. Life's stories scribbled deep in her lines of dangerous roads walked. Maybe I hadn't travelled her path and neither was I going to fuel a short-lived confidence my meagre moves could save them from anybody. It didn't work that way, it never worked out the same. I could scrap with Jack and we would have great fights, but in the end if he showed determination, I would not have stood a moment's chance.

"Look," I say to her softly, "I'm not a saviour, okay." I do my best to make her understand. "I'm not this... *answer* everybody seems to think I am. I might help out with reading and writing but that's it. I can do that I can't do the other stuff. I don't want to run the wing I don't want to teach judo. I'm not the one to change your lives that way. You women are starting to look at me like I can do anything, well I can't...I won't. I don't need it. I just want to do my time and be left alone, that's all."

~

That was not all.

For a while things were permitted to run smoothly as another Christmas approached and my parents left a super-sized hamper for me with the wing-governor. Its contents ample had everything any detained person could wish for so the annual special were enjoyed. A spicy whole-chicken required microwave heating within forty-eight hours so it would make the twenty-fifth of December, and all the other trimmings, black pudding, desserts, fruits, mint chocolate, and several mini-liquor bottles which were naturally confiscated by the guards, I shared it all out when Christmas came. My refusal to teach judo-wrestling long forgotten as each and every one of us delighted in the ambience of a good old-fashioned prison-Christmas, and even a large tree got hauled in and was decorated frivolously by a couple of overly-merry ladies who had successfully gannet grabbed a few of those liquor bottles while attending the guards' office to clear up their tea-making facilities.

My mum and dad's offering engaged us all to embrace a merry old time, and for once my 'snobbery' brushed off on to hardened others even for twenty-four hours, because there flew no swearing, nor malice looks, only a desire to hand out joy and sing carols. And after noticing our two swaggering tea-ladies hiccup through tinsel decorating, the pious guards allowed us the remaining mini-liquor bottles to be had, plus several litre-size bottles of malt from the staff cabinet. I gave away my spirits and watched this special day come one not to forget. I hadn't bought anyone's affections I just knew that that was the way most of them wanted to be.

Chapter Fifteen

It was our first entire summer together alone and I was inducted to fruit pieces that could benefit me in other ways than just eating.

We moved down to Hertfordshire. Jack brought a small place, two-bed newly built, in the midst of a block of four on a growing estate. Upwardly mobile young couples were homing in with an optimistic view of everything. In fact they all seemed to *have* everything; a car each, good jobs, ten credit cards, and family and friends who flocked to their abodes each month to have backyard barbecues and dinner parties. Our little community endorsed a set of feel-good factors that I thought hid open truths. Nothing portrayed so perfect with all that was really going on underneath. The pubs were full, the hotels packed, the town's nightlife buzzed at weekends bringing in those looking to get better upwardly-mobile to come join in. Our regular social invites were taken up some thirty-per-cent as I couldn't see myself fitting in with this loved-up pack. I say that only because none of them had children but were lining them up, and they all spoke in a manner I found bloody off-putting. Carefully correct lingo at times during a champagne-filled dinner or the brute honesty of beer-swigging barbecues rearing unshod chat about women-in-sports and new-immigrants flocking the country.

"We could do with some cheap labour at my father's packaging factory," a voice announced, cheered on by male laughter on the veranda of our neighbour's home.

The twenty-something group were showing off yet another modern purchase of this beautifully crafted pergola on their back lawn. Adding to their garden shed and latest model car in the drive, I thought they were insane with all this debt they were accumulating.

"Oh, the pergola's on H.P!" our lovely lady-of-the-manor, Jill cried, "We'll pay that off by the end of the year."

I say to Jack, "End of the year?" as we make ourselves back round to our mortgage-heavy little home. "They're flipping nuts, the whole lot of them. All that monthly payment stuff, it's stupid, just a never-ending battle to pay bills on things you don't need."

He compresses me to his chest and peers down in to my eyes looking up in to his. He's grown a smart beard and his hair shows bundles of high curls covering his head. I liked that look on him.

"You know we could get H.P. for a few things to better the house," he mentions, "Might be worth looking in to."

I pause as we start up our paved drive passing his Suzuki 350 and my '80's Mini Cooper. Each cost under a thousand pounds and we paid cash. What we could not afford I did not want him breaking in to Hire-Purchase for.

"Jack, we've got the mortgage, that's big enough without adding more things we don't necessarily want."

"They'd be for the house," he enthuses, fetching out the front door keys, "It would improve the value of it too."

His neighbours' exuberant displays were getting to him, I could tell, but I didn't want him becoming another clone of them. I wanted him to still *be* him. He had no need to change by imitating others to impress me.

"We don't need new stuff, Jack. The house is fine. Let's just be okay for now, why get things we don't really want?"

Materialism was alright if you could splash-the-cash and not be concerned. We weren't broke or anything, I liked to be comfortable and stay focused in our work. Nothing was a struggle and I wanted to keep it that way.

~

Being brought up, my parents were frugal though we never went without. Not once did they seem distressed about monies nor look to borrow to make ends meet. I understood times were changing and your 'flexible-friend' had much to answer, but I also believed you did not have to take up every offer open to you.

~

I could have said the same with Jack.

He was poking round his bike briefly captivating me with his finicky hands assembling and disassembling wires and bolts and singing aloud lyrics to his own created melody. He was a song to be sung and I helped him along, wetting his vocal chords to a tune of two peeled oranges on a saucer. A late summer's afternoon of '95, I'd finished fixing up Sunday dinner that had everything roasting slow inside the oven. His mum would have been proud. The smell filling the house wafted out to the garden and the juiced fruit would keep up his appetite till it was time to eat.

Half-an-hour later whilst washing-up utensils, I stared out over the back yard which bore a neat cut green and an adult double-swing given to us by his brother Joshua. Yes, he'd driven down from The Lakes and assembled it precisely, attaching two green painted, weather-treated lorry tyres hanging from warship anchoring rope. It was a thing of scrupulous beauty and several neighbours shared abashed enquiries as to where they could purchase the same and equally as to whom was the bear-sized hillbilly putting it together.

We never let Joshua in on what they called him but Jack felt the remark out of place and I said what did he expect from those, 'non new-thinkers'?

A novel mode of people were permeating the beaten track with the assist of credit, mortgages, and the like, and a fast growing trend saw many with a new car every couple of years. This recent set was banding together, and me and Jack relieved we stayed free of their bustling nest.

From tinkering about his bike I heard him walk in the kitchen and place the saucer with three uneaten orange segments on to the draining shelf. He joined me washing his hands in the soapy dish water. I turned my head and pecked him on his beardy cheek.

"We could go for a swing later," I mood out as he takes a tea towel to dry his hands. "It's been a while since we sat on that thing."

He places his chin on my shoulder to garish his brother's gallery piece. "Mm," he hums thoughtful, "how about we enjoy a *swing* right now?"

His well-equipped muscled torso brushes up behind me as he flakes a now dry, right hand, and grabs hard my crotch, his middle-finger pressing firm in to my lipped centre. I so loved the way he performed that, it was intelligently delivered with the exact amount of energy applied not to hurt but to arouse. A shot of air was released from my lungs, like I just missed a step, and he held his left arm, tight, high over my chest area.

"Jack?"

He says, "Em!"

The graze of his beard tickles while brushing along my nape craftily shifting my hair aside for him to guzzle the underneath of my chin. Continuing, he combed his way along my shoulder, his right hand opening a life all its own and taking hold of my left breast with an intense squeeze that is frankly pain inducing. I reach behind and grab a handful of those zealous locks crowning him, equal to the intensity and ferity with which he took my breast letting him know I feel the calculations of his arithmetic.

Left dazzled I am for within seconds he escorts my jogging pants, minus any panties - it's Sunday for chrissakes - to my knees, and switches upward, fast, grabbing bunches of my hair in one hand. It feels like he is about to break me.

If you must show me something then show it, you...

His right hand flips to my crotch again and fierce, far fiercer this time, he grips hold of my vaginal area like there is urgency to crash open its door. A quick fingered entrance piled in a single force saw him hurtle me round to look up at him but my face hit his chest first and my teeth grip a mouthful of his oil-stained T-shirt. His soft yelp explained he'd been bit hard enough to feel my incisors pinch his skin serving to ingratiate him further. The surprise of his rocky, bike-tinkering hands, muscling me on top the draining board, a second's shock of cool aluminium smacking my bare backside while he shoved cooking utensils back in to the soapy water and we charge the three pieces of orange scattering seductively. He captured one and manhandled my legs open, inner thighs creeping wet from his crotch grabs to a lay open of his mastery theatre.

The scripts unscripted, the stage reworked, and no words spoke to the end of an invisible audience.

The segmented orange pressed my parts, its juice forced inside to wet myself more. Jack's fingers crumbled the piece to sqeeze fruit ingredients firmly in to me. As vagina on vagina, a flame of bright colours, moistening, entering, my clitoris squirting juice of its own.

Jack shoved his head fucking hard at my chest like a wrestler's head-butt then came up around my neck and across my face. It felt as though this folklore's giant thumb were kneading and poking me so I met him for strength and he suddenly upped his game with my feeling the masculine pressure of his higher genetic force.

I said nothing as he took another piece of orange and ran it over my hips before connecting with my vagina then breaking it up to have the soggy fruit marching tenderly in to my hole. His finger followed through forcing the broken fruit deep inside and he played a musical composition I had not felt before. The music swarmed to a beat of its own, rising and downing, its melody meeting my succulent inner that creaked noises from a cunt he knew well. The beat unfinished, Jack un-played his finger, because it was left nicely wet, before he sucked it dry.

The final segment of orange he reached for then opened my thighs as far as they could go. Surprisingly, he gave the fruit to my mouth which was barely open from my lips pressing together after feeling this recipient's sensual. I took half the fruit between my teeth and Jack swallowed up the other half while dancing fingers around my vagina. His tongue raced in to my mouth and I almost choked trying to manage him and the half piece of orange at the same time, when suddenly, he leaves me alone upstairs and goes to brandish about down there.

Perfectly supported by the draining shelf, Jack's famed hump, lift, and spread of my legs caused me to fall back against the window ledge as he scattered more utensils and anything else barring his way. Soon his mouth began to work wonders on my pink-rower and all were enhanced by the rich smell of a Sunday roast permeating everything.

~

I did wonder how he invented such stuff. I mean, out of the blue he would do me in ways I did not expect nor did I question, however I got curious and went nosing around one day while he was out on an errand and saw if I could find anything incriminating. I mean, call it paranoia, but when your man is so inventive at times, your wonder brightens as to where he's finding his light.

All men stashed away their porn, didn't they, but I found nothing anywhere belonging to Jack. Not even a newspaper bevvy of topless girls.

His nose was in the financial section one morning sitting at the kitchen table as I brought him coffee. He could be a quick-fire type sometimes and I'd shield his back before reaching round to play with his scrotum. Like a jellied sack of delicate balls they were in my hand and I squeezed and played as violently as I could before his cock stood up then I began playing with that.

Such a sensitive trio of membranes that ugly mess between his legs I'd wished able to hurt at times, you know, show him who's boss, punch it, bite it, dilate every part red till he couldn't breathe; literally take his bulk like a wrecking-machine to a building and fuck him up so my *six-million-dollar-man* could be rebuilt.

Broken down and fixed up, fixed up and broken down.

How brilliant would that be?

They say we find it hard to truly cohabit and understand one another. I thought of those couples who made separate homes yet their partnership worked and worked well. It crossed my mind when the times you fell ill and needed to wake up with tendering hands saddling to mend you. It was a balance few achieved great but when you witnessed it and saw how powerful a pact it could be, you strived for one yourself hoping to emulate those emotions naturally, because if it were force-played, you both would know about it.

~

Our special Saturday lie-in from another week of work neither of us were particularly keen on, I watched him on his back reading this strange novel by *Frank De Felita* and saw the image of a beautiful woman in the bottom right corner with her posture clearly saying, *'No!'* I saw what it meant and an idea I hid from long ago emerged.

"Jack?"

My wholesome guy glimpses me direct before returning to his book and makes me part of his space, cuddling an arm round the back of my neck bringing me closer.

"Uh-hmm?" he says, re-focusing his read.

"Jack..." I grade his book and make that quick look in to his eyes that forever shone green. "Do you ever think about...you know...maybe sneaking in on me one day and... You know..."

He stops reading and amazingly checks me out, "Eh, what?"

Fuck, I've fucking shocked him!

I fast run my hand across his haired chest, thick and fraggly curled, like his full head of hair.

"S'okay," I smile bashful, "it's nothing."

He puts the book down and gives me his complete attention, "Hey, Em, what? Come on, just say it?"

I hold his look and realise I cannot tell fibs. He'd know. He knows me so I had to tell him this, right? Well, no, I didn't need to. Yet I wanted to go against everything and just say it.

So I do, with the uncertainty of being.

"Why don't you ever," my words cross suffocate, "pretend to be a...you know, a bad guy or something, and sneak up on me...you know, like you're going to...be a bad guy and do something?"

The eye contact is meticulously chosen and he's making sure he's reading me right, as with a book, the words written are there to be read.

He's unhorsed, "Seriously, Em?"

Detective Charles gets it!

I measure to bring my play-book down, "Look, it's just a thought I had."

I worry I've hurt everything he holds dear.

"Lots of women have it," my hurried chuck in. "It's just a fantasy we sometimes get."

He looks like he's been shot.

Fast, I rub my palm over his chest and mate with his wavy hair like an apology is needed. I didn't think one did but I wanted to show his not to be offend.

"Is it because of this?" he asked, picking up the *De Felita* novel.

I complain, "Christ, no! You think I want a fucking ghost doing me?"

Nucleus annoyed I sit up and feel he needs to be more in touch and get what I'm saying sometimes. I never enjoyed this having to spell it out all the flipping time. And anyway, why the hell didn't I just say it out loud in plain words for goodness sake. Why all this creeping round the mulberry bullshit!

He sits up too and strokes a hand over my hair then shuts the book away and holds me tight. Together we fall back on the bed and he hugs me even tighter. The ridges of his flesh with areas hard and areas soft, I snuggle dominion to him like a second-skin while he clasps me mushily.

"After what happened before," he begins with the mood of a *Sinatra* emblem, "I wouldn't think you were in to stuff like that."

I crane up at him. "You're not a stranger, Jack. You're the man I'm living with, the man I love."

Now he's been shot *twice*.

"Did you just say...?" He settles like a bloodhound given scent. "Did you just say *love?*"

I smack him on the arm and snatch roughly at his tummy. "Stop it, you prick! I meant it!"

Encouraging that giggle from him he sells up and rolls on to his side giving me his all.

He's so big, so strong, his hands could break anything. He was a throbbing cell of niceties and passion and I loved every part.

"I've been careful," he utters, *Sinatra's* crescendo, "I've wanted to tell you that since forever."

We look in to each other and I wonder what he sees. The budding floret from secondary school, or the matured university grad who helped try and change the world, which is it?

"Since when?" poking around, because it was important to me.

"Since I first saw you in the boys' toilets," he says, and I see he really means this, "Since I first laid eyes on you...that first time...I wanted you back then. I thought about you when I went to college and when I saw you were there too, I could have died. I couldn't believe my luck."

I get comfortable for an upcoming *Jackanory*.

"Why didn't you tell me?"

"Yeah right," he sends out, "and if you'd not felt the same I would have looked a right prat, I wouldn't have been able to accept it."

"Jack?"

"Come on, Emery!" he sings, stroking my arm as I watch his muscles and tendons beneath the skin, "Everybody liked you, most guys fancied you, I thought I never stood a chance but when you liked me...I knew I had to make you mine. I knew I had to get it right...exactly right with you."

Finger-touching his midriff I smile for him, "You should have told me."

"Tell you what? We were young, naïve, growing up through all those changes and in the middle of it all I just wanted to take you away and love you forever. I didn't want anything to stop me from making that happen. Not anything could have broken us up, not for me! I would have gone anywhere after you-anywhere in the world."

A long drive of male emotion made him even soppier and I was drawn to hold his nerve-red cheek.

"Just say what you want, Em," he refreshes, "and I'll do it. Anything you want. I'll do it for you."

Shit, I just asked my perfect soul mate to fuck me in sordid fantasy and he in reply says I am his everything from the beginning of our moment's meet. I wonder why, under the circumstances given, the special connection which held between us, and captivity with my Jack, would never wane.

"I love you so much, Emery," he says brilliantly.

And once more I say I love him back.

Chapter Sixteen

He told me my dad sternly asked that he never hurt but to take care of me. Said in no uncertain terms during my graduation at the small celebratory-party dad had organised at a nearby pub-restaurant from the university, it left me curious when the two men cocooned in a corner sharing a pint among exchanging wisdom. From their body language mum even passed by to see if things were going well before crossing back to the our little group as we downed another round of tequila-shots. Seeing my parents end up tipsy and my sibling's parade near certified drunk, the day was enjoyed by everyone, especially me, because, after all, it would be a while before we all managed to make a family gathering in one place again.

~

I'd swept up Jack's love of bikes when he revealed his passion with a trip to Donnington after taking up work in a motorbike store. They were truly becoming a thing of art with increased interest in this bespoke style of 'moto' racing. There were differing levels to the sport, something I never really understood fully, but I appreciated the participants and their drive for the love of competition. TV coverage of it was growing in popularity and a graceful swell of budding beauties in equal rise came along with it.

I didn't mind the two-three-hour TV race shows on at the weekends that filled Jack's time as we both worked all week and had Saturdays and Sundays to rest easy. My hands-on guy did not belong at university and I wondered why he ever bothered to go in the first place.

"So why did you?" I ask, resting my head across his thighs in our long cushioned sofa.

Busy peeling a ring off his canned bitter he takes a sip. "I knew you were going," he says, wiping his mouth with a brisk hand.

"What?"

I sit up and fold my legs to touch him.

"I knew you were going," he repeats simply.

"But..." my start, grasping at reasoned shreds, "I thought...*you* wanted to go after college?"

He shrugs a man's shrug. Nothing complicated here, luv, it's you gals who complicate things.

"I was happy with college," he states, pulling me in to him, a resolute arm fixing round my shoulders. "I didn't need any more paper-chasing after that."

Once again he leaves me stupefied.

"Jack," my almost breathless by his will to roll out honesty and shock in the same state, "are you saying that was all a front for me or something?"

He lets go a deep sigh like he wants to say nothing but I free myself of him and gesture he carry on; this, not bulletproof, another revelation to me.

"Jack, are you saying university was all bullshit and you only went because *I* was going?"

A cool deciphering emerges, "My ideas about a lot of things got screwed up," he says, sipping bitter. "I had big ideas, wanted to make changes, saw things should be better but I couldn't change a thing."

I reach for the remote-control and 'mute' the TV set.

My philanthropist!

"I never had any power," he continues reflective, "I couldn't change people I couldn't do what I really wanted."

It was never up to him to change anybody; people had to want to change themselves, why couldn't we see that in one another. Women tried to change men, however men never seemed to try; it was the women who in fact changed for them.

"I wish you hadn't done it," said self-accusatory; I mean, really, like it was *my* fault.

He endorses a rueful glaze, "Then we wouldn't have continued seeing each other, would we."

"Yes we would," I'm thinking, "We could have made it work."

"And see you living in some other part of the country while I'm stuck renting a flat years away?"

Wow, he had followed *me* yet I believed I had followed *him*.

"That was stupid," said told off, "Really stupid! You forced yourself to do something you had no interest in doing at all. You hurt yourself to be with me."

"Hell, I didn't care," he puffs his chest, defiant in the social regulatory, "I was going to do my best to win you, no matter what I had to do, I'd have gone anywhere."

I pause and remember just exactly what he *did* do. Jesus Christ, what had he done!

Damn, this was crazy!

"The test-papers," I regrettably put, "You knew you couldn't pass them?"

Making each other's demur eyes he seems to break down before me. Something was eating him up and I grew afraid of what we had unwittingly opened.

"There was this girl," he starts, contemplative, "She was a friend, a really good friend... I was eleven and she was twelve... She loved riding BMX bikes cos she was always borrowing her brother's but her parents never bought her one and I really liked her so I went and stole one from a shop and I walked out with it and gave it to her..."

My mind was flipping spinning.

Thief as well as cheat!

Goddamn.

"We went to take it for a ride and she was doing these amazing things with it and we rode about near this steep railway embankment and she told me she could do wheelies, so she did this wheelie and she was going good but then she slipped and fell and..."

By now there is a lump in my throat that has grown to tear filled eyes. I fought hard not to let him see me cry. He was a wreck himself and I could not believe my ears.

"...I couldn't get her arm. She'd fallen down this edge and was holding on by this twig out the ground and the bike was gone in to the rocks by the stream below and she was struggling to hold on and I couldn't get to her. I mean, I climbed down as best I could but she was too far down and she couldn't hold on, and she...she couldn't hold on and...and I couldn't save her."

If Satan told me this I would have shaken my head no.

"I couldn't climb down enough cos it was too steep and I couldn't save her... I just couldn't save her, Em."

I go numb.

Belief in God, belief in spirituality, belief we could cross over and others swore of a beyond. As humans we were nothing on this amazing planet.

"Her parents blamed me for stealing that bike and causing her death...they never forgave me..." He trails off remembering it all, the canned bitter held in such a way it helps him remember the little girl. I never ask her name. "That's why my parents sent me to live with my aunt and I ended up at Montery," he recalls, "Before that I couldn't handle stuff, I became a tearaway, kind of...self-destructive. If I hadn't stolen the bike to try and impress that girl she would still be alive. And if I hadn't taken the test-papers to try and impress you, I might have done alright and hung around and...and maybe Knowles wouldn't have tried anything."

I feel like I'd been hit in the gut because I knew what that felt like and such epoch affecting words matched.

"Christ, Jack..." I'm inside-out, "Don't blame yourself for Knowles, he was a flipping creepy bastard!"

He nods, "Yeah, but if I'd been there..." drifting, he sinks deeper, "If I'd just *tried* and failed at uni it would have been better. I let you down by cheating and getting thrown out. I hated myself. I hated being a failure."

With such a mortal-changing spiel this litany was practically apocalyptic in its path.

I felt hit in the gut again.

Shit!

So, Jack, after all, *you* followed me, *you* cheated for me, and *you* were carrying this nightmare tragedy with you. Why, because you're a man? Trying to be honest while either male or female was something genetically problematic. So I thought; it was far easier being female.

Fearing bound and speechless I had no words for him, not the right kind of words, not right now, I could locate none. I suppose being female wasn't always easier.

"I'm sorry, Emery," he says, and I take hold of his bitter-clasping hand.

Don't worry, I was sorry too.

~

Jack surprised me when we arrived by rail to his first home in Hertfordshire. After working relentlessly the last two years in bike supplies and sales, the money he was making good enough to support the two of us but I wouldn't let that lie as the need to pay off his mortgage would be assisted by my working as well. It eased any burden his carrying everything and I saw to the utilities and insurances while he paid for the house. My job as a legal secretary was fine and that too paid well. I enjoyed the mix of people in need of help who came to our offices as we mostly categorised legal-aid but we also shone for those crooked who sought creative minds in getting them off clear guilt: 'We don't choose our clients," my boss's adage, "We represent and practice law." Yep, and sometimes it stank too.

The dinner parties thrown next door - and the next - clearly competing for who could throw the best, always reared up legal questions as our upwardly mobile neighbours constantly sought legislative information. I should have charged for the privilege as it got tiresome and there was too much focus on me at times. Weren't their own careers interesting enough?

"Guess not," Jack said, our arriving home carrying each a slice of home baked tart so deadly delicious we asked for seconds to eat while watching the sports highlights on TV.

"Think I should start running a legalities tab," I mention on entering our hallway.

He stirred, "You'd make a lot more money doing that kind of work."

I make off to the kitchen and take out custard for our second helping of dessert.

"You think so," I pay heed to his words, "Make money out of doing that?"

Smiling, he takes, breathes, and polishes two bowls and two spoons. "The way you're so charming they would pay *just* to look at you."

I give him a funny look.

"Don't say you haven't noticed, Emery," placing down the twin bowls.

Me, innocently, "Notice what?"

"Jill's husband can't take his eyes off you!"

"Eh?"

"Come on," he steps closer and dangles his long arms over my shoulders, "And *she's* no better either," whispered sensual.

Mildly, I hit him in the chest. "Oh, stop being a prat!"

Laughing a laugh, he says, "Hey, I'm serious," as I spin round to tend to the dessert prep he keeps his arms hung over my shoulders and lacily cups each of my breasts, "She's watching *these* closely."

"Shut up, Jack!"

But he goes on, "Like Caroline and Emma did...watch these buds of yours close."

I elbow rough his belly and he laughs again, holding me tighter.

"They're probably in there thinking of you right now," he starts to tease, "Mm, heavenly threesome, Jill, Paul, and Emery Pearson getting sent right up to-"

"You shit," now irate; "Stop it okay, I'll be blinking paranoid the next time we're over there."

"Don't worry," Jack disentangles me, "I'm sure they're already *paranoid* when you turn up."

He joins my side and starts helping ready the dessert. I grow quiet as he fumbles about, my chewing over his assumption. Jill and Paul, desiring me, really! He long thought my university dorm mates wanted to sleep with me but I never indulged anybody that way. Threesomes left someone out of the play and I did not want Jack, or myself, left out of anything like that. Besides, another woman, I didn't think so. Though Caroline and Emma's armour was a thing of beauty I did not desire another female sexually. I could *admire* minus the sex tab, and yet, Jack had grown quiet too. Now I wonder.

"You ever think of me with someone else?" I asked whilst placing the tart inside the oven as Jack puts the custard to heat on top the stove.

He breaks from his pattern and stands in front of me like he's about to do something untoward.

"You, my dear, Emery," fond, he mentally charges my breasts, my lips, and finally my eyes, "are a dream. You don't know it but you are. Women like you, men like you, and you can't seem to notice that. Well...that's okay. You underestimate your beauty but I know it's there, and not just the physical side, your inner beauty comes out and you can't even see it."

He tends to the custard pot while taking a tea-towel before fetching two glasses out the top cupboard to indicate we enjoy opening a bottle of red as we await the dessert to heat.

I grow somewhat quiet as I ponder his render of me, then he reaches out with the tea-towel slung over his shoulder and takes me by the hand leading me toward the living room.

~

"Emery, darling, could you glance over this, please? It came yesterday and I'm afraid Paul didn't even bother to look at it!"

My neighbour in exuberant fashion stands with determination at the front door and a foot positioned ready to enter our home. I cannot say no as she appears flustered to get an understanding of this paperwork off her chest. It's Saturday and Jack's down the local watching 'live-sports' with his work mates and I'm busy being free.

Inside the kitchen, yes, Jill's a fast walker when she needs to be, already seeking to make us coffee as I peruse the letters about passing over deeds from holder to custodian, explaining the fact that Paul, her husband, was being granted award of his parents estate. Things seemed to be in perfect order as far as I could tell so I inform her she has nothing to worry about as it looked like they could make money from any sales or boost any loans tied directly to the estate. It was a definite win-win and she should chill about it. Their future assuredly bright and financially stable as Paul's parents had him late in life and they were looking to downsize, so the large estate, now unmanageable, was fashioned to him. It bore more questions though.

"With such accumulated wealth he could leave me," Jill said dire. "We share our home but he could be free of that burden at any given moment."

I meet her half way with the steaming coffee.

"He wouldn't need me now," she irks, and grabs a taste of gold-roast. "He could easily buy me out and still have enough to purchase a second home."

Things were *not* as upwardly as they seemed.

"I mean," she whips round to determinedly flake me over, "he always goes on about that Mini of yours, like it's an antique that should be in a museum, this treasured relic he would pay anything for because the model was being phased out and bought up by some German people. Lost The War so they want to own or businesses...can see that happening."

Leaning back against the worktop I flash down at her papers. "You'll be fine," I try out, "Paul loves you. He isn't going anywhere."

"And how would you know?" she says not unfriendly. "He doesn't love me the way Jack loves you. I see it in his eyes, the way he looks at you. I can tell that's real love. A real love story's in there between you two."

People never fail to surprise me. Who would have known our upwardly charging neighbours envied me and Jack.

"Oh don't get me wrong, Emery," Jill feeds off fast, "We love the way you two are so in love it's wonderful to see. You have youth on your side and that's going to help you go a long way in the future."

Didn't know what she was hinting at but they weren't exactly old hens either.

I play a little with her letterings as she sips her coffee like a munchkin searching further inland. Things interchangeable were to be found.

"Have you ever thought," she begins, folding one arm over her waist as she handles the coffee cup, "about Jack ever cheating?"

The legislation papers a planned ruse to go elsewhere. I was waking up to her.

"You've a brilliant mind, Emery, and some men can get intimidated by that."

I'm in a playground so I play.

"Not Jack," said confident, "He's got a brilliant mind all his own."

"Yes, but bikes and oil aren't the same as law and aid."

No, didn't enjoy her pejorative staleness nor did I think she ought to offer it.

"He's happy doing what he's doing," I defend, "Not everyone can be academically driven."

"So he never went to university then?"

It wasn't my place to tell her I didn't think, so I made something up.

"He decided against," my sweeping tale, "He got in but he knew it wasn't for him."

She offers this broad grin. "Opposites attract so they say."

"Yeah," my leaning off the worktop and finishing the coffee, "They do."

"But still," she interjects, "don't you think about him ever cheating on you?"

I answer brisk this time, "No, I don't," putting down my cup, "He isn't like that."

"Okay." She moves back and puts her coffee cup next to mine. I feel her steel is about to become molten. "I mean," she begins naturally, her 'woman's-hour', "so what about you then...would you...cheat with someone?"

I hand out, "What, of course not," my movements hasten across to the sink and she comes after me with both cups in hand.

"I was just asking, Emery, you don't have to get upset."

"I'm not upset," but I was, "I just don't get all these questions about Jack."

"Fine, alright," she ties up a tad haughty, placing the cups in the sink, "But something tells me you're not exactly the type to be afraid of using the word *cunt!*"

Remember before I said it felt like being hit in the guts because I had been; well, this, another of those bleeding occasions.

"Oh don't look so surprised, my dear," Jill lingers ravishingly, "You're a fucking great tease and I appreciate it."

She snatches up her paperwork with the flair of uncharted elegance and heads out.

"Thanks for the advice. I'll let Paul know he can fuck off but to leave me financially secure."

Chapter Seventeen

I couldn't let that woman in to my home again. Sufficient excuses were made to give her the hint she was no longer welcome. Funnily enough she and Paul continued happily inviting Jack and me to their socials but often I did not attend explaining a bout of the 'monthlies', or some other plan that could pass. I neither told Jack what had happened that fruitless afternoon despite his knowing something must have gone on because my continued excuses to avoid that toxic couple was obvious.

After one garrulous, rapturous evening, Jack totted back from an event even he said was beginning to push things. A unisex fed lingerie-party had the four-house block in turmoil with everything overheating and then - and only then - did Jill forward her suggestive collection of nudity to Jack. The French bubbly helped her fibril moves on my man and his being a tender drunk his self, admitted her exaggerated pout flew close.

I didn't play the enraged; I was.

"You what?"

"It's alright, Em," he scuttles, "she never managed to."

"But she bleeding well *tried!*"

"Yeah, but forget it, it was a silly little incident."

"Silly!" From the kitchen I follow him in to the hallway as he's making to evade but I stay with him and stay pursuing, "That woman's a snake and so's her husband. They're an emotional wreck waiting to haul someone's arse in to their bungling cock-up of a marriage."

Jack freezes and hands me this 'what-the-fuck' type look as I brace in front of him.

"What do you know?" he queries fevered.

"I know Paul's come in to a wad of money and Jill's a mess he's gonna leave her and they want to cheat on one another with someone willing and able and whoever takes their blinking fancy they make moves on them!"

"Hey, Em," he takes me at arms-length, "I would *never* cheat on you."

"Christ, Jack, I'm not saying you would. It's those two. They act like they can buy and sell anything."

"Round here it seems like they can."

"What do you mean?" I take myself out of his caring hold. "Have they tried something with you?"

"Hell no, Em, I'm just saying," entering our spacious living room, "They've got most people eating out of their palms around here."

I dig him for his evidence.

"Like who, what have they been up to?"

"I don't know," his slack arms flung wide before he sinks in the sofa, "Bleeding everyone they meet. It's like watching a full blown seduction at times."

I huff as that is not what I want to hear but specifics, times, occasions, however Jack doesn't deliver, or perhaps he doesn't want to.

"Are you not telling me something here?" asked I, sitting close to him I won't let up; "I mean, has Jill said anything to you...you know, anything strange?"

Edgy, he feeds me those emerald greens and I want him to take me hard, really hard, right there, right then. His male easy-to-wound a treasure inside for I enjoyed that weakness before brute strength.

"Wait a second," he gets comfortable and is Jack, "What did Jill *do* to you, Em?"

Shit!

"Nothing," I pitch, "Nothing, it's..." I sit up straight and he makes all over me like I'm tonight's prey.

"What the fuck did she do to you?!"

He's unhappy though I bring him back cool after explaining our little conversation over deeds and legacies and he claims back an ease non-threatening to our neighbours.

Relief, for I did not want any reprisals.

"That's why you've not been going over there, cos of that?"

Nodding my head yes, he pulls me near and gives me one of his almighty hugs that nearly cracks my spine.

"I wish you would just tell me everything sometimes," his placed words accurate of dart throwing, my heart pings at his concerns. "I don't want anything bad happening to you, Em, I couldn't deal with it."

I ache at his ending. Goddamn it, my want to have told him this earlier and stop all of these footling outbursts easily avoided if honesty in me was more forthright. I would try and comport accordingly. If our relationship was to be truly successful, we needed better communication, and on my front, I would try to do more.

~

We had to stay away from them and of that we made sure. Several others from our dubious neighbourhood asked why we never made the barbecues or dinner-parties anymore and our answer being we were cooling things but did not hate them or anything. We politely made the usual 'Good-mornings' and social etiquette, and that's as far as it went. Word got round Paul and Jill was missing our company and agonised for a friendly return, but as it turns out, he was on the cusp of leaving her for an older model socialite. Jill was breaking up inside and I did feel sorrow for her. A flagellant appearance highlighted her comings and goings and I wanted to pay her a sympathy visit. Jack warned strongly against, fearing I might get sucked in to a family drama I would not be able to get out from.

So I stayed away, however not after paying Jill a last visit to express my dolour at the break-up of her marriage, and Paul leaving for another woman.

Purple-passion, she stepped outside herself, "Gloat, why don't you, you fucking bitch!"

My God, I wasn't gloating!

"Jill, I am sorry."

"Sorry!" she slings a rampart growl as her make-up runs with tears and lets spill so readily. "All he could do was go on about you and that frigging car of yours and that hunk on a bike who was probably fucking you blind every night because that's what Paul would have done if he had you! You-you, you fucking hippie-type with your model body and your no fucking make-up! You-you, you think you're better than everyone cos you *aren't* like everyone and you just think you're fucking it! Well, finally, Emery Pearson, fuck you! Fuck you and all that you bring with you! I hope you have a great life and leave me the fuck alone!"

~

My mood wasn't good for a few days after that and Jack of course sensed the need to give me some space. Around a week later, I don't exactly understand why this came to be, but a miss-timed act from my other-half had his read of the situation off by about a gazillion miles. Yes, I was upset over Jill and Paul though the assist to gladden me over it all was not well assessed by a sudden and alarming decision to act out a long forgotten fantasy.

Yes, it had been put out there, however things took a drastic about-turn with Jack's outpoured feelings over his tragic past. My own revelation too, later on, was poorly timed, yet it clearly left a quagmire draining deep inside Mr Charles that he would let it stew until the right moment to dish it out.

And that moment was all so very fucking wrong!

It could have been the beer, it could have been the testosterone boiling in him, or he could have just meant well, of either three I did not know, and we never discussed it till days later.

Coming from the kitchen on an autumn evening it was time for an early night as I was exhausted from a hectic week at work and felt fresh that Jack had gone out with his mates for their frequent Saturday 'live-sports' drink. Heading for a planned long soak in the bath with a novel tucked under my arm, I saw the front door had peeled open and believed I hadn't closed it right comfortably thinking the howling November wind eased it ajar. Mind you, I did look outside and checked nobody was there upon closing the door then called out to see if Jack was home. With no reply I wandered upstairs for my eager visionary hot tub when some twat smashed in to me from out of our bedroom and slung me up against the wall.

I couldn't scream as the eyes beneath the bloody balaclava wearing thug briefly shut before my metamorphosis in to a fighting cat, clawing and kicking at my assailant till he yelped and let go. I scrambled inside the bedroom maddening to shut the door but this guy was good, he was fast, and got a hold of me and hurtled me on to the bed.

Belly-down, shoving my face in a pillow, I couldn't breathe as he machined himself on top my back and grabbed my hair, forcing my face further. I tried turning to grasp air but my head was held vice-tight as he roughed down my jogging-pants. All my nightmares stashed in to one I hadn't believed this was happening nor would I let it because Benjamin Knowles would be a first, and last one, to attempt that.

I sensed this bastard's body loosen when he rubbed a hand up and down my torso, feeling over me like a parcel to be opened but I would open him first. Forcing my head to suck in air I screamed something foul and whirled round to un-gum him off but he buried his head in my chest and attempted to snatch hold of my wrists. I manage to crab and paw him fierce getting a grip of that damn balaclava and wrestle it off his head. I thought that was a big mistake as it could have made him a tempestuousness I would not be able to handle but my heart sank when I glared with stopped breath in to Jack's green eyes.

"You fucking bastard, get off of me, get fucking off me, you fuck!"

Apoplectic, he jumped back, a look of sheer horror embedded.

"Emery!"

I punched his face. I don't know why, I just did. With everything unleashed I punched him.

He reeled back falling off the bed and I dived on top of him premiering an uncontrolled flurry of punching. I *know* what came over me but I couldn't stop punching.

He yelled for me to quit as he covered up though I wouldn't stop so he changed keep and monumentally reversed the attack.

His strength was magnanimous, outdoing mine, caging my arms behind my back and crashed my body against the bedroom wall. Still I would not give in, my fury blind and unstoppable till Jack ducked down to evade my fists and he hit me with curbed perfection really hard in the stomach. I was totally winded and it stopped everything.

The pandemonium died as fast as it begun.

On my hands and knees, trying to draw breath, I couldn't move as Jack knelt down over me.

"Christ, Emery, I'm sorry, I'm really sorry!"

My attempt to look at him I cannot as I start to clutch my gut. That was some punch he threw and I was thinking, fuck, was that his only option? Hell, Emery, you would have kicked in his nuts if you could so why are you complaining.

I gag and wheeze a little easier as my breath mends a small return so Jack feels it safe to place a careful hand on to my shoulder.

"You went crazy, Em, I couldn't talk to you, I couldn't get you to calm down, I'm sorry about this, I'm sorry about what I did-I just..."

Finally I look up in those eyes. He's amassed bundles of tears matching blood from his nose. I say nothing, slowly rolling on to my back where I lie quiet, curling my legs up to my waist. Seconds later Jack's frame settles beside mine and quadrant's a soothing arm over me. Fantasies were fine when you had an inclination they were coming but such an awkward and frightening surprise was never ever welcome.

~

Grabbing me across the middle as I prepped another Sunday roast, I remained sore from our recent tussle and Jack spun me round lifting up my shirt top to snuzzle his nose in to my tummy. Peeling potatoes whilst he continued a frothy nosing around my waist, I tried getting back to my dinner's sorting but his hormones wouldn't let me. It was difficult trying to get anything done when Jack succumb me from behind playing with my body, needing not to say anything nor whisper a word eared, he just played, and eventually ended up with a heady hand wrapped between my legs. There was never any point trying to contrive myself free as his hands magisterially got me wet and I'd put the peeler down before intertwining our build's, ready to compose, construct, and cook something of our own.

He always satisfied. Even when touching and rubbing gently my arm, he always satisfied. I didn't need an open fire, hot-water bottles, or radiator to warm cold bones, because Jack, for another untold reason, read my needs keeping me cosied. Our play-fights were a different matter, my usually winning due to muscle-memory of my wrestling and judo days, so when he came up short, a quick jab to my ribs meant he had a chance at victory but predominantly I got him round the neck and choked the living daylights out of him.

After pottering with his bike one bank-holiday morning, he suggested we take a ride in the swirling country lanes and find a pub for a quick bevvy before returning home. He was a safe old chap. I would down a couple of brandies while he stayed drink-free as we rode. That was my maximum when we hit the lanes. I relied on Jack to keep off any influence while I maintained a level of being capable to hold on to him. Each time we arrived back, our bodies stepped off one throbbing machine to another as we ended up somewhere in the house fucking each other's brains out. Mostly we made love, though on occasion we fucked and I found myself never wanting.

During the week as I drove to work the growing radio talk-shows discussed plenty of unhappiness. Unhappy marriages, unhappy families, unhappy whatever's and I thought mine and Jack's relationship was pretty good because we hadn't bumped in to those 'unhappys' yet. We never complained bitterly, there was no abuse from either side, we took in to account each other's feelings and I truly believed we loved one another and not many people could honestly say that.

He knew to wash his smelly feet when he took off his biker's boots. Sometimes with the cheek of a child he'd lift them up and drop one of his size-ten's in to my dishwater. Men had to act the fool but I didn't mind. I never got angry at his babying antics because I grabbed his every all the more coy to toy with.

A favourite time savoured is when we'd read together out loud a paragraph from an article in the Sunday papers or a magazine or book. I got goose pimples when Jack finished his piece and would ladder me before I began reading my part. It was another characteristic of his I had no words for but longed to see again and again: A brief glance, a turn of eyes, to blink, to see, a reminder of me.

The U-bend needing fixing under the kitchen sink became another favourite. Couple times a year it clogged and required hands of skill to keep it working thorough. Opting for the job every time I think Jack knew I enjoyed his masculine play of building maintenance. I mean, really, who wouldn't. *Superman* hands of steel which precisely mastered his Suzuki and in relate, could master the piping under the sink. Afterward of course, you know what he mastered.

I could never get round his play of my vagina either with his tongue or fingers or a piece of fruit. My zone down there capable of spouting out a new-born could also leave a woman unbelievably messed up, with her soul on fire falling in to a pit. Dark murmurings followed me and Jack from college to now but it was not something we deliberately sought to create. It happened. It just happened and I got it that if you tried to force a love's flourish, you were on the road to nowhere. Emma and Caroline's warn about Jack dug at the back of my mind but I could see nothing to hint in, around, or through, that he would hurt me. We were strong together and sometimes weak, we could row and we could talk, we made our own bed and would lie in it, and shelve blame on no other but ourselves.

~

Winter of '96.

The house had been burgled when we came back from a brief stay at Jack's family home in The Lake District. They'd hit Jill and Paul's too. Fortunately the bloody gits were caught by neighbouring residents and held down till the police could arrest them after they got hold of Jack's Suzuki keys and tried starting the bike to ride off with. Knowing we were out of town for the week the neighbours knew something was off and maraud the uninvited two. I had my car's keys with me so that prevented them escaping in my Mini. They got a good haul from both homes, broke plenty of equipment, and violated what they could. Knowing Jill was approaching 'divorcee' and up for selling to move out, a short time after the burglary I wanted to leave. Those creeps depredate left a nasty taste and Jack soundly understood.

"Maybe it is time to move on," he coats warmly, looking over insurance claim papers.

"Yeah, but where?" I was feeling hopeless. I was angry too.

"We could go further south, or maybe head back nearer your folks?"

I loved my family and missed them but I needed to be me. Hanging on to my mother's coat-tails was not a good idea. Twenty-seven-years old and Jack twenty-eight, we had to manage together and meet our own challenges. Mum no doubt would want me closer to her and dad, and not dismissing having within reach any family support was always a good thing.

"We could do," I start thinking.

"We'd be nearer my family too," he adds hopeful.

217

I smile suspiciously, "You're not a mummy's-boy are you?"

"Who me?" he laughs, "I'm an *Emery's* boy!"

He pulls me in to his arms and smacks this almighty kiss on my cheek.

"Anything for you," he said, snuggling my neck, "Anything you want, anytime, anywhere."

Putty-in-my-hand, candy-floss from a baby, though I would never take advantage of him; we were a partnership and expected equal and fair all round.

"What do you want to do, Jack?"

"I want to do what Emery wants."

"No, come on," I make him stop kissing me and watch my eyes, serious moment for thought. "I mean it, what do you want to do, move further south or head back up north?"

"Families are back up north," he says, "but greater opportunities down south."

"We could both get jobs."

"Yeah...but what kind," he feeds off something, "Credit driven lifestyle or sometimes work we half enjoy?"

He'd turned on the tap of reasoning. I step out from him to go look outside. The street we were accustomed to, the neighbours, our jobs, everything simple. Suddenly break from that and head where? What to create now?

The burglary did my head in and I could tell it unsettled Jack. He wouldn't say so, maybe because he was a man, but I could tell.

"They only broke in because we weren't home, Jack," I say openly. "They knew we were gone, just like Jill's, that's why they broke in."

He comes over and takes me inside his arms. "And what if you were home, what if Jill was home, I'd hate to think what could have happened."

On that he was right. The thought leaves me cold.

We could find safer, better, be at ease. Our lives had been rattled and it did not feel okay. Sell up, move on, and start over, for we had youth on our side. Whatever future I wanted it would be with Jack, and his very words told me the same.

"Emery, you know I love you."

The beat of his heart, coolth from my mother's bosom: I say I love him too, and, "Okay, Jack," meeting his macarise greens while tossing a coin inside my head, fifty-fifty; "Further south or head north?"

Chapter Eighteen

We headed down two Boroughs south and mortgaged up a quaint old number, this picturesque, detached, two-bed cottagey home in a quiet Enfield suburb. It also allowed us to reacquaint with Emma and Caroline who came up from East London to attend our house-warming. Both were milking successfully accidental careers in theatre-land, London's prime West-End; Emma a stage manager, and Caroline, a freelance director of independent theatre productions. Still together, they bought a flat in the Hackney Borough and were looking fine with their winning attitudes and incomes.

"So who's the hairy Neanderthal putting up the adult swing then?"

Joshua came from The Lake's and was re-erecting the green-tyre swing. After dismantling, driving it down, and rebuilding the morbidly beautiful thing, he stayed on for our week's end house-warming.

"That's Jack's brother, Joshua."

Emma gold's me one of her unique, 'what-the-fuck', faces and beams encouragingly.

"Jesus, he's *huge!*"

I make out like what does she mean by 'huge', and she hugs me warmly.

"You wouldn't need a fucking guard dog, would you?"

Jack enters the kitchen and we baste him our female eyes. I know he's heard Emma's exclamation so I broad smiled. Looking dandy in white T-shirt and dark blue jeans, I'd no choice but to admire the way he strode in with such butch-ness and ordain the space we address him.

The depth of male vocals: "You two lovelies talking nice 'bout my brother?"

I liked Joshua, but he wasn't Jack.

"Is he coming in to get some food?" I'm worried he's staying outside too long, shadily avoiding the southern folk because they were not like northern ones. Joshua fortified his element back in The Lake's but down south, he always shifted uncomfortable.

"He's just finishing up," Jack says, fetching more beer from the fridge.

I cross over and affectionately prod his newly fetching beer-gut. "Think there's gonna be enough?"

Clanging the bottles, he graces me a lip kiss and says sure; my turning round to carry on with Emma's curious chat.

"He's some character, isn't he Jack?" Emma ignoring me, side looking at my beau, "I do love the swing."

"Go out and try it when he's finished," the cool offer. "Just don't make out you're sniggering behind his back."

Emma, half-offended, "Oh, I wasn't! I was just saying to Em, I think he's well put-together."

"Put-together?" said, lacing my old friend a mistrustful eye. "Thought you didn't notice those things?"

"Jack!" I intercede, sensing he wanted to have a little dig, "Emma was only saying."

For him not so easily the giver-upper, "Well," he pokes goblin, "I thought it was women you more noticed."

Emma's retort was a little bold, "Err, Jack my dear boy," sudden defence, "I may *prefer* my lady friend here, but I'm not blind to a well-built guy doing guy-things, and cos I'm queer doesn't mean I'm dead!"

Now get between.

"Okay, you two," my timed entry, and checking out Joshua in the back garden noticing how largely framed he really is, "let's do without the university griping. This is meant to be a happy house-warming."

Jack shakes the beers and kisses my mouth before a fast glance at Emma then heads back to our handful of guests. Neither of us wanted any tension and I hoped things had ended there, however Emma had to get a last word in.

"Guess he never got over the fact we were your close dorm mates and not him."

~

But he was. Jack was my close dorm mate despite not sharing my room, he was my closest. I did not like beef between him and Emma though undoubtedly it was there. Her suspicions about him test-cheating proved true but I never revealed to my uni friends why he felt the need to. That revelation of his childhood tragedy gone so deep, I still wondered if Jack had even begun to start coping with it. Something told me his tough, country-worn parents would have scoffed at counsel over such internalised matters. He was a kid seeing another kid die, a best friend, a young girl too, which could only have been crippling.

His parents joined us for a couple of nights stay after inspecting our new abode of which they vastly approved but something else told me they did not enjoy their second son being pulled farther away from them. Mary and Jake shuffled around consistently, wandering through the small cosy garden and ended up on the green tyre swing involving intense chat. My ears burning, I made a self-promise not to make love to Jack while they were around.

Oh-no, not anywhere, for any reason, our sexual urges to be kept hidden till Mary and Jake fell well away.

However they would not fall away till the middle of a second week. They loved being in our cottage so much with the vauntful woodlands in view it had them enjoying this home-from-home feel. Great! Mine and Jack's hunger was satiated little with a walk through the woods and a quick fuck against an oak, but it had to do until we got the place to ourselves again.

Upon their welcomed - though not rudely wished exit - Mary and Jake baked us a current-cake that could have fed all the local school kids and fixed up a roast pork-shoulder joint lasting well after several days. Stocked up, full, and looking forward to a warm brandy by our open fire, waving goodbye to his folks on the train I mention that Mary spoke of marriage and that real relationships were not complete in the eyes of God till consummated. Jack shrugged and said that was typical of his mother but still I wondered if he carried old traditions in a part of him.

Not thinking over old traditions as my leaving him with a sore penis after heavy, biting led fellatio and cunnilingus, we were too sensitive to move and let the open fire heat our souls to the point we fell asleep.

Urinating next morning while preparing for work, I found it hard to straighten up as my crotch area felt the effects of last night's munching.

"Shit, I'm fucked too," Jack crooned, joining me in the shower.

"Bastard, you were too rough," I lay cross, trying a degree best to wash my bits properly.

He disagrees, "Me!" jabbing my ribs, so I hit his balls and he drops to one knee.

Over breakfast I make out I'm not sorry so he apologises first. Children making up, he kisses my head then I take and squeeze his hand expressing sympathies which in return encourages him to fondly grab me round the throat and pretend to choke me.

We marked new employment; his in a bikers' sales-and-parts shop, and I, a clerk to one of the Justices in the town's magistrates court. We remained passengers to what we knew, becoming familiar, adjusted, and creatures of habit, and with our jobs, okay looks, and approachable personalities, unwelcome attraction too, grew.

I was left a bunch of roses on Valentine's from a person unknown and it kind of freaked me out. A fellow employee or visitor to the courts, who knew! The bloody thing left me recalling the incident with Benjamin Knowles as I had never been the wiser about his state of feelings toward me. When feasible, Jack followed me home from work on his Suzuki or sometimes came by bus so we drove back in my Mini. I felt presidential in my car when he tailed me on his motorbike, stopping at traffic lights pulling alongside and ensuring a check that everything's okay.

Fear of anything untoward happening was soon forgot as weeks passed and nothing sinister, prophesied likely. My paranoia reflecting past events having needled my conscience to increased awareness, I mean, it wouldn't have felt so bad if I had an inkling whom it were.

~

Jack sculptured his own unsought interest to others, especially a couple of local women who made it their obligation when he tinkered with his bike on a Sunday morning. Lifting up and inspecting under my Mini's hood, ensuring the plugs, the points, and the battery were fine, I ogled him while sipping a fresh brew and fine-tuned a slightly older looking of the opposite gender saunter his way from across the road. Appearing to have neared the end of her morning's jog, she clocked Jack and orotund to his attend.

Unable to hear their words, though I could tell it included banter as they burst out laughing, anyone outside of that gathering would have thought they were actually a couple. Hell, I watched intrigued as he crossed back to his bike and started explaining some things about it to this veleta female who could have stepped off any American soap-opera with its bevvy of damn fine looking mature women. And yes, a tad jealous - me, this femme appeared to be getting herself quite the acquainted.

Ascertaining I had none to fear yet unsteadily I felt so, I believe women were taught subconsciously to inherit those insecurities further and level a distrust of other women toward their men. I knew Jack wouldn't cheat, I was sure of it, yet why did I think he might or that he could develop feelings strong enough for another. I shut my eyes hating the thought. I shut my eyes seeing him kissing her. That self-hate or blaming a menstrual cycle for increased tension, I did put it down to ovulating, and that made me feel even worse.

The filing to rest of her hands on his shoulder while he shared his face with his bike did not stop her obvious glance up at the cottage bedroom window though I was certain she could not see me spying. And had she, that wily, girly, flick of her heel, like cheerleading practice were nearly over for another week, made me heave.

"Who was that?" I freshened upon entering our small hallway.

"Oh, some lady living up the street," mangling his hands on the dirty bike rag, "She's been here a while, saw us coming and going and thought she'd say hello."

I'm not buying, "Oh yeah, hello to *who?*"

He stops and gives me a Jack-so-simple look; no reply.

"Come on," I push, "Who is she?"

We brighten the kitchen and Jack begins to run hot water in the fantastically large sink after applying mechanic soap to his greasy hands, and avoiding my question indagates me more.

"Jack!"

"What?"

I understand I've prickled him but he better answer cos I wanted to know.

"Well, what's her name?"

A moment's absorption says should he tell me or not. He had no choice as far as I could see.

"Emily," he replies, "Her name's Emily."

"What's with these Em's," I ruse, "Emma, Emily, *Emery!*"

He beams whilst intertwining frothy palms, "Yours is the best though."

"Mm?" my lips pressed.

"Emery Pearson," sing-sung, "Emery, Emery..."

"So what did this *Emily* want?"

Jack won't detract me from my detection. I still wanted answers from this *innocent* meet.

"She didn't want anything, she was just saying hello."

"Just hello?" my lean back busk by the sink's edge. "Women don't just come from up the road and say hello."

"You saw her," he pranged, "she was out jogging."

Oh, like I really needed him to stand up for her, give me the answers will you.

"Jack!"

"Christ, Em!" He jumps to the indecorous mode and I don't give a shit cos he was going to give me what I wanted. And I wanted to know what this Emily was playing at. For godssake, she was older, and Paul leaving Jill crashed at the back of my mind. Older women had to be watched out for.

"Well what did she want?"

"Why, what, didn't you hear?"

I smack his arm. Not hard.

"Don't be such a smart-arse!"

"I wasn't."

"Well what," I furnish him, "you're thinking of fucking another woman?"

Snatching rash a tea-towel to dry his hands, he mixes my eyes with a simmering disquiet of his own.

"You're being stupid," he says, and brushes past me clipping my shoulder quite rough I start to boil.

You want to hit me, mate, come on, hit me, we've fought before!

I go after him.

"Hey, big man," untamed, grabbing his arm spinning him round, "You want to do this, let's do this!"

Perplexed lain business, "Do fucking what?"

"Oh, you're swearing now, great! Losing control, Jack?"

"You're being silly," he shouts, and whirls to storm off but I won't let it go.

"Me? Silly?"

I grab him, and it's a nasty grab, scratching his arm. I don't care. Shit, I suddenly didn't care.

"You want to get fucking angry, Jack, get fucking angry! You want to turn this in to something then turn it in to something!"

"Take a fucking pill, will you!"

Cheeky son-of-a-

He breaks to flee again but once more I grab his arm and haul him round and slap his face. Pronouncing my anger more I shove him in to the wall. I want a reaction, I want something from him, and then I get it.

My wish may have wanted to address him far harsher but he disengages me, jerking my hands off of him, to flash, and brutally, crushingly grip my biceps, turn me round and slam me up against the wall. It was rushing hell ferocious that a hanging picture crashed down at the side of us.

"You fuck!"

"Look, don't be a stupid cunt!"

That was it!

"You shit bastard!" I holler, "You want to fucking hit me, Jack, is that it, you want to hit me, well come on then, fucking hit me, go on!"

There is *Hail Mary* burn in his eyes and I have woken some kind of demon because I did not recognise my Jack, yet I was the one who summoned it and continued to stoke its flame. Why, I truly did not know, but truth incumbent, a moment with another woman and the way they were, left me fuming. For heaven's sake, why!

I lash to start a pointless brawl however he simply cages me and my savagery comes excessive.

"Fucking whack me, you bastard, come on, whack my guts if you want, fucking hit me!"

Wriggling like fish out of water an escaped hand of mine grapples him round the throat and I feel his *Adam's.* Knowing that I can hurt him there he hurricane's a manoeuvre imprisoning me hard, keeping my arms from fray, his body pressing with alacrity against my own.

"Don't you fucking get it!" he screams, bewildered, "It isn't *me*, Em! It isn't fucking *me* they want!"

I breathe close his face, his breathes close mine. I cannot move; he stays his command. What was he saying?

"They want *you*, they *all* want you! *She* wanted you!"

What the-

"Don't you see?" He crush wraps me so I struggle beneath his frame. I wasn't scared, just a little panicked.

"That Emily was asking about *you*, Em, she was asking *all* about you...not *me*, it wasn't about *me!*"

I feel him lessen, feel his weak. I think about my arguing and look to empathy.

"Eh!" my jolt, "What?"

Seeing reflected in his green eyes, the demon gone and bright stars stare back.

"I wouldn't hurt you, Emery," he says moonlike, "I wouldn't cheat on you I would never do that."

Slow, he releases my arms so I breeze myself loose and trace my fingers over his cheeks. He could drag me away, punch me even, instead he chooses to kiss my mouth and I open for his scent of breath to husk with mine. My hands ruffle his hair, cup the back of his neck, and gloved him in to me; a signature to ravish, maraud, use me fit, leave me bruised and torn, I press him to grand-centralise, I press him to care.

What followed come a scene of beastly sensuousness and I never halted the callous with his calm. Love was one hell of a crooked road with a life-psalm all its own, poetic in destruction, from past to fucking future.

~

Jamie told me over our managed fortnightly phone conversations she'd found a fabulous guy, some junior doctor specialising in geriatrics. Instantly I wondered if she were indulging in great sex like Jack and me.

I often masturbated in front of him.

Well, why not!

I discovered too my smelling better as I got older. Wasn't sure if it was a hormonal thing or God planned it so. I mean, increased wrinkles, cracks, and slowing athleticism, I think God was trying to compensate for us 'approaching older' women to have some bodily benefits welcome waiting. My youth held much imagination but when I hit thirty, damn, my blood sauté for more and greater sex. Demands in performance excelled though not an orgasmic finish were called each time. A higher level deemed needed in all aspects relating from embraces to train-wreck sex. Hormonal or otherwise, I found myself playing with my clit frequently, and sometimes Jack discovered me in that moment of come.

"Why didn't you join in?" I gasp, practically doubled-up from the zenith of orgasm.

Tossing his bike keys aside from a hard day at the shop, he straddles up a movie-cowboy-walk-on over to me by the kitchen sink.

"Didn't want to disturb such a wonderful scene," he says, and whips out his cock.

Leaning back by the sink, I watch him start to give that thing some pull as he manhandles a fist full of my jumper front to complete his artistry. I lavish him crane those greens all over me devoutly pulling off his penis. Christ, men could work their organ flipping hard.

When he climaxes I smile exoterically. He takes me by the hand leading me upstairs where we drop knackered on our Elizabethan-style bed. Both watching the ceiling, both undressing our tops, he starts to tell me about his day and I tell him about mine.

~

What was it with other women?

Emily 'bumped' in to Jack another given Sunday and I'm again at the window with yet another cupped brew and this time she looks up and waves.

Smooth cunt! I think courtly.

Here stood this older female who had no idea about the accelerant fuelled argument her presence induced only weeks ago, acting out her usual niceties and clandestinely pretending her interests were those of good neighbourly. Good neighbourly my arse, that's if Jack's interpretations of her stop-overs were correct. Fuck, we were all strange! Did she think it feasible I would sleep with her while I had a partner? I mean, cheat so overtly? If she were invited round Jack would clearly know what was going on. Maybe she didn't care but I sure did, and the bleeding assumption that I'd be open to sleeping with her anyways was too much pretention. Confidence is one thing and actual belief someone may so 'no' to your charms, another.

Overloading thoughts circled my brain about women's attraction to me, those I already knew of anyway: not standing alone Emma and Caroline, but other university friends, then Jill, now this Emily. Had the emotion mutualised my experimental side might have indulged but never was there *that* feeling. Admiration, yes, that's all, and that's where it stayed. On my part, maybe it was the 'no-make-up', a jaunty swagger, and converse any subject landed. Whatever the reason, I mused them all and found nothing out the ordinary, just women being that - women.

Though all said and done, and careful not to encourage anything untoward from my latest secret admirer, for Emily I did wave a limp hand back.

~

"Should we tie the knot?"

I react to billowy biceps clung round me as his fingers played a tune upon my tummy beneath my jumper.

On my back I was laying on top of Jack's stomach, our bodies slapdash in the sofa. The football match humming low from the TV, my hesitant question doesn't stir much action.

"Mm," he mumbles, "what do you mean?"

I gesture sideways at him, his fingers continuing to play.

"Get married," I say floaty, "You know, make it official?"

He's quiet: Thinking.

The movement of his breathing massages my neck. I could fall asleep.

Stroking kind his thigh, nudging for a reply, his thoughts would be welcome.

"What for?" he asked sudden.

A little taken back, I mark the situation turning round on top of him with my face turned aside to catch the game.

"It would please your mum," my words seeking some sort of approval from one I know we shouldn't consent.

"Why?"

Jack starts playing with my hair, gently twisting and turning my locks, like figuring out what they were actually for. Mood deep, he measures uncomfortable.

"I'm just saying," my hinting unimportant, but really I thought it was. I wanted to know how he felt. I thought it was important to discuss. A future together with or without papers meant something.

"Well don't say," he moons easy. "We don't need a certificate to be like man and wife."

Soft, I rub a hand over his chest.

"But it would seal-it," I say to his cuddly belly.

Cosying me tighter, he takes a clump of my hair and entices me to look up at him.

I do.

"You want to get married?" his ask.

I shake my head. "I don't care."

"Well do you think it would make us...better?"

Again my head shakes.

"Emery," he lifts my chin to meet studious eyes.

Whatever he wanted I would do.

"Do you want me to ask you to marry me?"

That makes me smile. "I don't care, Jack," folding my arms across his adorable middle, "I'm with you," my chin dips in his belly, "It doesn't matter if we're married or not."

He sprinkles a shimmer of clean teeth, "To you or my mother?"

Mary influences my question from time. If not for her *consummate* label I would have forgot.

"I know she still bears down on you," hopefully he gets it, "And I just thought you might be thinking about it."

The man fizzes up as I shake inside his bottle. Reaching, he coaxingly pulls me level right on top of him without any effort. Our faces come close. His frame belies a tremendous strength.

"You want to get married, Em," he says, "we'll get married, otherwise, I'm okay. We don't have to be like our parents, we don't need their approval. A piece of paper saying something doesn't mean I should love you more, I already love you over everything."

Why does he have the right words each time? Why could he make it all come together?

I wanted to be like my parents, seeing them tied, looking at one another like they really felt it and really meant it and understanding their love could not be undone no matter the circumstances. Theirs was true. From a love only they knew, I felt I had that with Jack. Right now, I knew we meant true, and no one, could make it not.

"I love my mum and dad," he adds, almost sad, "but they're not *us*, Emery. They're not living my life for me no matter how much they wish they could...or were ever hoping to."

Swelling, I look to share his un-comfort, "Jack," watching close his green marbles, "I'm not asking you to choose anything here, just tell me how you really feel."

"How I feel?" He makes himself content below me in an old-fashioned flirt's way, "How I feel is everything you've given me, Emery. It means my world, and I'm not bee-essing you. Just you being with me and loving me is all I need. We could live anywhere, do anything, you'll always be my everything. I just hope I'll always be yours."

He must have been a poet in a past life because his renditions of theories close to the heart masked a distich-like quality I had not broached upon before. Don't know if riding that big bike kept him in touch with Mother Earth, but there was definitely a unique stance to him no other could muster, not even briefly, because Jack was perfect, and perfection ought to be worshipped.

"You know what," I said, snuggling my head in to his gentlest breathing chest, "I don't think I deserve you sometimes, I really don't."

"And you know something else, Em," beginning to play around with my hair once more, "we don't have to be anybody." His deep vocals reverberated round my ears resting close above his heart, "Let's just be us, okay?"

Again I glance up at him. He's craning down at me. I see an absolute. It's all I need to see.

Chapter Nineteen

The burden hung around my neck to keep myself safe and avoid at all costs any friction possible. I'd been pencilled in to see the therapist in two weeks' time concerning my emotional web. I could see things going fine and that my filling in the relevant psyche-assessments would get my sorry-self out of this haunt in due course. HMC Maidenhall, my unchosen home these last four years. I had come along well and been selected to assist others in their literacy development wherever feasible, though of course my help needed to be sought first. I would not have volunteered my services unless Miss Trimble guided me. One did not need a 'bettered' detainee insisting the 'lesser' do things her way. I mean, you could have signed your own penalty phase. The irony in Maidenhall's stamp: *Her Majesty's Corrections*. What a crude slap in the face. There felt nothing 'corrected' about prison unless you included a good beating from the guards that aided a digestive system to expurgate unwanted food, or perhaps shown how to commit latent female rape, 'corrections' was an ill-thought-out word. I wondered what our long standing Queen actually thought of her *nom-de-visage*. If she really viewed what went on here at times, she wouldn't exactly call it being corrected.

~

My chance to start believing I could soon be free beckoned.

Two weeks is all it took.

My burden fell heavy.

Keep clear nuances of fear, assail, or enmity, anything whatsoever, and see how this therapy could actually get me the hell out of here.

I never breathed a word to anybody about the pending sessions so I was surprised to find a tornado-faced guard at my cell door furtively pushing me back inside for an unscheduled one-on-one chat.

I tightened my abdominals expecting him to hit me but he chose to stink out my face with an unremittingly horrid breath. We had basic fluoride toothpaste so you'd think he could use some if none were to be found at his home.

He pressed a huge fist in to my ribs and I let him, I wasn't going to argue with the guy. He could make my life hell, accuse me of something, chuck me down the block, or plain old beat me up. This, I wanted to avoid.

"Got your smug self some therapy, eh, Pearson," his reviled feed, "Well you'd better make good use of it cos we all think you should do the full twelve for what you did."

What I *did* he could never understand: Brainless stone-age twit, stalking this place daily, looking to hurt someone! You had to have feelings for what I did and he never showed an iota of any.

"You walked in here with that stink of 'I'm fucking better', well you're not. You didn't want to make friends you didn't want to fit in. You really thought you could do your stretch without flinching? Well we made you flinch, didn't we, you fucking flinched alright, you cocky cunt. Soon put you in your place and you *stayed* there. Well you'd better pray this therapy works, cos if it doesn't...well, you'll still be ours to continue fucking playing with, you, and your fucking books."

After that hateful spiel he couldn't resist could he as he stepped back before upping his huge fist in to my belly that knocked the stuffing right out of me. I dropped to the floor but it never stopped him from hauling me up on to my feet and thumping me again.

Uninvited, he additionally spread the word that I would be getting this help as several other women would approach myself - most of a friendly disposition - and left positive reflection in my ear.

"Use the time well, Pearce," one woman hoped, "That shit's good if you use it right."

She informs me she was in therapy on the outside and had she continued getting it - lack of personal funds saw her giving it up - she might not have stabbed her cheating partner to death. He had messed with her head, she said, and pulled all the right strings to get her wound up, challenging her to stab him after grabbing hold a kitchen knife in the middle of cooking this bastard's dinner - her words, not mine - and the judge gave her nine years. Hell, it stunk of misogyny alright, I saw men walk away with probation after killing a 'nagging wife'.

~

My case got mentioned from time to time when related matters were discussed in the media. Five days before my scheduled first meet with my therapist, I was talked about in the local media due to what I had done and therefore interest lined up three 'specialists' wanting to review my case. Unless I'd held up a great train, or broke a copper, celebrity idolising remained unwelcome in here, though some with broader, non-judgemental thinking, believed in what I did and offered support. Saying they understood where I was coming from, I got the gist they would have acted the same given the exact set of misfortune. Who am I to say different, I couldn't be the only woman to have done what I did in the moment. We were emotive creatures, and love was the biggest emotion.

~

Searching to give advice, or receive some, cometh everyone: Christ, I didn't know where to go at times, like the women saw me as some type of philosopher who could get them distinction to include time off their sentence or good credit. Finding myself a most prized Apostle, I tried to stay un-lined. I couldn't even escape during our classes.

"What are you gonna do, Pearsy, play it nutty so you get sent to a pampered head-hospital?"

"I don't think I'm a head-case," I responded, shuffling up a pile of papers the class completed for marking later.

"After what you done," she dribbles back, "you don't call that nutty?"

Could I be bothered to explain, no, no, I wasn't going to stand there and defend any action, not that she would have come to understand either way. This would be what the therapy entailed: Explanations of everything anything. Sounded like a mountainous challenge afore me.

"You got a man looking inside your head or a woman?"

Shoving books back on to their shelves, I didn't know. Eager to help me pack up after class, three 'extra-hands' were busy probing the topic instead of doing their opted duties. Smithson; in for armed robbery with intent, bulldog build and attitude to match, Keane; fiery Irish lass, who thought we were related in some bizarre way, failure to pay fines, and Heathcote; embezzlement worries, all three overlapping questions I couldn't get a chance to answer; oh yeah, okay, I wasn't going to.

"You know, you play your cards right, Pearsy, you might get some nookie if it's a guy."

My God, the thought was repellent.

"Well it's not like you're in to the *ladies*, is it!"

Where this line of chatter were heading I did not want to visit. I tried to finish up fast to get out of the library before my head exploded.

"You know," Keane looking keen, "just play it cool, Pearce. Some of that good fortune can rub off on the rest of us."

"Yeah," Heathcote, stood near, "You've done alright by yourself. You done alright by others too, now's the time to get yourself out!"

I glimpse my two fellow teacher's-assistants as they finish up for another class. My three helpful hands pat me on the back before leaving and I'm guessing, from a muted response off of Thomson and Harriot, I was becoming more than an example to these women. I was sounding like their game-changer.

~

An unfortunate delay held up my meeting. Last minute appendages interrupted the day's play. I heard final plans were in place from the three squabbling specialists to hand in their proposed methods for me. I was no notorious detainee but they really wanted to hunt round inside my head and all this internecine nonsense between the different therapy fields was coming tiresome.

I waited patiently for a new date to be allocated, however I were having doubts about being made some type of notoriety. The media were eager to get their hands on me for a live-TV-chat and others started to show concern for my well-being.

"Don't take it to heart, Pearson," a surly guard offers, "You'll be out if you do things right, just don't get ahead of yourself."

Ahead of myself: everybody seemed to be ahead for me!

"So how long do you think it'll take, a couple of weeks or a few months to *fib* yourself out?"

I wasn't putting a time on anything, they could surmise till their hearts content.

"You don't say a lot do you, Pearce?" I got asked grumpily, "Won't be any flipping good then to a bloody therapist will you, not saying much."

I felt need to reply, "They chose me, I never chose them."

"Oh yeah," her splash back, "you never choose anything, do you, Pearson, it just buzzes toward you like fly to shit."

"I never asked for any of this!"

"No, you just expect it because of the way you look!"

"No I don't!"

"Yes, you do, everybody thinks it."

"Well they're wrong then, aren't they, cos I never screwed anyone to get any favours?"

"No, of course not," she unevenly prunes me, "But you push it out there, don't you, and you know you do."

For once this exchange got under my skin, "No I don't," razor cut, "I've never done *a thing* to show that I look for favours and I never will."

She motors, "Too much of a prude," staring hard, "You don't have to spread your legs to get the upper hand, Pearce, you just use your head and bat those eyes of yours. Clever cunt! But we won't hold it against you."

"That's because you can't," I remoulded, "You can't say a *thing* about me cos I never did shit to anybody in here and I never went looking for it!"

Again, her search over me is unnerving. "So your shit doesn't stink, eh?"

Now I move toward her face. It is not like me yet I do. "Like everyone else," my begin slow and careful, "my shit does stink." I lick my lips and blow cool because I was showing cool, before saying, "I just don't go smearing it all over the bloody place, that's all."

~

With so much cross-movement happening I realised this therapy was a guarantor of early release. No doubt it smacked of politics, prison reform, and the added gloss of a 'handsome bandit' at the fore. *'The cruel beauty of reason'*, I got called after my case, and a lot of critics had their own quips, each involving the state of my physicality's as well as my attire; fascination for the discerning fashionistas following my story in the daily rags. Nothing I wore were high-end designer labelled, however my trim build enough to send tongues wagging and women's health segments supposing my dietary lifestyle. Simple jumper, blouse, and pants; all items of clothing fuelling gossip of that taut waist and saucy bottom. Purely down to paternal genes, nothing more, yet it was given credence to any proceedings in court. I never claimed aphrodisiac goddess but the country heralded a growing waistline and some perceived 'evil' being of 'supermodel form', enhanced all quota of interest. I was a human aphid in most households up and down the country greedy for gossip to help pass the day along. And days passed were good. I was able to see my parents, friends, and barristers, and I could come and go from the courthouse to home. Weekends I managed being me until I was handed down my fate. No one expected such a heavy twelve-year sentence and none of us prepared to accept it. I lost an appeal but the barristers would continue. I lost a second and after three years the therapy idea got brought up. An underhanded scheme to get me early release, my barrister thought so, as did Governor Barron and my family wanted me to go for it regardless. I agreed with them all and would play my part when the time came.

~

The three sensationalist head-shrinks were doing their media rounds claiming I should have got the help in their institutions not a HMC Gaol. Maidenhall had all the facilities to assist me during my sojourn so Barron gave her account of where things needed to be. She strongly recommended this proven therapist who had worked change-rounds on those forwarded to her, and with a track history Barron lavishly approved, pushing forward any suggestions in relation to mental health reflected well on her standing. Improvements were drastic in all marked cases but surely that was because women *did*, and *said* anything to get better conditions for themselves or to simply get out early. I knew I had to do well. Of course I'd throw in honesty and make my point but I couldn't risk fucking this up for anything.

Barron gave me a heads up the first meeting was now scheduled in forty-eight hours' time and I should make sure all my classes were up to date with paperwork complete because it would show me in good stead. Reflect efficiency, a well-balanced aptitude, and an understanding of the help being entrusted. Cute, regulatory words I could vomit at. The old gal's beautifully maintained machine kept working perfectly and that's the way the Governor liked it. It was too the way corrupt guards and their contraband loving power-players stayed efficient. A little of something good could influence a lot of things bad, and with my media interests mixed with the detainees sensing change for the better, it got the insalubrious-set really hot under the collar.

Without need for greater expression, it was never me which needed sorting out. Abusers enjoyed abusing as word spread my presence in here was upsetting the norm. No wait, hey, just another excuse for looking to do me over one more time.

I got the sense a minority dislike were waiting for me in the wings. My awareness tripled after my first beating and growing eyes in the back of my head only worked half the time. If they wanted to get you, they got you. And they wanted to get me.

I mustn't say I'm used to getting beaten up, nobody is, you just expect some kinds of pain, 'debilitate' or 'left-standing' type, but no one ever gets used to it. I thought I'd been dealt my fair share, however I assumed wrong.

~

It threw down cold winter rain the first week of December, 2005, when the code-blue alarm hit everyone in the visiting-room. Following the drill in place and kissing our loved ones goodbye till next time, we watched them file from view as the guards ushered us detainees out for mandatory lockdown.

My mum's customary handing over of the upcoming Christmas hamper was safely locked away along with other relatives' goodies from that day's visit. Straight away I felt a shiver. From the start things were wrong, the way the alarm was given, no one sure of the emergency, and where its allocation, all pretty unusual for an institution get up.

My cell mates also felt something 'smelt off' but we couldn't pinpoint what. Maybe an escape planned, a whole lorry load of contraband smuggled in, or it was a genuine code-blue. That meant anything to fall at your feet for an explanation must be open to interpretation. Lots of deceptive shenanigans occurred and no matter the reason, detainees kept their mouths shut.

"What was all that yesterday?" I asked my fellow teacher-aids before the start of second class.

"Why'd you want to know, Pearson?" Harriot almost berates me, "You never share your information when you get any?"

I felt punched in the face. It wasn't like her to be such a snide shit. Yes, I kept family and personal matters aside, but any crap that was liable to badly affect the other women I would have a word to utter. Intended or not, we helped one another when Maidenhall etiquette allowed but you never stepped over the line. You never breached detainee rules everybody knew that, so I couldn't believe some still held a grudge over my not teaching judo or basic wrestling. The sting of resentment hit my very bones. I got my warn.

It had been reconnoitred from days past when I was heading to collect a box of new literature and notebooks. My escorting officer said to wait a moment while he checked for corridor clearance at the side wing leading to the kitchens and gym hall.

When he left unlocked the gated cell area, immediately I knew it was no mistake; he brought me here not only to fetch the new materials because they had been ordered, but I was to get some 'physical-education' along the route.

There were five of them. Three faces I recognised, the power-women and two more genus's.

I had no inkling how far they would go except I had serious pain coming. It wasn't typical of a location in here for you to get sexually brutalised but I knew what was heading my way would be equally horrid. I tried not to panic, I wouldn't shout out, there was no alarm to alert, and my mind thought the week's previous code-blue somehow related.

"You know you guys don't have to do this."

All five of them looked at one another like they'd just heard God talking to Moses. Who was I kidding? They couldn't *wait* to do this. My therapy would be delayed yet again, and now I got the growing resentment. The one perceived receiving special treatment, who strutted round like a seventies-pin-up, masking talents she unwilled to share, needed to be bought crashing down. I thought about slagging myself off for them but I knew it wouldn't stop their plans. Nothing was going to prevent this heavy mob from dealing me their prepped desserts so I decided this time I wouldn't take it lying down. I wouldn't just brace and accept it. No, fuck that. I was going to fight back.

They rushed me sudden and sensing their un-worded actions I managed to chop down two of them, one with an upper-cut elbow to the chin, another, a perfect side punch to the jaw. I don't really know what the hell I was doing but it took a good few moments before the other two could get control of me as I'd rough-housed a third, bashing her head up against the iron-bars before I got dropped with a series of implete body shots.

After that I didn't remember much except feeling my torso take one hell of a kicking and being pulled up on to my knees with my arms held back and my front left wide open. One of the still-standing powers got a hold of my hair to kept my head sweetly in position and kneed me several times in the face.

I heard the code-blue alarm radioed by my 'trusted' guard and tried to see what was going on but my eyes quickly swelled shut. My ribcage pulverised, I fought to inhale a proper breath while my hands hurt from what I were later told savage foot stomps to them.

Inside the infirmary under observation and sedation to aid quelling my pain, days later I recalled hearing a beautiful voice that worded a melody of kindness in my ear. Soon Governor Barron spoke then the special 'voice' spoke again and I sensed it come closer to my battered face. I tried to see through a mass of broken blood vessels and swollen tissue but I could only hear words. I was safe for now. I could do nada about a gang jumping me, I wouldn't be around to see the women revise and pass their exams, I got comfort from Barron expressing genuine concern, and I remembered that poetic voice.

I let my right forearm drop so they knew I was awake.

The unknown hand gently curved round mine which was heavily bandaged from a knuckle dislocation and two hairline fractures.

If I had not known whom this new voice belonged I would have believed my mum was in the room with me.

I wanted to cry but didn't.

I wanted Jack to say everything would be fine.

I wanted my mum and dad, my brother and my sister.

I wanted to be okay.

I coughed from stabbing pain in my ribs and this new voice came closer whilst touching a healing hand upon my chest. With both lips split I couldn't speak well and so let all my pain strain through.

"Who..." I successfully whisper, and I'm told *who*.

"Hi, Emery, I'm Susan. My name's Susan James. I'm going to be your therapist."

I make to smile but all the pother consumes me, then, as though guided in slow motion, I begin to snivel.

Chapter Twenty

From that moment I had found a friend. I knew it. Not a therapist or white-coat wearing detachment, no, a friend. Susan made me feel special from the get-go and it did not lessen.

"You know what's needed," she addresses me, fixing back a strand of hair after her bun-pull.

Everything from her I heed would be put right, said right, and done right.

My say is conclusive, "You know I want to get out of here. I couldn't do another year."

She ginger-bread's me, "You shouldn't have done a single year in the first place."

I cock a brow.

"Let's not play with each other, Emery," she said, like reaching to smack a naughty child's wrist, "You're well aware I thought you should have been given probation. After everything that happened with your case, you shouldn't have done hard time. They could have opted to put you in an open-prison for a couple of years."

My smiling isn't a piss-take, it's genuine. "Pay some type of recompense?" I ask.

She puffs, unimpressed with my circumvallate. "Recompense," she derided, "After I saw what they did to you that was recompense *unfair*, way more, than enough."

I sit up straight and glean my good companion of these last few months. She cared, and my spine tingled. No, not like that, more affable, more obliging, more being her.

The books I'd read, the lessons I helped penned, writings I commented on, my own 'real-life' book held page-opened to a detailed, acutely driven kicking, and Susan began to read.

~

"When do you think she'll be out of here?"

"Another week," the nurse tells my awaiting therapist as I can just about see her for the first time through an opening in my repairing right eye. "They beat her up pretty good."

My bandaged hand slipped across my stomach as this nice woman advances to peer down at me.

The nurse mentions, "It got leaked to the press," and Susan kindly berates her.

"You don't have to let her hear stuff like that right now," but my ears have heard and I know my family will have too. "This poor woman needs to focus on getting better so she can get back on track to getting herself out."

"Yeah, well, we all get it," the nurse shields, "This Pearson's done a lot of good in here and she'll be missed."

"Missed?"

The nurse approaches and I close my eye like I'm still out of it so the two of them continue talking.

"Word is she helped a lot of poorly-read women read and write properly."

The new female within-these-walls is scented, "This lady, here, Emery Pearson?"

"Well, I wouldn't exactly call her a *lady*," responds the nurse, "I mean, she can handle herself with some kind of fighting skill she has, didn't tell a soul about it till she was found out a while ago."

Illicit more, so said: "A soul about what?"

The nurse reaches descriptive, "That she could have probably taken over the wing and made it a better place with her *given* talents."

Susan's interest grows. Peeking open my right eye I see her stand to address the nurse face to face. Intrigue!

"Just what did she *do?*" the therapist enquires, crossing her arms and probing to score high.

"Well..." the nurse, shifting comfortably, "that's just it. She didn't *do* a damn thing."

The mind Doctor's motions group for more.

"Kept herself to herself most of the time," the sister professional, "Word spread she was a snob so some women messed her up. Didn't like her, taught her a few hard prison lessons."

"She was bullied?"

"You could say," replied effective, "But it got round she was pretty tough and wasn't averse to taking a right old hammering."

I glimpse Susan uncross her arms and turn to give me a mothering look. I wanted to tell both ladies I was fine but remained still, and as Susan returned to sit by my bedside, her usher soaked inside me. I kept my busted eyes shut.

"I didn't know all this trouble was happening to her," she says mindful.

"You know how it is," the nurse refreshes, neatening needles and swabs in to a medicine box, "You're an outsider from the beginning so they'll bloody well let you know it."

"They could have just left her alone," Susan, upset, "They didn't have to hurt her."

"My word," exclaims the nurse, "who are you kidding! If this lot couldn't *make-out* with her then they were certain to go the other way and enjoy doing her in."

"It doesn't have to be like that." I think my mum is speaking. "It doesn't have to be so spiteful."

Again the nurse steps across to where I am laid and gives Susan a blessed hand on the shoulder. Words to follow; a hint she was a naïve little pup.

"My dear, you can take wild hogs from their pen but they'll always be wild, and when someone like this Pearson here proves an exception to the rule, she's going to get singled out for special treatment."

Susan could sing an elegy and I would keep my eyes closed. Couldn't let them know I'd heard every word.

"It's bad enough all the violence out there," her quaint protest, "Then you get women hurting other women on the inside too!"

"The system makes them what they are," saddles the nurse, returning to her spread-sheet desk. "These women look to inflict their own deep seated pain on one another if they can."

"So that makes it okay then, we accept all this stuff because the system says we *should?*"

The nurse looks back as she fiddles around with her nurse-things in her hands. "My dear," lusciously condescending her address of Susan, "you're only visiting a couple of times a week to these places. *You* stay and work for a whole year then I'll hear your opinion. In the meantime, let this tough-cookie rest and I'll inform you of any changes so you can schedule your - meeting."

~

Must have been hard on old Susan seeing me for the first time, and after hearing her words and minding my thoughts, she felt like family. I let them down before. I wasn't going to let Susan down now.

"So you're happy with everything then, you don't think we might need a plan to go over anything?"

"Sorry," I say, "but what's there to go over?" thinking all ground met covered. "You know how I've survived in here you know I miss Jack and my family and how I'm going to make amends."

"Are you?" Susan jumps in, "Going to make amends?"

"Well" looking to traverse, "it's not like I'm going to swagger about like I did nothing wrong. I'll do whatever's necessary to get forgiven and hopefully move on."

"It won't be easy."

"I know it won't."

"You're going to meet some tough challenges, Em."

"Yeah, I know."

"Do you?" she breezes, "Do you know what's really waiting for you when the time comes and you do get out?"

She smells like it's a done-deal. "So you're convinced I *will* make it?"

"I'd like to think so," spoken true. "My report will recommend your release and I'm sure the Governor will endorse it. You simply have to make the right moves for the preview Judge and his team."

"They won't hold it against me?" I asked, knowing of the in-fighting during my incarceration to look inside my head. I remind her, "Lots vied for my attention."

She smiles, "Well...now they'll be getting it, won't they."

"Yeah," I recall, "but it wasn't right from the start."

Coolly, she puts, "I was recommended by Barron, Emery," tilting her head so nice, "She knew about me from past associations so the board shouldn't let that get in the way of an honest report, or the strong recommendation you get paroled. Barron really liked you."

I pull a face.

"I know, I know," Susan cuddles me with her words, "She can come across as an old battle-axe at times but she's from an archaic system where borstal days meant harsh, *was* harsh."

I enjoy her excuse for the Governor, yet say, "If today's anything like yesteryear we haven't come very far."

I watch her ponder. "You have to admit, Em, your input here made things a little bit better for some?"

I grin inwards, "I only know that they're bang-on about lunatics running the asylum."

"You don't mean that!"

I go to say I do however I stop. I had to conduct mself properly and be 'their' sincere to reach my goal. It was within grasp and all I had to do was stretch.

"You've helped me get through what I needed to," sited like to close things.

"Have I?" Susan shifts her elegant blouse and leans on top the desk again. There goes that inviting pose, shoring up my ideas of how seductive she can be, not realising, yet perhaps so, she *was* a distraction as well as a honed point forcing one to recollect. It worked each time.

"You say you've missed him, Em?" her shifting focus, "Have you, have you really missed him?"

Is she trying to get my back up!

"Did you ever stop to think about his family and how it would affect them? It seems you never considered their feelings and you were going to make that choice for them. I mean, the assumption you could make that choice in the first place is obviously self-absorbed?"

"Self-absorbed," I branched, "No, I told you," and now ready for her but instantly I see this reaction is incorrect, "I told you why I did what I did. We couldn't deal with it."

"*You* couldn't deal with it?"

"No," amplified, "*We!*"

"So you'd do it again, Em, is that what you're saying?"

"No!" blinking trickster, "Just no, I'd never do that again, not ever, I couldn't!"

"Why not, Em, think you're above it now? Think you can control yourself if something like that happened again?"

"What?" I laced-up strong, "No," but clearly a bit confused, "No, it *couldn't* happen again!"

"Why not, Emery, why couldn't it happen again? Are you saying things would be different next time?"

Different! They couldn't be *any more* different!

"What?" I scratch my head, "No, of course not!"

"Really?" she poked.

"Well, no," I tried answering, tried getting round it, "There wouldn't be another time!"

"Why's that, Em, why not another time?"

"Because there just wouldn't!"

"Oh really, couldn't there be?"

I remember and I shiver, "After what happened, no!"

Small doubted, "Never?"

"No," I clasped, "I wouldn't let it!"

"Why not, Emery, what makes you think you can control it now?"

Where is she going, "Control it now, yes I could!"

"Could you?"

"Look, there couldn't be a next time!"

"Why couldn't there *be* a next time?"

"Why?"

She slaps hard, "Yes, *why*, Emery, why all the control all of a sudden, you needed it when you did what you did to him, why couldn't it be someone else just the same, why only him?"

I remember the eyes, I remember the look, I remember it all.

Oh God!

"Come on, Emery, tell me!"

"Tell you what?" I fumed, "That it was fucking Jack, alright, *my* fucking Jack, there's only one Jack Charles there could never be another like him and I could never do that to another man! I could never love someone like that again, not ever, never!"

Fuck, shit!

And fuck again!

Goddamn, what was this!

She hands me that great mountain I have climbed. I was over, triumph, but I wanted to lash out with a denouncing that I would have soulfully regretted because she had pulled out my intestines and I could not gather them back.

Her test! It was a fucking test!

You fool.

I flash up and angrily slap my chair against her desk and in doing so she jumps up, my explosion shocks us both and I grace her with sorry eyes. Shit, this was not good. But Christ, it was me!

Gesturing to make a cautious approach, my friend Susan, but I hold out my hand to her: *No! Don't!* I moved back till I hit the door then slid to the floor in a cloud of shame. Had I just turned everything inside-out again, or outside-in, hell, I didn't know, my only thought was that I'd regressed back to a year ago, letting anger slip, not accept my feelings, or perhaps I had, I just didn't get it, but Susan, I think, got everything.

Slow, she crosses over to me and is unconcerned with the spoiling of her neat attire getting ruffled, and equally considered, joined me on the floor.

She put her arm around me.

I sobbed briefly.

She squeezed my shoulder awful tight and I looked in to her turquoise eyes. The tropical colours made me think of an island somewhere, in the equator, alone, the middle of nowhere, misunderstood. Yeah, that was me. Thirty-six-years old and still I were getting to know myself. Mother of God, define me.

My tearing ends with my world crumbling and disappearing at my feet. "I'm still not ready," I said miserable, "I'm gonna mess this up, aren't I?"

A reassuring hug nestles my deflated form. I'm surprised by her read of the situation.

"On the contrary," Susan smiles sultry, "I think you're going to do brilliantly."

Chapter Twenty-One

I never thought so. I laid awake that night thinking over the mistakes I'd made, the man I loved, the family I left behind, to the life I were living now. Unforgotten suffering at times by other detainees' hands, I lay hoping to make certain I received parole. I needed out. I could not risk another beating, another week in the block or being placed on any type of report, all stains to hash up my early release. My nose would have to remain on the up if I were to make that final hearing. I understood the ticking of boxes would guarantee success, however I had to ensure my character wavered on top till I stepped foot out of here.

I needed to succeed.

God, please, I needed to.

Nothing quelled my thirst for freedom except freedom itself. Nobody was going to push my buttons and get me situated to mess things up. I could take anything, couldn't I? *Sure,* as my only true friend in here was able to shove me over the edge. How the hell did I let that happen, I mean, couldn't I see Susan was winding me up, like the preview board might next week? I incredibly flew-off-the-handle and wished I hadn't. Letting her down this penultimate meet, I was left prostrated and hugely disappointed. After eight months of therapy with two of them sat healing from my battering, I should be a cool head by now, though approaching five years locked in this place, remaining cool at each aggravated turn; impossible. But it was Susan. Susan James who literally held my hand and picked me up each time I fell. She carried me to a safe haven inside my aching head and led me down a path, dare I say, of righteousness. Shit, I hadn't *found* God, but what I'm trying to say, is I found *something*. In fact it could be God in disguise, a moment where he touches you and you feel it in an offhand way. Those beatings I absorbed was possibly his way of telling me to stay strong, turn the other cheek, delivery awaits. I played my part with helping literacy improve and was thanked in part with spilt blood and bruises though I never let them get me down. I don't know, maybe I had, maybe I'm kidding myself thinking I deserved all I got. Hadn't I? My own selfish actions rewarding of this place I should be thankful they never killed me. Perhaps my lost cool said I should serve the whole twelve, then again if I were male, I'm certain I would have received less. I know I moan about such stuff but all one had to do was look around: Perceived racial injustice, the sexes sentencing differential, and a class system that always fucked the lowers. If you were going to get shafted then you were going to get shafted *real* good. Forget the red hot poker it was more like a pile driver covered in hydrochloric acid. God, I hurt. God, I'm sorry I keep talking to you tonight. I'll stop moaning if you help me get through the week, I promise. Stave off the unwelcome towel-wrapped hands of the guards and any power-women seeking to place a crowbar in my works. I know you'll look after me cos I looked after others and I never sought to do harm. Always have the upper hand, Jamie said, so my refusing to become one of the hard-cases dealing out uncontested power-rules means I had succeeded somewhere, didn't it? Look, I never implemented their brutal regulations. I saw too much pain, witnessed mental breakdowns, and had my own woes flung in my face. No one ever saw a quiet dusk come down from being inside.

Hell, I needed to look up and stay looking up. Susan floated over me indicating my family were not far away so all I had to do to complete the reunion was steer clear of every damn thing that could corrupt it. So, God, because I know you're listening, here's to helping my sorry-arse make it.

~

Following my three weeks in the infirmary, Governor Barron rebirthed to a fine concerned citizen; she personally checked over my healing hand fractures and requested to know if I wished to have a single-cell. I said yes, of course, and with my rapidly healing body made it back to the wing with increased vigour. The old girl had been highly praised for her successful treatment of the women's literacy classes and their own successes at passing the country's certified exams saw the anachronistic Governor hop up a notch with the prison authorities. A huge political golden ticket for her she'd beamed for an entire week after that. Some of her colleagues even guessed it was what Barron secretly desired from her contentious career. The hard-woman rehabilitation persona deeply held a desire for the less fortunate to do better, and our literacy classes saw that happen. There was only one fail in the year's group total of forty leaving the singular detainee heartbroken. The more others tried to console her the less she felt about herself, and of my own unsureness, I made over to congratulate her mammoth efforts to which she happily accepted, and after her sudden grab of my body and much repressed emotion, she kissed me hungrily on the mouth then apologised.

~

I checked a heavy choice not to pursue anymore teaching.

I'd had enough and lay eternally grateful the women all done so well. Barron wanted to keep the classes going and brought in a second qualified teacher to help roll our prison curriculum along. She would also try to gain a third class to be incorporated. At least Thomson, Harriot, and me left a mark like no other: Continuing education for those who wanted it and a less frightened bunch of detainees ready to make improvements in themselves if they chose to. The end of the line never stopped, you could step over it and start again. And so being detained at our Queen's pleasure, though I'm still not sure she would approve of such menial crap but grander efforts all round, it did not mean times were at an end. My own chances to improve and change were also welcomed so I'm feeling I should be ready for anything. Yeah, sure I was.

Unwanted news headlines for what I'd done never easily forgotten I would not hide from my critics, of which there were many. Thomson and Harriot thought I was insane, however they started to accept who I was, what I'd become, and offered support in any way to help with my upcoming parole hearing. Remember, offer support in any way they can.

"You know Abrams is looking to do you in again?"

Do me in again, hell! I'd been done in so many times I forgot. Abrams, the top-bitch of the power-three, okay, now what!

"Pearson," Thompson flew concerned, "you need to watch your back, I ain't kidding."

Watch my back, I couldn't watch my front!

"Listen," all nicely stated to my past teaching assistant, "I'm staying out of her way, there's nothing she has on me or will do to me."

Thomson acts like she's been stabbed. "You don't have to do anything, Pearson," she trims, "You're cannon-fodder and you know it!"

Cannon-fodder, awful expression for getting beaten up attune to being blown to bits on a war field. Suppose it was a little like that, your insides feeling as though they've been turned upside down. Guh!

I wasn't worried. There were too many applauders on my worn down side and Abrams would be treading a fine line if she thought beating me up again would ever be accepted by anyone. Let alone me.

It was simply not going to happen.

~

Like my hearing next week I would not accept defeat nor be taken down. I was going to be on my best behaviour and project uprightness in all its forms. Susan told me in advance everything I needed to know about my panel. They were mainly family men and women, evenly split, two of each, both men middle-aged cronies but easily won over if a detainee exemplified their self in the grandest of etiquette, and two well-chewed women who shored-up for the crime afore them not to get repeated. Well, there was no chance of that happening. What needed to happen was for me to rebuild severely broken bridges and calm the rushing waters beneath. Clichés, but they worked. Things sided new not a good indication for a worn weary panel who'd heard it all before. Simple, honest truth the way forward and a heart of regrets appreciated. I couldn't believe my love brought me here. I mean, had it? Or perhaps I wanted to believe that it had. My memories of Jack a broken wing from that tumbling bird rolling around looking to get up and fly again, and if the wing stayed broken, I stayed here. The healing need cometh from within, from in me, and I was certain I'd reached there. My routine life these past years all hinged on next week so I could re-comfort those who cared and tell them my love never died. It just lay stored before pastures new.

~

All the emotional tide gathered and swept out to sea I wondered about my efforts and what other clients' tales played on dear Susan. The minds she saw each day, the collapses, the rage, the ones who fell madly in love with her, surely in amongst that she would need help of her own. Only a machine could take on such responsibility and not crack without some sort of aid. I thought of her supervisor who oversaw her. Susan carried a massive debt to us all and she needed to prove successful. Whether we were her preferred pet-project or someone else's, success upon these correctional shores integral to her own stability; I mean, if all this talking and working out other people's minds wasn't manageable enough, her world would crash too, right? If her mental health couldn't take it then neither would ours. Of the crimes and thoughts behind every single person we were each different yet the working of our minds revealed the same emotional mine-field: Criminalities' deadly sins, jealousy, greed, hate, and love. Inside stoked the answers to every act we perpetrated for whatever reason, and we, or another, tried to work it out. I hoped my time with Susan did not greatly consume her. I felt she thought I was special from the beginning. The moment you are introduced to a new client left broken in half from a heavy beating had to invoke a higher feel over your 'less-beaten-up' ones, and after my healing was almost complete, yeah, I still bathed faded bruises and a marked lip, among wounds you could not see, our official first meet came cloaked in distrust - from my side at least anyway. Was I to be a waste of everyone's time to make me look good in a report my sad self could cope with its silliness? And silliness perhaps it was. I'd taken on a role far wiser than myself, and now older, pressures of being me, changing and mending the web I'd broken, my *silliness* explained through one-on-one therapy. Only I didn't think it had but Susan did. Coming from the infirmary escorted by two female guards, my presence in front the women on the wing garnered several to nod their heads like they approved of my gallant return however it was never gallant. I had to come back here I had no choice, and given one I still would have come back. Jack didn't run from anything. Whatever was to be, he faced up to. He'd shown me the same. Face up to everything lain before you and if you could change better the matter at hand, then do so. I was going to change this present matter for the better and getting escorted to my new single-cell be it the start I need.

Thomson and Harriot engaged me as I sat down on my spine-meddling mattress. I hadn't rested my head before they told me they'd packed and bagged all my things for my new, highly-sought after abode. Lacing my letters inside ribbon-tied envelopes and placing my books in alphabetical order, I smiled at their fastidiousness. I also appreciated it as my hands were still tender from the hairline fractures, and my two ex-teaching-assistants expressed sadness about my being there no more. Afterward they passed on regrets from the other women who were looking forward to a Pearson return but they too were deprived. I honestly did not expect myself to have been *that* popular. Still, they couldn't rely on me and I wished Thomson and Harriot the very best for the future and their hurry to explain the second professional brought in to assist the growing literacy demand was not exactly unattractive to sigh over, so, things were *really* looking up.

My first therapeutic crash, I call it a crash, I was still inflamed from the princely beating I'd taken and Susan could see this. She sat for most of our first session watching me look to avoid answering anything because I was still a wreck and found it bloody hard to come down from my annoyance. The moment I saw her I thought her beauty was misplaced in this hell forsook dungeon but she lightened it with a special lamp deflecting any Tudor-ness with her strong held angelic glow. From then on I wrongly believed she got off on it so I held back more than I should of. It was petty stuff on my part though after my status came elevated while other experts fought to get inside my head, I grew receptive to a genuine belief she wanted to see my early release. I wasn't featured material for any future book, not that she would be writing one, but her concerns for all her patients was clear. Yes, her beauty dazzled, it also furthered you to open up and accept her help.

"Well then, Emery," her politeness remained after our introductory sixty-minutes, "do you think your first session went okay?"

Through all the villainy encompassing, through the leers and the guards of maltreatment, this one among many came gilded from above and there was holy-water amid this hailstorm. Real, I brooded awkward, sought to oppose, but I wouldn't cometh the next time.

"I didn't say much," my truthful reply, "and I know you'll write that in your report."

Her smile matches Adam's Eve. "I'm not here to trip you up, Emery," she says light, "And I won't deceive you either. You've agreed to this course of therapy and I'll do all I can to see you get everything you need."

My mind foxily grabs the most important to me: "A way out?"

That fantastic smile of hers forms again. "Well, Emery," the way she says my name of no other, "that will be entirely up to you. You have to show those concerned you want to get out."

I could lie, could act, I could play the role needed of me, yet somehow because of this Susan, I would head for genuine truths.

"Okay," I said, and she outstretches her palm. The reach of friendship is made.

"See you next week?" her ask.

I glimpse the manicured extreme with its offer to pull me through these tough times. It is a gesture unavoidable, affable, and wanting. This kid wasn't kidding around and neither would I.

Pleasantly I shake her hand. She's warm. I feel good.

"See you next week," I said.

Crossing to the door she lets me know she's still here.

"These sessions will work out, Emery, trust me."

Little did she know; I already started to.

Chapter Twenty-Two

The events which led to me being detained merry-go-round inside my head. I couldn't let others' actions pay my burden so this event would see me act out on my own.

With fractures to my hand mended I built up my strength doing press-ups. The second month after seeing Susan, my head was clearing certain things out and holding on to bits anew. Stacking fresh thoughts over time, I leisurely read my own choice of books and exhibited far more relaxed when family visited. My unusually happy self, saw word get round the therapy sessions must be working however my jolly nature actually hid a tremulous fear as a new-student to the prison's curriculum gladly informs me over supper-time, "You were mentioned today in class about getting special treatment and all that therapy."

Trying to spoon a beef-broth inside me halted as the younger woman glued my eyes.

"After what you did gave you all that publicity and now everyone's trying to help you, some are saying you don't deserve it."

Oh yeah, I wondered who, cos my ears were constantly frying.

"They're even saying you're some kind of prize, Pearson, and a few are thinking about getting a piece."

Thanks, like I was butchered meat hung up in a shop; I'll take that slice, please.

"Who's saying it?" my making out the obvious.

"You know who," she courts, dipping buttered bread in her broth, "Just look out for yourself," she adds watchful, "A lot of us think you should be left alone."

I could be. I only needed to do one thing.

~

For weeks now after that vicious ambush, payback stoked under my skin far more than when Benjamin Knowles messed me up. From what I remembered of that incident left thoughts much worse toward the five women who'd cruel handled me. Knowles' comeuppance shifted round inside my head. Sometimes one needed to strike back with less severe repercussions after turning the other cheek. Depended upon your own wiring, you chose your route with abandon. I chose this one extremely careful because I had to get it right if I was to pull it off successfully.

The ninth of Susan's sessions ended with a thumbs-up and I was making my way back to the wing when my male guard escort informed he needed to make a brief detour while I waited in the corridor leading toward the humming boiler room. He gave me this look and I understood. I would be alone, he would say nothing, and this, whatever this would turn out to be, would stay among us.

"Pull out your shit, Pearson," he uttered embroidered, "Fucking end this and fuck her up!"

I didn't fuck people up, though some say I did with my pussy-tease, sexual desire, and unaware crushes. Those fuck-ups I could deal with, but this shined mactation would be measured in accordance. So I thought.

He turned the short corner leaving me alone and mere seconds after Abrams emerged in the opposite direction ensuring no one was behind her as she positioned herself squarely in front of me. A tigress out its cage, ready to tear apart prey, I searched for my sling and pebbles to drop this goliath.

"You sent for me, Pearson, so...here I am!"

Stupid, yes I know, but it was the only way I could get a fair fight. I called her out in yard-time through a hand gesture we meet and she accepted. I wouldn't run scared anymore and I refused to look over my shoulder for the remainder of my time in here. I lost, I could expect more beatings, I won; I would be left alone.

"You're brave, Pearce," she says, making fists of her hands as though I was about to feel each knuckle, "You think that judo shit's gonna help you?"

She had no idea of my capabilities yet I was going to show her not judo, not grappling, but me: *My* release, seeing *my* family, becoming free. *This* is what Abrams would now see.

Of course I was afraid but I had to overcome, and even if I lost here today, I'm sure I would gain her begrudged respect for having called her out. No one ever did.

"Let's just get on with it, Abrams," I said simple.

She laughs like a kayaking beast. "What, you're not mentioning any rules, no eye-gouging, no hair-pulling, no biting, no-"

Cleverly done, a good attempt to divert for she saw me flinch then ran at me full speed but I was speedier, stepping aside and pushing her face first in to the unequivocally lined floor-to-ceiling iron-bars. I'd never heard someone whelp this helplessly as she emerged with a loss front tooth and lacerate dug mouth. The rage that engulfed her summoned me to be cool and finish this for I drew her blood and she was fumigating to draw mine.

At that moment, my then thirty-five-year old body had been unnecessarily pummelled, smashed, and trodden, and I would not, if I could, allow it again. My healed hands still possessed their muscle-memory from my wrestling-come-sex days, and the judo with Carla during college, fondly recalled.

Whoever set this up timed it right because I could not have been with Abrams in the spot where we were without the approval of a head-guard or other. And I suppose wherever Abrams and I were to meet, the outcome would be the same.

No matter what!

I remember everything but I won't boast. You don't boast about hurting someone even if it is in revenge. I had thrown Jack around before and could handle him but if he ever got violent with me I would be incapable of pulling out a victory. One correctly placed punch is all it took and I would go down, so I made sure Abrams was not able to land such a punch.

By the time she curved round to charge me I dropped her with a kick to the back of her knee and set myself up to safely coil through her flailing limbs and crank back her right arm breaking her shoulder. I heard the bone snap and a chilling cry exploded however I managed to silence her with an effective throat choke. Keeping her controlled, keeping myself clear, I emphasised my point.

"We're even, okay," I breathe hard over her left ear while applying pressure to her neck, "You lay off of me and I stay away from you *and* your cronies or they'll all get a taste of this judo shit, do you hear me?!"

Bloodied, loss tooth, a broke shoulder, she manages to nod yes but I demand, after a surge in pressure to her neck, that she say it out loud so she does.

Fast, I release her and she collapses while I leapt up and headed down the corridor.

I turn the corner and bump in to my escorting guard who airlessly steps over to me and firmly takes hold of my arm.

Thinking I've been double-crossed and going to get kidney-punched, I braced myself as he said naturally, "Hey, Pearson, when's your next therapy session?"

~

Governor Barron paid a surprise visit to our wing a few days later. On her exit after briefly looking round, she made sure to catch my eye for a telling couple of seconds. Even in her position having secretly accepted my actions, no matter her new-found respect for detainee Pearson, I would entrust no soul. As with the nurse from the infirmary who stopped me upon passing through the canteen doors whispered delightfully that Abrams wore her warning well.

I hadn't looked for accolades or congratulatory back slaps, I just wanted the violence against me to end. And it did.

Susan however was far from impressed because I spoke of nothing.

"We've come a long way in just ten weeks, Emery," she reminds me, "what's changed?"

"Well..." I stow away momentarily, "Can't there be ups and downs sometimes?" my huffed response motions a narrowing of her awesome eyes.

"Did I offend you with that," asked and answered, "taking a step backwards after your success thus far!"

"Success of what," I groan, childish, "telling you how I feel?"

"Being honest about *how* you feel was the beginning," folding her arms upon the desk, "Being honest about your *actions* is furthering."

She's digging for truth to rumours about my vengeance. She could dig. This would stay buried.

Mindful, she probes, "You want to talk about Abrams?"

I want to shout, *Christ, no,* though shrug lackadaisically.

"You *did* hear what happened to her?"

I shake my head, "So what?"

Susan flits unhappily, "Her injuries were pretty horrific."

I act insouciant, "And?"

"Emery!"

I know I was sounding harsh but I felt that about the power-women. Their leader unfortunately received what she dished out and I wanted it left at that.

"You know Abrams made a trip to the Royal's A and E before being sent to the infirmary," my hard-play got informed like I ought to be sorry for that pig-lug bitch. Shit, I was turning in to one of them.

"So what," reacting a little discordant, "I'm meant to be worried for her? I don't know anything about it. I've got my own stuff to deal with."

"You don't know *anything?*" Susan measures her question frankly, "You didn't *do* anything to her, Emery! You never paid her back for anything, something she may have done to you in the past or one of your cell-mates?"

"I don't have cell-mates."

"You did once?"

"I don't have them now."

"Really, no one at all, nobody who even likes you a tiny bit and you like them back, no one in here is a *friend* to you?"

My friends were out there, my family, and everything else.

"These are just people I know," put offhandedly, "They're not my friends they're acquaintances."

The word is pejorative and I ache having said it. Friends cleaned me up after I got bashed, friends stayed quiet when I broke the rules, friends saw to it I got a good breakfast after feeling rundown, and friends offered sound advice when they could. I had friends in here; I was just being a bitch.

"You know what you did to wind up in here shows similar circumstances with what happened to Abrams."

Like being told off in school I want to tell her to mind her own business but I don't. "I told you I had nothing to do with that."

Susan behoves me. "I get the rules, Emery," she greys firm, "I know you have to say what you say but you need to understand something right at the off," I pay attention to her wonderful ire, "I'm not here to play around and mess you about and you need to know that whatever you tell me stays with me and I would never put anything in my report that I felt the authorities would unfairly exploit. If I get a whiff of uncontrolled violence I have to say something, I have to speak out, but if I sense the actions of somebody desperate to end horrors against them, I'll speak up for that as well but please hear me out! Don't treat me like I know nothing about prison life and its secret rules because I do! I've done this sort of work for seven years now and I'm no stranger to the retaliatory actions of those who've been harmed. I saw what happened to you and I can understand your desire for revenge, just don't take me for an idiot who sits behind a desk and listens to other people's unfortunate woes. I want you to be able to talk to me, Emery, to please trust me! I'm not the enemy, I won't go gossiping behind your back to make myself look good. I told you before I'm a friend to you in here and I wish you'd just trust me more."

Damn!

Well, if there was ever a real kinship moment, that was one of them. Playing the tough attitude did not wash and I admired Susan for stepping down my throat the way she did. At that moment she could have pummelled me something rotten and I don't think I would have minded. The fact she stood up to me like that and was unafraid if I walked out and said goodbye to her therapy held her in good stead with me. She wasn't scared of the rules and would break them herself if called upon, so yeah, we hit common ground. I liked her. I liked her lots, and I would begin to tell her everything.

Chapter Twenty-Three

We gloved a Saturday afternoon spat and Jack got me over the sofa and fucked me real hard from behind. I was in a bit of pain and couldn't relax enough for him to begin eating me down there. Because that's what he did. He ate me like a good old sweet-pudding as he once poured warm custard over my vagina and carefully spooned me out. It was great his prudently measuring each spoon before coming across my labial then tipping the head of my clitoris. Afterward he used the end of the spoon probing inside my hole like a surgeon's special delicacy. Jack knew my body better than I so I was in debt that I didn't enjoy his penis as much as he'd eagerly wait my detecting to discover more about the damn thing. I mean, what was there to forage about a man's prick. It got erect, spurted out semen then fell limp. And that sack of wet balls hanging beneath could be toyed with or even bitten but you had to be careful not to raise him impotent. There wasn't a time I didn't enjoy his making love to me. It need not be perfect either with neither of us coming each time, it just needed to be.

~

'96 saw our very first holiday across the Atlantic address sun-drenched Miami. Avoiding the hurricane season we arrived in late October where the temperatures continued to soar and a year-round continuous vacationing feel gripped us both. We stayed near South Beach where Jack and I occupied a middle-of-the-road hotel and enjoyed our own purchased bottle of champagne. The bubbly was overrated twaddle however what Jack did afterward with that French Grape was pretty unforgettable. I mean, in general we didn't use implements to further our sex lives, just sometimes things came to hand and we found ourselves indulging other items in to our game. They worked uniquely well in foreplay and could get our juices flowing long before orgasm. The feel of a chilled two-litre glass bottle pressing against my mushrooming clitoris was enough to force my head's erupt. Jack enjoyed seeing the veins in my neck pulsate beneath the skin and strangely I liked the ones gracing the side of his temple when he burst his spurt.

For a couple who often talked about sex and played in other areas to spice things up, we never went over old ground when things didn't exactly pan out. Those were left in the past though sometimes I wanted to explore them further. Remember my so-called fantasy had been thoroughly quashed that night when Jack mistakenly thought my desires should be ingratiated. He'd been drastically incorrect and misread the entire situation. I never helped by feeding out obscure details about what I would have probably enjoyed anyway.

The holiday saw us strengthen our relationship. We didn't argue, never bickered, but discuss one another's choices. Still in accordance kids were not in the picture, we would continue living our lives while putting the other first. And so his puppy-greens lifted to scamper in anticipation of us hiring a Harley-Davidson for a week and taking to the wide roads for miles and miles, cruising like Hells-Angels straight out the Sixties. Jack could employ his little-boy-want so long as we'd stop to catch a dropping sunset across the ocean. In agreement we whisked up each other's delight and set off for that long ride on the two-wheeled beauty. I finally got why Jack loved these throbbing beasts. That engine chucked out a sound one couldn't describe and I could not get over how smooth the machine was, even the dirt roads were eaten up effortlessly as I held his leather-jacketed waist whilst hearing the sounds of America. We could have made the covers of a Seventies LP or soft-porn flick. Jack loved that.

Slowly dressed too was my tomboy side when we stopped to check the sun setting on the East-Coast. I perused the black-gold's working engine like I was Jack on given Sunday mornings, maintaining his bike for the week ahead. The experience of this holiday made me think about leaving my job and take to traveling the world. It was a big decision; the house, our mortgage, family, all would be left behind, but we had our own lives to live.

"We could do it," Jack suggests, sat holding me from behind perched on the bike's rear seat.

I glance over my shoulder and see the setting sun inside his greens. "We've got a lot of commitments," I remind him, though I see he's pondering the options.

"Maybe we could rent out the house for a couple of years, come back and find new jobs? Who knows?"

I squirm, "Someone else living in our home?" but he's okay about it.

"Come on, Em, I don't feel like being homeless either when we got back."

It was something to think about. We worked hard and selling up to travel the world seemed extreme in today's climate. A home was immeasurable.

Squeezing me tight through our leathers, its sound of a tightening lizard ready to pounce, I get the urge to swing round and throw Jack on his back then sit atop him while the sun disappeared. Riding back to South Beach would have to wait till morning because I could have sat there all night watching his face looking in to mine. I intertwine my fingers around his and he squeezes me tighter. The sun beginning its fading descent, he says in my ear, I love you.

~

Getting home early winter from another State-side trip, I decided to see in the approaching millennium with a new job and new prospects. Jack, happy with the work in the bike shop and enjoying his time there, would carry on as normal. I joked he should upgrade to a Harley and it wasn't long before his brother Joshua, arriving for an extended weekend stay during the Christmas of '99, agreed.

"I could see you both on a Harley," he gushes, chomping salivary on reheated turkey, "You could live in a caravan and move round more and not be tied forever to this place."

"Hold on," I act in, pulling Joshua's late-presented out of its paper wrapping, "I like it here, and this is our home."

"Yeah, Emery," he smarts, gnashing away, checking over my revealing his gift to us, "but you could be freer to travel and see more."

"We still travel," unravelling a hand-crafted wooden picture frame with carvings so intricate it should have been in a museum. "We're still free," I add, handling Joshua's masterpiece.

He says nothing then asks, "You like it?"

Jack steps across and caresses its shape.

"It's absolutely beautiful," I tell Joshua, and immediately see he has plans for what should be placed inside.

"Family photos look great in that."

Another crunch of turkey between his large country-fingers and I glance at Jack.

"We're not thinking about starting a family, Josh," Jack unloads, cautiously putting the frame on top the mantle-piece above our open wood-fire crackling away. "Em and I are okay with the way things are."

"You know *I'm* not gonna get married," he asserts, now licking his fingers, "Mum wouldn't mind a grandkid."

I laugh and Joshua looks at me like I snatched his turkey from him.

"Come on, J," that's what I called him sometimes, "you don't have to get married to give your mum grandkids."

Pausing mid bite he absorbs what I've said. "Well…that's the proper done way, Emery… I'm only saying."

His sweetening old fashions are a delight. "J," I begin charmed, and lean down to grab his bushy beard followed up with a warm hug, "it's soon the next century and I think we can broaden our horizons a little."

Now he checks me like I've cut off his nose then relaxes and nods his head while coming round to the possible idea things were a flexing.

"You could be right, girl," he kicks down, and bites an even bigger slosh of turkey, "But I'm stuck in my ways."

Ye ole country folk!

I kiss his cheekbone wishing him a Merry Christmas as he revels to finish the rest of our hearty leftovers.

~

By the end of that week, Joshua decided to leave before the New Year came in. I thought he should stay and see it in with us but he was adamant about returning to The Lakes and spend it with Mary and Jake. I could see his point. Family was too important to ignore at these special times and I regretted not seeing my family for the first time in a long while: Their synthesis of voices over a phone-call not the same as seeing their faces and holding them close.

"How are you and Jack?"

"Oh, we're doing great, mum. We had Joshua over after Christmas and he's going back tomorrow night."

"What, New Year's Eve? He's not spending it with you two?"

"No, no, you know how he is about family and stuff."

"Talking about family, Lucas has got himself a nice Officer girlfriend."

"What," I shriek, "about time too! He's so busy getting ribbons he's missing out on living."

"You know he's career driven."

"Yeah, he'll be head of the Air-Force soon the way he's going."

"Says he loves you, Emery, and misses you, we all do."

"And I miss you as well, mum. You know I'll come up next year, we're just a bit busy down here, that's all."

"You're okay financially? I know it's getting tough with things."

"Hey, honestly, we're fine, things couldn't be better. I won't give up my job till I find something else first."

"Don't waste yourself, Emery, you're smart and you're young."

"Thanks, mum, I won't. I just don't know what direction I want to go in right now."

"You'll find something, you always do."

Time for mood change, "Hey, how's Jamie, heard from her lately?"

"She's here. She came over last night."

"She with anyone?"

"Nah! Even if she is, she hasn't said anything to me."

"She's probably waiting to surprise you at any moment, married with kids!"

"Oh lord, I don't need a heart-attack, I need to know you're all okay."

"Mum, we *are* okay, all of us. No matter what, we'll *all* be fine."

"Really, Emery, Lucas the pilot, Jamie delivering babies, you and Jack so far away...I worry."

"Hey, mum, come on, we're adults, stop worrying. You need to let us live our lives. You don't want us to be unhappy."

Interlude too long!

"Are you happy, Em?"

"Mum...I'm more than happy. I love Jack, and I'll *always* love you too."

~

Loving was everything. It entailed respect, trust, care, and desire. I loved Jack and he loved me, and every detail in between was a part of it.

Noticing Joshua's small suitcase ready and packed by the front door of our little cottage, I would make my way upstairs to say goodbye before calling him a taxi but I wouldn't call him a taxi this New Year's Eve of '99.

"What the hell did you do, are you crazy?!"

I stopped midway on the narrow staircase and, unnoticed, saw Jack slam in the guest-bedroom door, its purpose for me not to hear a thing.

The soundproofing of the old cottage held well and the two country brothers' muffled angry voices were stifled steadfast. I crept up three more treads and craned to listen but could not make out clear words. However both men sounded fiercely defensive, Jack more so, and I wanted to know why.

He never got angry with Joshua before and this was heavily new. I could not understand the fury because their relationship never so much as hinted of one. Yes, siblings clashed, but Jack and Joshua?

The bedroom door yanked open and there was no millisecond for me to leg it downstairs as Joshua halted and matched the stunned look in my eyes.

Fuck! Double fuck!

A twitch shook the corner of my mouth, my embarrassment evident at the situation. Joshua let a smile leave his lips then aimed assured, hurrying past me, fast squeezing my arm and pecking my forehead before grabbing his suitcase and slipping outside.

Of his usually slow, lumbering form, I never seen him shift so quick and neither had I Jack, who motored on after his brother.

"Hey, what's going on?" seizing Jack's hand on passing me.

"Forget it, Em, it's brother stuff!"

"You call *that* brother stuff, you sounded like you wanted to take his head off."

Unresponsive, ripping his hand from mine, Jack tails after Joshua, and I tail after him.

I stop at the front door as Jack stalks over to Joshua who's stood next to our parked car and motorbike when he spins his elder brother round for further words.

Their verbal exchange like drowning at sea I do not hear though read the heat rising between them. Whatever happened effectively broke Jack and I hated to think what it was. I just hoped the family were alright.

"What the hell was that?" I demanded after Jack's return ushering me inside and banging the door shut. "Jack?"

"Look, leave it, Em, it's nothing, just something between Josh and me."

"Just something, you were flipping angry at him!"

"Yeah, and it's over now!"

"You call that over," I field his body *savoir*, "You're still fuming."

"Look, let it go, will you, it's none of your business!"

That enraged me.

"He's my family too, Jack. We might not be frigging married but I still see him as family."

"Oh yeah, *your* family, smug and self-assured, the Pearson's, neat little package wrapped perfection, well Joshua isn't fucking like that!"

I could have slapped him.

"My family *isn't* like that!"

"Aren't they?"

He stormed in the living room and I followed, pissed right fucking off.

"You have a big shitting row with your brother and take it out on *my* family?"

"Oh, give it a rest, Emery."

"Give it a rest? Are you fucking kidding me?"

"I wasn't having a go at your family!"

"Then what do you call it, Jack, a fucking song-of-praise?"

"Shut up! You have to make everything about you!"

"Jesus, what did you just say?"

"It was a private thing between Josh and me so you don't need to know, okay!"

"I don't eh? Then why'd you bring my family in to it?"

"You brought your family in to it, not me."

"I was referring to J as *my* family, Jack, not anything else."

"Oh yeah, *J*," gnawed back, "J, your name for him, so fucking cute!"

I forgot to breathe. "Fuck you, Jack!"

"No," he blasts back, "fuck you, Emery!"

I punched his chest. I couldn't think of anything to say so I punched his chest, hard, and he staggered backward holding his breast area. My anger portrayed scurried higher as Jack, duty bound, turned his back on me.

He wouldn't walk away, no, I wouldn't let him, and using both my arms I whirl him round to face me. He must have anticipated my action because he shone full force and nothing told me what was coming as he back-handed me across the face. I took the blow and my nose started to bleed. Shit. I perked up straight to lash him with blazing words but he punched me with his best everything right in the stomach. Fuck.

"Is that what you want, Emery, for this to be a fucking fight, is that it?"

On all-fours, trying to gulp in air, I failed to look up as I was damn hurting and he knew, and although I had nothing immediately forthcoming, I was determined not to let our argument end this way.

Chapter Twenty-Four

"So, Emery, you ready?"

The week had flown by since my semi-final session with Susan. The female guard wore a nice smile as she stood at my cell door awaiting my unsure self to be escorted to the office where I would meet the preview panel. Family people so I would show family values. My selfishness from past would not rear its side and my only focus was to latch on to everything that should see me past the gate.

Parole: My goal.

"All nice and neat, I see."

The female guard checked me over with a look that said she wouldn't mind a rumble in the sack but I was over all the lewdness. In fact, I was humbled by it. On notice that at my age many still found me attractive was something I grew to appreciate. I only ever loved Jack and it would undoubtedly remain that way.

Pulling crisply at the smart cotton navy blouse and skirt my mum delivered for the meet, I looked professional, engaging, and felt it too. This a must-win all round so every angle usable to gain favour would come in play and be assisted with words of a rehabilitated convict able to sail back in to society. I could feel the ocean breeze in my face, the early sun beat down on me, and all kinds of spoken language whizzing past my ears, so with this, I rose in to the air to be carried across the sandy beaches to a new life without concrete walls. So much of you disappeared in this place and to recapture it again would mark a beginning struggle, especially if you were looking to get over your past.

Fidgeting a final time to ensure the fit of my blouse looked good, I turned to greet the guard with a bashful grin.

"You'll do okay, Pearson," she flatters me.

"You think so?"

She beams. "You're a hot-shot, girl...and you know it."

I think I did. Everyone kept telling me that so I must have done.

"Come on, let's be having you."

Approaching her with a flow to freedom; the sea, the sun, the world's human faces, I step out from my single-cell to an orchestra of applause accompanied with cries of, 'You'll do well', 'Get your arse released', 'Burn it to 'em, girl', among more selective prose. I grinned at the whole lot of them and picked my head up straight as the guard escorted me to the wing's locked gates.

As she gestured for the supervisor to open up, Susan appeared beside the entrance gate and smiled at me. I smiled back and the rushing sounds of yowling mouth-whistles from the audience of women was deafening.

Was I ready? You bet I was.

~

His words matched an emphatic applauding, like those jeering execution crowds baying for blood.

I stayed on my knees grabbing my gut from the devastating impact of Jack's fist. We'd been here before but it was more mutual. I laid in to him, I wanted to fight, and I could see he got fucking turned on with the big scraps that we had. Don't worry, I did too, but this right now, he was angry, and I knew it. Therefore no, I would not look to hit him back.

"You get your way with Joshua, with Jill, with bloody Caroline! You even get it with *me!*"

Trying to make me sound like some B-movie femme-fatale didn't take as I toiled up on one knee. I crammed a thousand things I wanted to say but accessed none as Jack leant down and hauled me up on my feet.

"Fuck, Em!"

His sorrow was clear. His damning of his own actions made me stay cool.

"Christ, I'm sorry!"

The young boy emerged, the one who picked up snails and placed them safely on to dropped autumn leaves and who put himself out to help others and who'd stand up for the ill-treated...

I hated the contradictory but we all had it.

I gagged and coughed and Jack gingerly placed his forehead against my temple. I really didn't need any hugs and kisses right now as fighting to regain my balanced breathing was uppermost in my thoughts. But with Jack's insist to press his lips upon mine lay foolishly unwelcome.

I tried to push him away but he remained jammed up, our chests touching, legs touching, and his lips forcing touch of my trembling own.

"Emery, please?" his receding mop of curls got brushed aside while his burning eyes tried to locate my sadly dimming ones.

He didn't get that I wanted to double over and try to comfortably breathe as I fought to escape his straightening up of my winded torso.

Moving nowhere was I and he wasn't going to stop.

"Jack," I croak, gasping, clutching my gut, "let go of me...Jesus, let me go."

It's as though he is deaf.

He forces yet another kiss smothering my pledge and mixes saliva with my bloodied nose however I did not want any of it. I *wasn't* being turned on, I wanted to be away of him.

"Emery..."

"Jack - fuck!" I hurled his way, "Fucking stop!"

I gain some strength and shove him back. I hear his heavy breath, sounds of a forlorn beast with regret amassing in abundance. Gripping my stomach, trying to look up at him, I simply couldn't.

So he shouts, seemingly bewildered, "It was Joshua, J, whatever you want to call him, I'm just sorry I hit you!"

This time I crank my head up and feel a tear splash my cheek. The big oaf was crying. Hell, I should have been as well.

~

Bravely, Susan blinked back a tear as we came in contact. Shouldn't I be tearful not her?

"You go down there, Emery, and win your freedom."

Grasping my hand with a squeeze that came from her heart, she willed me to do this, and I would. The applause and shrieks from the women behind began to fade as we made our way with another rugged female guard matching us stride for stride, and knowing they had to reflect tough, come on now, a little ease of a hard-bitten soul wouldn't go amiss.

Turning in to an adjoining corridor Susan releases my hand and I touch my chest. My heart maddened and my adrenaline flowed as the bang shut of an iron-door sent the yelps of the women on the wing to close silent.

We walked a further two minutes, turning this way then a next till we entered a brooding green painted hallway which saw a beautifully panelled oak door at the end of it.

This was parole etiquette.

"You'll be fine," someone whispers in my ear.

That someone was *not* Susan with my turn to see she's fumbling around inside her briefcase. Looking in the opposite direction I saw the rugged female guard has acquired the softness of a woollen teddy-bear. Even she was rooting for me.

"I can't mess this up," I say more to myself than addressing the two women accompanying, and I'm left stunned by a rewarding response.

"You won't," words reverberated back, "You'll fucking do alright."

Startled to see Susan with fingers-crossed nudge my arm after her expletive short in regard to these matters shocks me. Really, she left me shocked. I don't recall her *ever* swearing.

"You don't have to be so blunt," my new restless, and before she makes to knock the thick panelled oak, she takes my arm and squeezes again.

"Well," the James grin, "sometimes you just have to be," and I'm left spellbound.

~

"I didn't mean to take it out on you."

I at last manage to stand up and level Jack with 'you cunt' eyes. I try to step beyond his frame but he curls rough fingers around my arm to contain me.

"You know I'm sorry, okay," shedding another tear, "I shouldn't have let that happen."

"Jack, get off me!"

"Emery, please!"

"I said let go, will you!" I pull free and he steps off, that deeply engraved sorrow filtering each of his pores.

"Emery, listen-"

No, I shuffle past and turn for the salvage of the living room.

"Hey, wait!"

Reaching he seeks to maul my hand and again I wriggle free.

"Jack, don't!" I flip round and hold out my hands gently palming him away. "Don't touch me, please! Just let me go!"

"Emery?"

My gesture to escape he makes sure I can't by seizing both my arms and mangling them rigid to my sides.

"Jack!"

I think I'm panicking.

Start to worry!

His tone mashes extreme my face, "Em, just listen to me for a minute!" and emphatically bangs me against the wall.

Docile and recede I did not play.

"Take your fucking hands off me!"

"Em!"

Defensive cometh I; my literal digs a trench dashing Jack out of it. Stunned, he's taken aback and stood staring at me then flings his arms wide expressing he's open and sorry and ready for a slap.

But I wasn't going to hit him.

Wiping my bloody nose I simply go around him and aim for the stairs.

"Aren't we gonna talk about this?"

My hand fixed tight the baluster and I jump up a step then clothe Jack in my furnace I felt afraid uncontained.

"You fucking bastard, you think I'm gonna talk to you after that!"

"Christ, you started it!"

"Me?" I subliminally measure my step across to him. "You were arguing with your brother," I pointed out, "I just wanted to know what it was about, you're the one who got all fucked off about it!"

"It was fucking private, that's why!"

"Fucking private, you, your brother, me, fucking private?!"

His glowing picture covered full with a not-coping mechanism. I could see something frightening tearing him up but my fuel for their sibling argument leading to ours prioritised.

"There's nothing *private* in this house, Jack. You want to fight with your brother, take it outside, down a fucking pub, in the park, anywhere but our fucking house."

"It just happened!"

"So you beat me up for it?"

"Jesus, you came at me, you hit me!"

"You didn't have to fucking hit me, you know you're stronger, Jack, you fucking hurt me!"

"Yeah, and you hurt me, Em! You *always* hurt me!"

I hurt him, what a crock of crap. So he's looking to justify bloodying my nose and punching my stomach, well, I wasn't about to allow it.

"Take your feeling sorry for yourself and shove it down your throat!"

I bolted upstairs and Jack streams after me.

"You think you're all proper, don't you, Emery, you can't see the fucking effect you have on people, can you? You can't see past your own fucking nose!"

So I detonated, "Which you happily fucking bloodied, you cunt!"

Inside our bedroom I sling shut the door but Jack charges in to pursue his confront. I start to feel exhausted and I wasn't ready for this.

~

All four sat with authoritarian and unsmiling erect forms. Professional apparel with expertly prepped folders of everything they wished to ask, speak, or jot down. I'd follow their lead, measure their brows, study pursed lips, and see how quick they viewed their lined A4's. I wouldn't miss a trick.

First, Susan approached the sturdy desk seating all four parole members, and I, obsequiously, perched on the plastic chair gestured by the room's customary guard for my rear. My friend from this time said a couple of managed words for the panel after pointing to a few select paragraphs in her file before leaving, though not after a positive squeeze of my shoulder upon passing.

Now I made alone with four persons who held my brief future in their officious hands. I didn't play chess but chess be it the game this officialdom handed me.

After littered mutterings and glances held out, I took mental details of the power-grid four. Not dissimilar to the power-women who gladly knocked the love out of me, these four came viewed like the Tower of Babylon; differing language, misconstrued movements, and any threat perceived immediately overcome. So, all my aces were kept closely guarded.

Then: "Emery Pearson?"

I spark and stretch to shake hands with male-number-one who personifies a private-investigator out of the Fifties done good. Appearing around sixty, any second then I thought he'd get up and put on a caramel-coloured mac.

"I'm Donald Schmitz," he says, "One who's going to listen to you today and ask you some specific questions."

Formerly done I read him outright then smile and nod confidently. He was reluctant to marry, preferring to stay single but enjoy the freedoms of carrying on with one woman to the next. Marriage and the ties that came with it not important to him so I figure he had a broad view of life's misgivings. One assumed notch for me.

"Hello, Emery..."

This second male voice, leaner, less strident, an obvious call he was on my side, sat at the opposite end with the two females in between, perhaps indicating he was the cushion for a stricter pairing to come.

"I'm Anderson Perkins," fixing a thin bunch of hair across his head in an attempt to disguise a huge receding hairline, "Don't worry about me, I'm here to listen rather than to question you."

Nice. Two on my side: Next!

This woman smells of having an ingrown beef with detained women of loose morals: First sign of trouble.

"Miss Pearson," her firm address already says she displays a heavy dislike but I stay resolutely polite, feeding her a kind, unshifting look, "you obviously know why you're here so we won't waste anybody's time."

Err, hello, didn't catch your name? Mm, something niggling me she is opposed to this meeting altogether. Right, where's back up?

"Hi, Emery," a melt coolant cradles my ear and I'm quickly introduced to this younger, receptive, times-are-a-changing female who looked like she just stepped off the training bus. Good news.

"I'm Geraldine Bracken," tidily shoed, "and I'll admit I read a lot about your case before this hearing so it's a little surprising to finally meet you. I hope you're doing well."

Hm, harder to read, but she comes across as good natured and fair. I'll have some convincing to do with this one.

A capturing cough fills the room and we are all pulled to its insistence as Schmitz grabs control.

"Okay," he tolls, "Emery Pearson, tell us why you're here."

~

Three massive strides were all it took for Jack to marry up and I jarringly placed a hand across my belly in case he thought about hitting me again.

"Jack, don't!"

"You like J? You want to call him *J!*"

"You moron, you think I fancy your brother?"

"Everyone seems to fancy *you!*"

Hollered, "I can't believe your fucking insecurities!" I'm mad and I let him have it, "You shit yourself every time someone comes near me, someone hints that they like me and you go all up inside your fucking self. You're a grown man, for chrissakes, why don't you act your age!"

He throws back, "The fucking age when you're a young kid who knows how to flaunt *your* fucking self and tease all the boys in to liking you!"

Now that had the impact of him punching me *without* him punching me.

"You're gonna blame some childish shit on the way you are now?"

The manly contort of his build spells don't-mess-I'm-in-charge. "Everyone has to save you, Em! Everyone comes to your fucking side and bays all over you."

I stab him more, "Interesting sentence for a university drop-out."

"You-"

Not letting him finish whatever he was to say, I look again to escape but he crabs my arm, swinging me round to face him, and I face him alright with a charring instinctive slap. He backs up permitting a red flame to appear. So this was Jack and I wouldn't be intimidated.

"We can fight, Jack," intuitively sworn. "Now I'm fucking up for it!"

What did I do? I didn't want to fight and I wasn't up for it.

The animalistic snatch of my jumper front by his steel-cuff grip sees his superiorly slam me in to the bedroom wall. The glow of his teeth like he were to savour every part of me in only seconds.

"We could fight, Em," he claims, "but I'd win...and I think you'd like that. I think you'd want more saving from the next stupid prick to fall in love with you!"

"What's the matter, Jack, did Joshua tell you his manhood's bigger than yours?"

"You want to sleep with my brother?"

"Don't be a fucking idiot!" I screamed, "I don't fancy your fucking brother, he put up a fucking swing once, I don't fancy him, I don't fancy anybody, you twat!"

He gently, apologetically, senses to release me, after I, in turn, had hurt his. Oh, my wish to have not.

"So, Em..." the glum detects deep, "you've always thought you were better, haven't you? I was always less than you, right?"

Wiping at my nose the blood is smeared across my top lip. Jack was beginning to seem pathetic and I was growing resentful.

"Don't be such a soppy cunt," I tell him, "Jesus, you have an argument with Joshua and all this shit comes out of nowhere, what is fucking wrong with you?"

He slows down, steps away, and laughs this uncomfortable laugh.

"All of that, what," he begins, "new-thinking back then...it was just bullshit to you, wasn't it?" His wave of slight recede, near black curls is thoughtfully brushed away, "What was I...a wimp, couldn't really protect you-you always needed something more, right?"

I'm discombobulated, flipping discombobulated, and this was finishing somewhere unknown to me.

"Everyone thought Knowles deserved what he got and no one would admit to it."

I look for an in-way.

"Jack-"

His in-way lights first, "I quietly kept all the glory because everyone believed I'd done it."

Oh shit!

I try to stop him say more but he turns from me raising both hands to rest on top of his head. Whatever had burned him from past came to scald him now.

"It was Joshua who beat up Knowles, not me."

My hand covers my mouth. Not due to what J did but because it ate Jack up. His big brother showing the futility of his smaller who couldn't get revenge over something that nasty, well, however, in whatever tone Joshua revealed it, Jack no longer felt like mine. He didn't need to say it, I just knew. So, I shrug to simplify.

"You're gonna let *that* come between us?" Our eyes momentarily meet. "Your brother, *Mr Macho*, whoever said I wanted Knowles done in anyway? I never asked anyone to do anything for me, not to go and hurt him. It was done, over, I wanted to forget it."

"*I* wanted to hurt him!"

The stupid retribution gets bigger.

"But I never *asked* you to do anything, did I, Jack. I never wanted some tit-for-tat thing going on, that would have been insane."

He huffs and puffs like to blow my house down and I want to tell him forget everything.

"You don't get it, do you?" him lost and figuring things his stubborn way, "Some guy or some...*girl* thinks they can just have you! They're all over you in their warped minds doing what they want to you and I hate it...I hate them thinking about you like that, like you can be any frigging body's at any time."

Mad, mad, mad, pointless shit, all of it!

Shaking my head I can't believe he's boiled so much down to trivia. I refuse to see the broader picture, his hurt ego, his belittling off his brother, his inability to having protected me that night but it was nothing, nothing I couldn't handle, and I was begging for Jack to see it that way. Like his youth tragedy, now this twenties crap, he was thirty-years-old for heaven's sake and carried too much shit around. His pain smashed in to my heart and I reached to hug his excruciated soul. He pushed me away. I couldn't get to him. He wouldn't let me get there and I felt our love for one another leave.

~

I tell the four why I am here.

After spending near five years in this place, it helped me realise I broke the law rather selfishly. I'd taken away other people's choices and that had been negligent of me.

Though my approaching five-of-twelve saw me achieve good things inside, I worked hard, kept my head down, took hard knocks but never bit angry. I saw Schmitz nod his head and seem impressed. My shit was working.

Oh, back up, the un-named parole board member mugs me.

"You got attacked and badly hurt, didn't you? Why do you think you got attacked so violently?"

Well how the fuck did I know, I mean really, some people you resent their advances and they make your time a shit-storm, others were cool and sought friendship out of respect. *Restraint, Em, how could you put it less succinctly?* My eyes dart about and I scurry to place my words which were perspicuously dignified so the un-named of the four flexes a smile and stutters her late introduction; Mrs Skilton, ravishingly paraded, then she attempts to detract it with a shuffle of formal papers before scribbling a note on her A4. I hadn't grown bitter and twisted due to the violence I'd suffered and I suppose Skilton was trying to locate a miniscule of evidence that I had: The code of silence in this place fortunate at times because I'd be done for if they found out about my extra curricula Abrams lesson. Come on, it was a one-off and duly necessary to prevent my regularly getting pulverised. I wasn't proud of myself and would never speak of it so.

All four board members rest quiet a moment and I know I mustn't fluctuate.

Geraldine Bracken absorbed everything. Waiting for her moment she shapely leans from one side of her chair to the other, a very familiar trait that Susan adorned with an air of artistry. The gesture emitted so slight yet it exercised a flotilla for all your control.

"These reports," her begin, blending out any harsh in the room to bring in feeling good, "they speak highly of you. Governor Barron and your therapist, Susan James, couldn't be more appraising."

I know there's a 'but' coming.

"So...do you...Emery," a serious set now, "feel what you did to Jack was wrong?"

~

Jack practically crashed down the stairs after brushing off my advance to tend his fettered soul. I literally touched the air he left scorching my face.

I ran down to follow and he was already throwing on his biker jacket about to blitz himself outside.

Like a ransack I gravel in to him.

"Where are you fucking going?"

For the first time I'm frantic and losing it.

He whips round burying his head in my face.

"I can't even protect you from myself," he wails.

"Jack," I panic, "what are you doing, this is stupid! Stay here and we can talk about it."

Effort free he shoves me away and it feels like we meant nothing to one another, and all because of the assumption he'd taken the accolades from that vengeful assault made it even more stupid. Guys had crazy ways of viewing their reason. I didn't understand and perhaps never would.

"Jack, just stay okay, let's talk about this."

"I need some air, Emery, I need to get out!"

"You're shit scaring me, you're too fucking wound up!"

"And you're making me too fucking angry!"

"Jack, wait-"

I soak up the power of that growing male rage as he smashes me against the wall.

I freeze. He does too. Like the Walls of Jericho, we had come crashing down. Neither one of us it appeared could lean straight our pillars to remain upright. The decline of this day's revelation did not cloud over the love I still had for him. I hoped to Jesus he felt the same.

"Jack-"

A forceful finger seals shut my mouth and he kisses me vehemently. Determined to reshape this alternate display I look to shake him off but he begins to ferociously handle my breasts. The darkness colouring him I would not bear. His sorry state would not get his way and I broke in to the base of all my strength to grapple him off my horrified soul.

Our eyes met.

His beautiful greens blazon before me sought to explain to make right this wrong and cool the rise in heat yet to singe him. There was no more I could relay in words how devastated I felt so expressed a hazel coloured tear to leave my eye.

Licking his lips liking to speak something strong, I evade his every, and run in to kitchen.

He doesn't follow.

I only hear the front door bang shut and I close my crying eyes.

This day, what had we done to each other?

Chapter Twenty-Five

I looked in to his eyes and saw a pain I had not seen before. It was not churl, not a cut finger, nor a disentangled love, no, it was far greater a sadden matching the shakes of God witnessing his crashing Earth. I don't believe anyone could explain it. It was impossible to describe, for you could only feel it and that was all. You could not touch or retrace its sorrow, you only *felt* it. Okay, so how do I now communicate all that emotion to Geraldine? Whichever way my best attempts to discuss this end matter it would all sound wrong. I know it would. Then what's next for this panel's believe; my words or dictated themes from some 'professional psycho manual'? Maybe I needed to get both sets of interprets right, the professional dialogue mingled with my layman's take of things. I did not want these four thinking I was acting to claim my freedom. No, I wanted to be true to them and everyone who believed in me.

I say sullen, "How could it have been right? It felt right at the time...but now, now thinking about it... I knew it was wrong."

"You admit your actions were inappropriate and wholeheartedly against the law?"

Wholeheartedly against the law, give me a rope, why don't you! Sheesh, I took enough beatings in here without you four doing me over too. Damn, I try to reel myself back in.

"Look," a second start, and I must admit sounding a bit tense too, "it just seems that whatever I say you'll read it your own way. I could be an angel, or a cold blooded animal, you'll still see things your way. I can't explain how I was truly feeling that day nor can I make you understand my feelings back then, but I never meant anyone any harm. I was only thinking of Jack and what he wanted nobody else, not even me. I wasn't thinking about me, everybody thinks that I was but I wasn't...I really wasn't."

In problematic mode Geraldine lands three fingers across her bottom lip which instantly reminds me of the night I did the same when Jack ran out of our home.

~

It fell midnight when the front door knocked and I thought he forgot his house keys.

I mulled over about opening up but let him stew a bit in the New Year's cold. He'd been a bastard so his bastard could stay out there a little longer. The living room light was on so he knew I was still up and rapped the front door again.

I peeked through the curtains and didn't see his Suzuki.

I saw a police car.

~

New Year's Day of '99 he rolled me around the floor in a super soft duvet with its pastel coloured covering adding warmth to our freezing winter. The real fire in the living room heated the entire cottage and left the cosy feel of, 'All things bright and beautiful'.

Unrolling my naked torso from out the duvet he spread me across the thick wool rug in front the fire. He played with the dark shadows running across my form, training their way mapping all directions as he explored one highlighted ripple of flesh to another.

His hand toyed across my face then finger-tipped my eyes shut before he nuzzled his head in my stomach and blew a huge raspberry.

My whole body's laughter lit up shades and shadows that enveloped me whilst Jack smoothed himself on top.

His pouching belly flopped gently on to mine as he pressed his right hand over my vagina. The power of his large palm over my pubic region blew a protrusion of my clitoris wanting to be fingered to corruption.

The mere touch from him down there was enough for me to find anything he wanted to explore allowed. Choose a heated poker, leather bound whip, or hot wax. He never needed them. The masterly calculations of his hard-working hands were enough. His mouth peeled open my labial folds poking feverishly inside thus released a jellied flow momentarily stopping my breath. How he did that left me constantly surprised. I had not yet come yet he could make me spill deliriously. The orgasm came later after the heavily laboured tease, the boiling of my abdomen, his fingers pressuring my ribs, and natural teeth nibbling my breasts in foreplay that had me open my legs and yank his penis inside my vagina. The dance he danced unforgettable, the rhythm of his hips marvelled as though his penis kept separate from his groin. I never could explain two movements that existed as one in an area that did not exist apart. He only ever said that he just performed it and never thought about it because he liked moving around me that way.

Well, *that* dance, *that* way, came fulfilled each New Year's and never failed to guide the beads of sweat travailing our bodies soaking in to fleshy cracks and crevices. At times I could have died, however his treatment of me left me more than alive.

~

They told me he hit a tree full on coming round a bend at top speed. The winding countryside in these parts an unforgiving landscape if you didn't respect its scenic shape. We cut our roads in to its beauty and took the risks to make our way safely through.

Jack hadn't been safe. He'd taken a stupid risk and lain less a man in intensive care.

I couldn't believe it, and wouldn't, till I saw him.

Curious about the blood on my jumper sleeve and flakes of it around my nostrils, I don't think I cognitively answered the two female police officers questions as I was busy rushing on my coat and locating house keys in order to be escorted to the local hospital's emergency room.

They say it's like a dream but it isn't. You know damn well it's real, you just want your loved one to be okay and things will work out and be back to normal. The realisation that things won't is when it hits you hard.

~

"Your emotions were running high," Geraldine confirms, "You were playing around with a lot of thinking under difficult circumstances."

Playing, I wasn't playing at anything.

I slumped in the plastic chair now showing lost as I didn't know what to say. If anyone's emotions were not running high that momentous day then they were obviously freezing cold. Any heart would have had its strings pulled apart. No one person of any inkling could cope with such a needless tragedy.

Skilton pitches in, "Do you honestly think you didn't have any other options?" Her tone stern and objective I feel a whip lash across my shoulders. Clearly from the *Temperate-Era* mode of thought; a woman's place was a woman's and a man's a man's. My position that day would never be allowed if this were still the temperance age. Jack and I long broke those golden-era-rules. Never married, had no children, sometimes drank and fornicated without restrictions, maybe Skilton's thoughts must still be to punish this 'rule-breaker'.

Need to drag her out the stone-age, so I step up, "I had options," said with raised confidence, "It was just that I simply followed what he wanted. I did what he asked, and to this very day..." my eyes search the entire panel first before saying conclusively, "I wouldn't change a thing."

Of the four board members none move. Surely my statement did not shock, when, "But regrets, Emery?" Schmitz executes diligently, "Any regrets?"

These people had no idea. My family, my partner, my friends, many suffered through my actions and I wish I could take it all back. I'd dressed several strong teas leaving bitterness from each taste. I served destruct and pain of which I had no authority to, but it was all over and I paid a damnable price. Still, for some, I could carry on and live my life and what was left of it to be mended along the way. Regrets? Shit!

I cover Schmitz wearing eyes that say I understand men like him perfectly, "There'll always be regret," I give to him, "And I have lots."

~

I listened to the Doctor express words to the effect that Jack was paralysed from the neck down. The tubes and wirings holding him together shown deceptive because I believed he could get up and walk away. I believed he could stand and slam me in to the wall. I wanted to believe he could fuck me beyond running horses or make love during the flow of meadows. We could pretend string-guitars when a favourite song played on the radio, be free to ride through the roads on a Harley, and tinker with our vehicles each Sunday morning... Oh... No. No more I guess. We weren't.

Fuck, what did it matter what school you went to, or the grades you got, or what job you ended up doing being able to afford anything? None of that mattered anymore. Only Jack getting better mattered, only his being able to walk, ride, run free and be him, each a prayer sent God's way to allow him to be him again. But not this way, not a living useless man! No, God, no, you can't do this to him, not him. Where was an ounce of fairness on this unfair planet because I wouldn't accept it. I couldn't.

I was paid a visit and spoken to. Something crossed over and I listened to the world around me.

It said many things.

Yes.

Okay, we were okay.

He could get up, he was fine, sure, show me.

Come on.

The hand which punched me earlier I felt for it among the hospital blanket and safety-bar tubing. The palm was warm. It was so warm. I would give anything for him to punch me again, playful, he could do that. All he needed was to sit up, get up. We could argue, yeah, let's fight. I would give my all to have that again. He cheated to impress me before, he could cheat this too. Come on, Jack, get up, you know you can perform anything, achieve anything, create something. After all, you were mine.

A nurse mentioned words about family. I had to inform his and my own of the situation. What on earth would I tell them? Our stupid arguing led to him riding off and crashing in to a tree. My God, really!

The Doctor reached out to place a trusted medical hand on my shoulder but he didn't make it as I collapsed to my knees and started an uncontrollable sob.

Jesus, Jack, just get up, will you. Open your eyes and speak to me and get up off this bed, please, just do that for me will you.

Unwilling to see, a blackness shrouded round. I was falling from on high. Where was I to rest, what would my landing say of me?

I touched again his softness filled with warmth.

Soon the darkness let in light.

His hand I squeezed so hard did not squeeze back.

~

"You mean what you say, don't you?" Geraldine commands, with a dose of sympathy.

I nod yes.

"But what about the domestic violence that led up to the argument?"

"It wasn't like that," I jump in, "Yeah, we had fights but it wasn't domestic violence stuff."

Anderson Perkins makes his position felt, "Bruised stomach, bloody nose? Would you indulge in that kind of relationship ever again?"

"No," I say frustrated, "you're getting it all wrong, our relationship wasn't domestic violence, we loved each other, we had a couple of bad incidents but there was never abuse, not like that, not what you're saying."

"Leaving you bruised and bloodied isn't abuse?"

Pausing, I think this guy is insane, a real book-read-facts that everything gets labelled and placed in to neat categories. Well not everything could be labelled and piled in to files or explained. I wouldn't be pushed in that direction and had to make them see my side.

"Jack Charles loved me," I said humble, feeding all four on the panel my memory eyes after turning to my right and seeing my beloved Jack sitting next to me. His greens bore in to my soul and my body struggled to contain arousal and sorrow in identical time. "I loved him back," said, reconnecting with Perkins' query. "You have no idea how much I loved him and what I did will forever haunt me but it wasn't done on a whim. I watched him in that hospital bed and saw a pain I hope never to see the rest of my life. If I could go back and change that day I would. I would ask God to help us not argue that morning. I would ask him to make our New Year like before, like we always spent it, making love to our hearts content. When Jack rode off that day I never thought I would not be able to make love to him ever again. I couldn't believe he'd been in an accident."

Geraldine is seen reaching inside her handbag by her chair's leg and hands me an unused tissue.

My wetting eyes let a tear drop, and taking the tissue from the concerned panel's hand, I am unable to prevent a flood of tears leave.

The crying becomes so loud it called for a stiff knock to spirit the oak wood door and my sobbing self being crushed inside a strong embrace from Susan James.

~

Jack awakened after seven weeks in a coma. The swelling of his head and face still so horrific we were barely able to recognise him.

I sat in stilled waters of the brook by my parents' house and watched the frogs jump from pebble to pebble to safely reach the sodden embankment. Their freedom seen unmeasured, their joyous play fluorescing a life we humans could only dream of with nothing to fret except the dangers of other predators. Human lives were a constant worry of monies, having a home, working for something we weren't truly enjoying and then greeting death. Was it worth it, because I don't think this is what was meant to be!

A frog saddled my side thinking I must have been a grand muddy rush to clamber over for it came up close and opened those massive squishy eyes. Unresisting, I captured his slimy bundle and held him carefully. Damn, he must be thinking I'd tricked him but I soon let him go after the kiss granted on his big blinking visuals. He scattered away with an urgency reminding me of Jack when I'd kissed one of his eyes. He would grab me round the waist before setting about my body aptly handling it.

The brook's waters hovered around zero so I knew it was time to get out and head home yet I wanted to stay seated and feel the chill over what had become my life. My one and only true love could hardly speak, nor tend to his own body, neither walk nor move his hands for nothing. I wanted the brook to become deep enough to submerge my pain because I would not believe anything in this world could alleviate it.

Lucas shouted me from on top the embankment. He came to see how I was as mum was getting worried. It was cold, I didn't have a coat, and Lucas moored on down to stand at my sitting.

He shifted out of his officer's shawl and covered me with it before joining my side. Alarmed, I went to get up but he held me tight and said it would be alright, it was just a shawl and could be cleaned afterward then I buried my head in his shoulder and cried.

Everyone tried to see how I felt, everyone searched to understand. Everyone got it and would think no less if I chose to walk away. Four months in, Jack could manage few words. He knew what had happened and understood what was going on around him. He called it a mess. He called it God's plan but it was still a mess. His parents, Mary and Jake, asked him to be strong but he would just stare at me with this intensely sad look. Each time I left his bedside I cried till my head hurt.

Mum said I'd manage but I knew I wouldn't. Barely attending work, the cottage too fell neglected and dishevelled. I tried clearing it out one weekend but simply put, I packed a bag and walked away. My family said they'd help me with it but I wanted it sold and out of my memories. They eventually agreed.

Joshua came and dismantled the tyre swing. He must have managed five sentences before hauling everything on to an old country Jeep and looked to shimmy out of our driveway when I went and knocked on his vehicle window.

I wanted to explain I knew what he'd done and that New Year's Eve led to mine and Jack's argument. Instead I told him Jack never stopped thinking about his family and that he loved them. J simply went over me with eyes woven from pity then pulled my head close and planted this warm kiss upon my forehead. I never saw him again.

It was the tenth month in when I sat next to Jack's bedside and watched him fight through the hardship of trying desperately to say something.

Witnessing the struggle behind his beautiful opened eyes encased within tubes and wirings and a sense of pending doom, I made myself close to hear him speak.

He uttered words I thought I heard so I checked his eyes to see if he'd just said what I thought he did.

He had.

We connected inside with tears falling from our eyes and I gasped horrified.

Then he uttered it again.

No.

But I knew he was serious.

I shot to my feet and looked to hurry away though couldn't. I clamped a hand over my mouth preventing sickness rising and inhaled a deep agonising breath.

"Jack!"

"Please, Emery!"

The despair in his look was traumatising, the tears bubbling out of his greens too much to wipe away.

"Emery, please...not me, not like this...no. Not me."

The strength I could not find to leave and the power Jack had given me too much to comprehend.

"Em...you ca...don't leave me...don't leave me like this."

I couldn't. I had no right.

"I love you, Jack!"

His eyes implored me. I fell toward his face and grabbed him as tight as I could, so tight I even thought I'd dislodged all his tubes and wires.

"Jack, don't ask me!"

"Yes," he whispered, "It's the last...the last I'll ever ask."

Of everything, this ask to end his life was never greater.

My feet glued to the floor I could not make away. I could not leave him and be free of his burden. His pleas were holy, his pleas were true.

He tried to lift his head to make stronger his plea, then to my horror, using his mouth, he fixed to tear off the tubes and wiring attached to his face and all around him.

Determined I held both his cheeks in an effort to stop his antics when he pressingly held on to one of my hands with his teeth. The tears which poured from his eyes were a colossal sight to bear.

"Oh, Jack, please!"

He refused to let go.

"Jack, I love you!"

The definitive crunching down of his teeth said *every*thing. He loved me too and he let go his bite.

"Jack..."

He smiled blissfully, he smiled cool, "Love me, Em...then do it."

I crumpled by his side and grabbed him hard before climbing on to the hospital bed. All the while his sad murmurings to please end this, to stop the indignity and please kill him were making through. My mind swarmed with guilt, my emotions mixed fire and water and I asked God to show me the way.

"No," Jack whispered in my ear, "*I'm* asking you...please..."

My hazels and his greens come together.

His slight crooked incisors pinch a gleam as the flesh around his eyes squeezes tight. He's happy. I want to be happy for him. And I think I am. I watch his tongue struggle to wet his lips as I reach to touch his mouth. His words I listened never forgot. His movements felt my very soul.

"A last kiss?" he asked of me. "You'll be okay, Em."

Our faces so close his breath warmed my nose.

I kissed each of his eyes. He closed them.

I kissed his nose. He smiled.

I kissed his mouth. He smiled again.

I told him I loved him and he mouthed I love you too.

He could not see then that I mouthed, Goodbye, Jack, but he must have sensed it because he mouthed back to me, Goodbye, Emery, and I slowly reached for the pillow.

Chapter Twenty-Six

I was granted early parole.

Susan went out of her way to congratulate me in my cell while I prepared for a dwindling feel-good recreational hour in the yard. Clutching hold another self-help book off my brother Lucas, Susan naturally took it from me.

"'Mind, Body, Spirit'," she begins the title rampantly, "'How to Manage in Great Difficulties'. Did it help?"

I look to take it back off her, "I'm only a few pages in," said optimistically.

Quiet comes over us as I leaf through the book then offer up a smile. Susan stands there with a look of complete newness and I am surprised to feel her awkward. No more the patient and therapist scenario it clearly unfits her.

"You helped me get through it," I say, hoping she relaxes.

Practically shifting coy she nods puerile.

"You did all the hard work, Em."

"Yeah," I say unboastful, "but...not without your help."

"Okay," her merrily, "we don't have to stay thanking one another anymore."

I grin. "Oh, shouldn't we?"

Her gentle laugh fills my single-cell and I toss the book on to my bunk. My sensitive says she wishes to say a few things, remind me of the cruel world awaiting, the problems I will face moving forward yet had to remain strong. For her, I would show I could.

"You know, Emery," emphasis endorsed with a hand on her hip, "I'm gonna miss you."

Well I knew she'd miss something but digging around inside my head not one.

"How could you want to keep figuring me out?" I play down, "I'm a bundle of contradictions all the way."

"A little truth," she said, my words re-igniting her values, "I don't think everything you laid out was one hundred percent."

"Oh," I take surprise, "I don't think I conned you."

"No, Em," she shoots assured, "you just didn't tell me everything, and why should you? No one could be fully honest about themselves."

"But you have to know that?"

"Of course," she unlaces, "I know that, but it doesn't stop me trying to do my job."

I make not to show offense, "A job...that's what we all are to you?"

The step forward sees her staring in to my uplifted eyes and I see my reflection in those turquoise-blues of hers.

"No," she near whispers, "Not everyone is a job to me."

Nodding my head yes, I turn away, saying, "Okay then, so there are some who-"

Her hand which clasped over mine coils my body round to face the good friend I had known these past months and before I can utter a syllable or meet her fantastic eyes again, she takes a commanding hold of my face and plants the most insistent tender kiss upon my lips.

She did not let go.

I never saw it coming, and neither, I believe, did Susan.

Releasing me, the times I'd fleeted my kiss upon her from thoughts agone I did not think would come to mean far more than I imagined, for it merged every feeling I had encapsulated over my time in here. Her tendency told a story all its own and I would merely wonder over it.

"You take care of yourself, Emery," she ends beautifully, and crosses to the cell door.

I want to go after her and fire a hundred questions but can only manage to say, "Thanks," before those eyes of hers varnish mine and I see a million different things tidily folded together then, she disappears.

~

A week later I walked free from Maidenhall with the grandest of thoughts from Governor Barron. She found it hard to admit she'd miss me but she would never forget me. I'd never forget my experiences there either nor what I had done to be there in the first place. Taking Jack's life was hard to truly reason and in front of four strangers too, though in the end I convinced the panel of my rehabilitation and no possible threat of it ever happening again. I mean, how could it? A love like we had comes round only once. I would never seek to replicate it. If I were lucky to love like that again it would be with God's blessing but I somehow doubted it.

My release was a low key affair compared to my headline making 'sensationalist' crime. A couple of reporters wanted to do a follow-up story but I declined. My freedom would be appreciated each day and I would look to make amends in all corners of my life. There were a couple of things I had to face first, not that the brilliant Sunday dinner mum cooked was a starting point but Mary Charles asked to see me the following week.

"Are you going to go, Emery?" solemnly asked.

"I have to, mum," I said, "I have to face her about what I did."

She ceases drying the washed plate I'd handed her, and says, "She never came to see you inside, why not let it go?"

"I can't," shrugged, "not to her, it would be wrong of me."

My mum wolfen, "Jack's gone, Emery, why can't you let things be?"

Mary buried her son due to my hands, I had to show myself. "Mum," I breathe, "I took her son away from her. I did it. I made that choice and I left her out of it."

Terror beamed from my mother's eyes.

"You don't have to go up there. You don't have to face it!"

"Yes, mum, I do."

She sprinkled me with worry then fastened this tough look on her second borne.

"Okay," she said certain, "Then I'm going with you!"

It wasn't necessary but I wouldn't fight her. Dad said he'd wait in the car in case of any trouble. I told my parents that the Charles's were not like that and if they'd wished me harm it would have happened already.

Lucas and Jamie's words of support rang in my ears as mum, dad, and me, drove the three hour grind up to The Lakes. Jamie said I needed to make my actions clear to Mary and not be hardened by anything she said negative, and Lucas said he'd put off his officer deployment to Germany till things settled down for us all. I felt like an anchor round my family's necks. They could not move forward till I cooked grounded, and when that was done, they could move free from around my chains. Boy, one really did not comprehend the enormity of having committed such an act could influence so drastically on so many others.

~

Mary opened the front door on a very chilly morning in November 2006. During the five years I'd been locked away much had changed throughout society but The Lakes seemed to stay forever in time. As though I had stepped back through the ages when I approached the Charles's house, it had not budged an inch in style from when Jack first introduced me to his family all those years ago.

With no clue what to expect; a slap, a push, or told to die, the breath which left me upon seeing Mary appear like a beaten down beaver was heart-breaking.

"You came?"

Taking her son's life had taken its own heavy toll on her. I felt obliterate.

"Mary, I am so-"

"Stop...Emery. Just stop."

Her disembowelled appearance was one I would not forget. In a click, she left me standing alone in the doorway before returning seconds later with a distinctly black urn and gracefully handed it to me.

"You know," she began like a great storyteller, "he always told me he'd want you to have him wherever you were. He said no matter what, give my ashes or my body to Emery and let her do what she wanted with me. For some crazy reason he always believed he would die before you, and...and I guess he was right."

I burst out crying.

"Hush, hush, now come my dear child," said heartened with a reach and embrace of such kindness I felt undeserving of, and after my release from her country-firm crush, she strokes my chin the way Jack once did.

"You need to go," she said motherly, and sent a compassionate smile my way. "Joshua and Jake are coming back from the hills soon and I don't want you around when they do. They haven't really got over things just yet."

Stood maudlin, I could not believe the generosity she afforded me and could say no words.

Holding tight the urn that cased our Jack, I gave Mary one last smile and through the tears streaming down my face, I moved close and gave her a kiss on the cheek. She smiled again then waved me away before she would let me see her crumble.

~

Mum and dad drove further up The Lakes till we reached the Coniston Water.

Getting out of the car, mum decided to come with me but I told her to please stay. This was a moment I needed alone.

Clambering down several feet of the muddied bank to stand by the water's edge, I scanned the scenic colours of autumn's green-golds and a stilled black river that held many secrets beneath its current. Mum always used to say God's work was wonderful in her own unique way and I got to understand. If this were his wonder, I would question nothing.

Jack and I spent one of those afternoons wondering about things as we would soak looks in to each other's eyes before sharing a brush of lips.

I lifted up the urn and gave it a long last kiss.

Gently, I sprinkled Jack's ashes out to sea.

Someday I believed I would see him again because the man I last saw in that hospital bed was not the man I knew.

I would no longer miss him that way because that wasn't Jack.

The End

Do feel free to leave an honest review of this book to the relevant web pages.

Thanks for reading.

About the author

I never thought I'd write another *new* book at my age but continue to revise my old works and yet, I did. I loved every single minute creating the characters Emery and Jack and all the others. They made me laugh and bought a tear to my eye. I've no idea where they came from but I'm really glad they lay inside me to tell their story. This was a real love affair indeed.

Toni and Rebecca, thank you.   22nd Dec 2017.

Visit the website: http://anovel.wix.com/strongwords

Also by this author *Spilling Blood*

29721563R00188

Printed in Poland
by Amazon Fulfillment
Poland Sp. z o.o., Wrocław